by
Paul C

GW00776614

First Published in Great Britain in 2002 by
Barny Books

© Paul Carroll
All rights reserved

ISBN N° 1 903172 15 2

Published by Barny Books, Hough on the Hill, Grantham, Lincolnshire
Produced by: TUCANN*design&print*, 19 High Street, Heighington Lincoln LN4 1RG
Tel & Fax: 01522 790009
www.tucann.co.uk

Chapter 1

According to the old Seth Thomas it was five to eleven. Quite how the antique American clock came to be hanging in the bar of the Bell Hotel in Melbury was a mystery beyond the memory of the local population. The locals did know however, that it was always five to eleven at the Bell Hotel.

In fact it had been five to eleven ever since Larcum Todd, the landlord, decided to boost his flagging profits by never closing whilst there was still a customer in the bar. Sergeant Ellis, of the Melbury police, obligingly used the clock to confirm that the hotel was not in breach of opening hours. The fact that Sergeant Ellis and his colleagues rarely left the bar until after midnight was both a tribute to the broad mind of the law and an indication as to the character of Melbury itself.

Melbury was the sort of picturesque English town that should by rights have been nestling quietly between two hills. Quiet Melbury was, but nestling was out of the question on the flat Suffolk landscape, so Melbury simply dozed under the open East Anglian skies as it had done for about eleven hundred years, unaware of the bizarre events which would soon make it a household name for years to come.

Eleven centuries years ago Melbury was just a settlement on the river Bey. It found prosperity in the 14th century as a weaving centre and became the fourteenth richest town in England. The fine Suffolk churches and many beautiful buildings seen now, give testimony to the wealth and benefactors of this period. As the weaving industry declined so did Melbury and although local towns found new business and revenue, Melbury just became poor. Whilst new architecture sprang up in other areas Melbury had to make the best of its Tudor heritage. The result, in the twentieth century, was a town full of pink and beige half-timbered houses, which did their best to defy the efforts of their owners to keep them upright. Most of the buildings leaned at outrageous angles, on some the outside walls bulged threateningly and at least a dozen dwellings were only standing due to the cooperative support of adjacent houses. The overall effect was extremely pretty and brought more than a few casual admirers to the area on day trips. Some, to Larcum's grateful pleasure, stayed the night at the Bell Hotel, the beautiful 14th century timber- clad inn, that was the social centre of the town.

Ronald Finch was sitting in the corner of the Bell's bar studying his half-pint of Ixdon Bitter. He puffed thoughtfully on a briar pipe. Ronald's only drinking companion this late afternoon was Bernie Small, the corpulent town garage owner, who sat on one of the many tapestries oak chairs scattered around the old beamed room. Small was reading the racing times. He lowered the paper and called to Debbie the new barmaid.

"Ere luv be a darlin' and bring us another scotch will you?"

Finch resented this interruption to his thoughts and he despised Small's vulgar manners and coarse London accent. Debbie obediently took a glass of whiskey across to Small who was absorbed in the prospects for the last race at Market Rasen. Debbie put the glass on his table spilling a little as the old table rocked on its uneven legs.

"Excuse me," she said politely.

"Squeeze you? I'll squeeze you alright darlin." Small attempted to carry out his threat, but Debbie moved deftly away.

"Excuse me I said." Debbie looked annoyed and headed back to the safety of the bar. Even Ronald Finch could not help registering how attractive she was.

"You still seein' that fella from Ixdon?" The sight of Debbie gracefully walking back to the bar had distracted Small from his paper; he had mischief in his voice.

"That's not for you to know Mr Small," Debbie flushed and Small continued.

"You should try a real man, someone a bit mature.. How about Albert Stern; he's always showin' more than a passin' interest." Small chuckled. Debbie was annoyed and quick on the riposte.

"Mr Stern and I just like chatting that's all, there's nothing else in it."

Small laughed out loud now.

"I should hope not darlin," he must be all of seventy! Oh lord." Small thumped his chest as his laugh became a coughing fit. He turned his attention to Ronald Finch.

"What do you think Mr Finch," Small called across the room. "I reckon old Albert's got an eye for young Debbie don't you?"

Finch looked contemptuously across at Small.

"I am not the slighted bit interested in Albert Stern's fancies or for that matter the man himself."

Small winked knowingly at Debbie, downed his whiskey and set of out of the bar clutching his racing times.

"Put it on me tab darlin.'" Small disappeared out through the door, allowing it to slam noisily behind him. Finch, grateful for some peace, returned to his thoughts and Debbie, shaking her head after the closing door, busied herself behind the bar.

Albert Stern, thought Finch. Even the mention of his name put Finch's blood pressure up and everyone knew it. Every year since Stern had moved to Melbury, Finch and Stern had battled for first prize in the flower and vegetable section of the annual Beekeeper Show. The event was called the Beekeeper Show for historical reasons, but in reality it was an horticultural show, or rather to those of that persuasion, *the* horticultural show. The intensity of the competition between the two men at this event had become a cause for amusement in Melbury, but to Ronald Finch it was far from amusing. For a start he did not like Stern; in almost every respect they were opposites. Finch was an ingenuous Suffolk countryman, sixty-five years of age, although he looked older with his thin grey hair and lined country face. Stern however, was over seventy and possessed a natural urbane charm and mature good looks. A long military career had bestowed him with a swaggering confidence, which annoyed Finch intensely. Stern was too 'hail fellow well met' for Finch and to top it all he was a newcomer, having lived in Melbury for only ten years. The one thing the two men did have in common though, was a love of horticulture and ever since his arrival, Stern had taken Finch's traditional first place at the Beekeeper Show. The Show was in one week's time and Ronald Finch was in a state of agitated apprehension.

As Finch ruminated on the matter, the subject of his enmity strode through the door. Albert Stern dressed and acted for that matter, the part of the country squire. Today he wore a smart tweed jacket, his Jockey Club tie, cavalry twills with razor sharp creases, and a pair of old but highly polished brogues. Stern noticed Finch in the corner of the bar and greeted him cordially.

5

"What ho Finch, yer roses look good this year!"

Stern was, as usual, in buoyant humour. He did not reciprocate Finch's personal dislike, and this served to annoy Ronald even more. Finch grudgingly muttered an acknowledgement, then, pushing the remains of his half pint across the table stood up, noisily scraping his chair on the wooden bar floor.

Stern continued to be friendly.

"Looking forward to the show Ronald? Should be a corker this year!"

Finch hated the way that Stern patronized him. He started to make an exit and brushed ungraciously past his adversary. As he walked out Ronald also allowed the glass lounge door to slam closed noisily behind him. Unperturbed, Albert Stern shrugged and leaned across the bar to engage Debbie in conversation.

On the streets of Melbury the dust of the harvest filled the air and small black thunder bugs, displaced from the fields, scrambled for refuge. The blue August Suffolk sky spread vastly from one horizon to the other, allowing the afternoon light to bathe the town's houses in a flattering pastel light. Today Melbury looked charming and contented, as if the town itself was a part of nature, above any mere human problems.

Finch walked slowly in the afternoon sun and turned right over the old stone bridge towards his home. On another day he would have taken great pleasure in the sound of the skylark overhead and in the scent of the harvest, but today he was preoccupied. He was thinking of dahlias: pom pom dahlias to be exact. The previous year the pom pom dahlias had been the deciding factor in the Beekeeper Show. This year Finch thought his dahlias were pretty good. They should be. He had lavished them with every attention possible: weekly feeding programmes, foliar cocktails and almost clinical temperature regulation. Yet still he had doubts. Last year his dahlias had been good; very good in fact and yet still that arrogant fellow Albert Stern had beaten him.

Finch was a scrupulously honest man, conservative to the core and possessing a strong sense of fair play. Nevertheless an idea kept recurring to him no matter how hard he tried to dismiss it. Ten years of ignominy kept forcing it back into his mind. He just *had* to know what Stern had produced for the competition this year. He could not bear another day of humiliation at the show with Albert Stern preening himself in front of his leeks and carrots whilst he, Ronald Finch, stood in the background awaiting, to his mind, the shame of the 'second place' ribbon. 'Second place'! Ha! He would never even have contemplated second place before *that man* had moved to Melbury. He would go to spy out the opposition; he wasn't going to wait to be humiliated again.

Finch turned into the front garden of his small red brick cottage, instinctively picking the dead heads off the roses lining the stone path. His wife, a happy rotund woman, was busy making pastry as Finch walked in through the kitchen door.

"Hello dear," Mrs Finch greeted her husband and wiped her pastry-encrusted hands on her apron. "I'm making some cakes for the show. I did quite well last year."

Finch ignored her.

"Are you alright Ronald?" Dorothy dusted the pine kitchen table with flour and began rolling the pastry into a flat oval shape.

Finch looked at the tiled floor moodily.

"I've had enough," he said, "I'm not going to spend all week waiting to be humiliated."

"What do you mean dear?"

Mrs Finch was used to her husband's strange moods at this time of the year.

"I'm going over to Stern's place tonight: I want to know what he's putting in the show."

"What?" Dorothy stopped rolling the pastry to give Ronald her full attention.

"I'm only going to have a peek," he explained. "I just can't stand not knowing.."

"Not knowing what?"

"Not knowing if I'm going to lose or not of course." Ronald began to pace the kitchen.

Mrs Finch was getting concerned. She could see how agitated her husband was becoming. It alarmed her.

"You can't do that, you can't just go and trespass on Mr Stern's property, it's against the law for a start. What if you're caught?"

"Well," said Ronald stubbornly, "I'm going to look anyway, I want to see his dahlia's."

Mrs Finch was losing patience. "Don't be daft Ronald, it's only a show. Anyway your dahlias must be almost perfect."

Ronald stopped in front of the table.

"I thought that last year," he said, "and look what happened."

"They *were* perfect last year," said Mrs Finch returning to her task.

"It's just that.." Dorothy shrugged, "well anyway, it's only a bit of fun, you know, a competition."

Finch, agitated, paced the kitchen again. "I know, I know what you were going to say, my dahlias were perfect only Stern's were better. Go on admit it."

Mrs Finch hesitated.

"Well they were very good, I must say," she said reluctantly. "I mean do you remember that big blue one he had? It was rather splendid.."

"How could I not remember," said Ronald miserably. The image of Albert Stern, standing victoriously in front of his dahlias, had haunted him all year.

"Well it was very close anyway." Added Dorothy cheerfully, "perhaps this will be your year."

It was always close, thought Finch, but somehow Stern always won.

Throughout the evening Finch continued to be unhappy about his prospects for the show and despite Mrs Finch trying to be upbeat with her husband she could not prevail on his mood. Ronald would have none of it and fell into a silent sulk. That night, after supper, Finch donned his blue gardening boiler suit and prepared for his adventure.

"What are you doing now Ronald?"

Mrs Finch watched, arms folded, as the blue clad figure rummaged in her cleaning cupboard.

"Boot polish," said Finch. "I'm going to wear boot polish so that I don't stand out, like during the war."

"You were in public works during the war," said Mrs Finch. Ronald ignored her and continued with his search. Mrs Finch unfolded her arms and walked out of the kitchen.

"You're mad," she said, "I'll have nothing to do with it."

Finch prepared himself in front of the hall mirror, smearing his face with black kiwi polish. Finally, apparently satisfied, he armed himself with a torch and headed for the back door.

"Wish me luck," he called to his wife.

"Grow up!" Her reply echoed from the depths of the lounge.

Finch made slow progress through the woods behind his cottage. His torch cast an eerie glow ahead of him and he grunted and puffed as he tripped over roots and scratched his face on unseen branches. Finally Albert Stern's grounds appeared out of the gloom ahead of him. Finch crept cautiously around the tall beech hedge which marked the rear boundary of Stern's garden. His heart was beating fast as he eased himself over the short wire fence at the side. Ronald tiptoed along the narrow damp grass strip between the vegetable patches and sank to all fours as he approached the greenhouse. Stern's house was only a few yards away. Finch crept to the nearest window and peered through. The lights were on but he could see no sign of life. He began to doubt his mission and question these antics at his time of life. Still he thought, while he was here..

He tried the door to the greenhouse; it was open. Both frightened and excited he crawled inside and scanned the rows of pots.

"Rubbish" he muttered. "No contest here."

Finch was beginning to feel quite pleased as he realized that his own efforts this year had rewarded him with very competitive plants. Stern's carnations were good but no better than his own and in the battle of the pelagoniums Ronald felt he had a slight edge. He illuminated a few dahlias but again they were not up to Stern's usual standard.

"Heh, the old boy's losing his touch," Finch chuckled.

Satisfied that he would not be humiliated, Finch turned and was about to make his way back when he gave a gasp of astonishment. His torchlight had fallen upon the most magnificent pom dom dahlia he had ever seen. The plant, obviously singled out for special care, stood apart from the others. Its beautiful petals and huge bloom looked almost unreal in the artificial light. Finch had seen a few specimen plants in his time but never one such as this. This dahlia was a world-beater and Finch was consumed with almost tearful jealousy. He held the bloom, unbelieving, in his left hand and his right hand caressed

9

the perfect formation of petals. Without thinking or conscious effort, with no malice aforethought, even without registering the urge, Finch's right hand began to tighten on the bloom. He couldn't bear this; he was going to lose.. He pinched out a segment from the centre of the flower, then stood back genuinely shocked at what he had done. Had he intended to do that? He wasn't sure himself, but one thing was certain, there was no more contest this year in the pom pom dahlia department.

Finch surveyed the sabotage, and his mind scrambled for excuses. A beetle! A beetle could have done it! He looked at the chunk out of the bloom; yes it could have been a beetle. Suddenly a loud noise from the house startled him and Finch ran from the greenhouse and headed for the fence, tearing his boiler suit in his effort to get over.

Finch ran back through the woods and started as a young couple by a tree fell under his torchlight. He recognised Debbie from the Bell, held in the arms of a young man. Debbie was embarrassed; she pushed her companion away and smoothed the front of her skirt. She could not make out the figure behind the dazzling torchlight and held her hand in front of her face to reduce the glare.

"Who's that?" She called out. Finch ignored her and concentrated on negotiating his path through the woods. As he passed, Debbie recognised the silhouette and unmistakable gait as one of her regular customers.

"Good evening Mr Finch," she called, rather bemused that the old man should be in the woods so late.

"Evening," grunted Finch unhappily. He stumbled past the couple, and continued noisily back through the undergrowth towards the haven of his cottage.

Ronald burst through the kitchen door and Mrs Finch looked up from where she was busy rolling pastry.

"Ronald!" She exclaimed as she surveyed the dishevelled figure. Her husband sat at the table and put a trembling hand to his forehead. He had horrified himself. He was a good man, a righteous man; even as a boy he refused to steal apples with the other boys.

"I can't believe what I have done!"

"What *have* you done Ronald?"

Mrs Finch adopted patient tones and patting her husband's hands, sat beside him. Finch began to pull himself together; he would have to live with it: the shame of cheating at the Beekeeper Show would be unbearable if it became local knowledge.

"I..er..I just can't believe that I had to go to Stern's garden, I must have lost my senses."

Finch seemed so upset that his wife was beginning to feel sorry for him. She forgot her annoyance from earlier that evening.

"I think you are going daft Ronald. Now just forget it, no harms done. I'll make us a nice cup of tea."

Ronald sat mulling his half-truth and began to brighten up. After all, the damage could not be undone. Perhaps he could just forget he ever did it. If Stern was only relying on one dahlia to win the show it wasn't right anyway, after all *he* had two that were really of a very good standard.

"What did you see anyway?" asked Mrs Finch, placing a steaming mug of tea in front of her husband. Dorothy's curiosity overrode her disapproval of Ronald's actions for a moment.

Finch took a deep breath and looked vacantly out of the kitchen window.

"Oh, nothing much really."

Then, pausing, he looked at his wife.

"I'll tell you what though.. old Stern's had some bad luck with beetles this year."

Chapter 2

Mrs Cummings looked out of her window. Across the road Albert Stern's house glowed pink in the sunset. Beyond, the steeple of the Melbury church basked in the fading light. The picturesque scene did not concern Mrs Cummings. She was more interested in the arrival at Stern's house of Debbie, the barmaid from the Bell Hotel. Mr Stern had answered the door and ushered Debbie in, as if expecting her. What business could they have together? The church clock struck in the town and Mrs Cummings pondered the unlikely. Surely the old man could not be up to his old tricks with a girl so young. She felt anger rising but as always suppressed it and continued to watch the Stern house.

Mrs Cummings had moved to Melbury from Norwich a year ago, after her husband had died. The depression which had plagued her for the last twenty years had become deeper set since the death of her husband and she occupied her time with her home, the local women's institute and by gazing from her upstairs window. She paid particular interest to the pink house opposite: the residence of Albert Stern.

Bernie Small tore up his betting slip in disgust and stomped out of the bookies office. The 4.30 race at Market Rasen had proven no more lucky than his garage business. Melbury was feeling the effects of the recession and most of Small's regular customers were either servicing their own cars or having the work done by 'moonlighting' mechanics. Bernie strode back down the high street and turned right into the Bell. Larcum greeted him.

"Cheer up Bernie, might never happen."
Bernie pulled a stool up to the oak bar and accepted a scotch ungratefully.
"Already has mate."
He looked sullenly at the glass. Larcum, wiping a mug with a towel,

tried again.

"How's the garage doing, still having troubles?"

Bernie nodded. "Bloody right. I had to get rid of a mechanic yesterday, there's just not enough work. Now he says he's going to sue me."

Larcum looked interested. "Sue you? Who was that? Young Solomon Weinstein I'll bet."

Bernie knocked back the scotch.

"That's it, bloody 'Einstein.' Thinks I'm getting rid of him because I'm anti Semitic, silly bugger. Just 'cos I make a few jokes. Doesn't understand I'm just about broke. He's already been to a legal beagle in Ixdon." He pushed the glass across the bar. "Same again please mate."

Larcum took the glass and turning to the optic behind him, carried on the conversation over his shoulder.

"Your jokes can be a bit near the knuckle you know Bernie." Larcum turned back and slid the refilled glass in front of his customer. "Anyway out of interest why did you choose Solomon to go? I mean I know he's a bit intense, but he seems like a nice lad."

Small was not sympathetic. He shrugged. "Last in first out.. he only joined in May. Anyway, it's only a temporary thing for him. Einstein isn't interested in being a mechanic. He's too ambitious. He wants to study law.. probably why he's being all precious about getting the shove. I mean I've got others there that have been with me for years. He was the obvious one to go."

Bernie looked dejected again. Larcum decided to change the conversation to a more cheerful subject.

"How about card school tonight Bernie? I'm feeling lucky these days, that new barmaid's doing wonders for my custom."

Bernie gripped his scotch and looked darkly at Larcum.

"I'm doing no more card school until a few debts have been settled. I'm pissed off with people like old Albert Stern all lah-di-dah and not payin' up."

"That reminds me," said Larcum, looking at a notepad by the till, "your tab stands at fifty eight pounds."

Larcum looked amused but it was lost on Small. Bernie leaned forward and glanced sourly at the row of figures on the notepad.

"Yeh yeh," he muttered, "Ill pay you tomorrow. I'm going to do a

13

bit of debt collecting myself tonight."

Bernie downed the scotch and gestured for yet another. Outside the Melbury streets were quiet and the sun made its inexorable progress to end another day, growing large on the horizon as if unwilling to go.

Father William Simpson admired the sunset from the porch of his church. The main town church, an inspired design by Pugin, was silhouetted half a mile away, square against the pink sky. Father Simpson wished once again that it were still catholic. It seemed ironic to him that the large Suffolk churches, protestant since the reformation, should have neither the congregations or the resources to support them, yet three times each Sunday, his church, Saint Theresa's, a small red brick catholic chapel, was packed to the seams.

A few years earlier William Simpson had been a Benedictine monk, engaged in his first love; composing music for the liturgy of the church. A shortage of priests on the 'front line' led to him being rapidly ordained and sent out into the 'real world.' A young man, holy in the truest sense of the word, William found himself totally unprepared for the roles of sociologist, psychologist and councillor, which had fallen to him since becoming the Melbury parish priest. Nevertheless, he applied himself energetically to the ministry and after a nervous start he began to enjoy the challenge. Besides, Father Simpson loved the town itself and he also enjoyed the popularity that his youth and integrity had earned him. When not on official church business William rarely wore his dog collar, preferring to dress casually in an open necked shirt, or a baggy sweater. The priest was also conscious that this informality made him seem less stuffy and more approachable. It certainly made his parishioners more comfortable when he turned up, unannounced, on their doorsteps. Some of them had even taken to having a bottle of benedictine handy for that occasional glass that 'father' allowed himself. Much to his alarm Father Simpson was particularly popular with the ladies of the parish. Disarmed by his appearance and confident in the fact that he was a priest, they felt able to discuss their innermost secrets with him. This often left William blushing to the core, but this general gossip and the information divulged to him in the confessional, made Father Simpson the most well informed person in Melbury. He was quite aware of the intricate lives that were being woven under the surface of the quiet Suffolk town.

David Robinson stirred under the pale yellow duvet. With a start he snatched up his watch from the bedside cabinet, his body relaxing as he registered the time. How had he managed doze off for so long he wondered. Looking across at the slumbering figure lying next to him he threw back the covers and rolled his feet out of the bed onto the white sheepskin rug. His head felt distinctly groggy; it must have been the red wine. He looked again at the slim figure, which was now beginning to move. This, he thought, had to stop. Jackie White yawned, made a disappointed grimace and stretched her arms and legs at full length.

"Do you have to go?" she asked pouting.

David admired Jackie's cat like movements as she stepped from the bed and moved gracefully towards him; no wonder he could not resist her. She wrapped her arms around his neck and began to kiss his chest. David pushed her away reluctantly.

"Look, we've both got to go, Frank will wonder what's going on if you keep staying out. If he rumbles us we're in Queer Street."

Frank White was the owner of the largest estate agent chain in the region. David had been having an affair with Jackie, Frank's wife, for six months now. It troubled David. Frank White, whilst a good boss, was not a character to cross. He was typical of some of the London overspill that had become successful in the local area. During the rapid expansion of his business in the early eighties Frank had been ruthless with his opposition and a godsend to his clients. He charged half the commission of other agents and when his main adversary, Arthur Wells, resorted to some mild intimidation, Frank White had responded in kind. Some of Frank's London acquaintances had visited 'Wells Properties' and Arthur, who was struggling to stay solvent anyway, decided on balance to let Frank buy him out. David had little doubt about the result of Frank discovering the affair. Jackie had similar sentiments. She had wanted David the moment she had met him. How clever of her husband to employ such an attractive man she thought. She did not, however, wish to give up the freedom and style that wealth brought her. She no longer loved Frank but she enjoyed his success. Right now she liked things just as they were.

Jackie padded naked to the bathroom confident in the assurance that there was little to criticize in her thirty two year old figure.

'Perfect' thought David, marvelling at Jackie's body as she disappeared behind the bathroom door. 'How do I give this up.' He absently pulled the bedroom curtain open an inch and peered at the world outside. Albert Stern's house was offset slightly to the right, beyond that the town lay peacefully. 'A perfect night' he murmured. A full moon illuminated the slight haze from the river and the mirage of a sunset hung in the night sky. Just as he was about to drop the curtain he noticed a dark figure flit across Albert Stern's lawn.

Jackie White looked into the mirror and held a wet flannel over the lower half of her face. The temazapan she had put in David's wine had obviously worked as he had not noticed her absence whilst he slept. She looked at the black frightened eyes staring back at her from the mirror. Then she thought about the situation. What a mess. Jackie had chosen that night to visit Stern because she had a perfect alibi. Her husband knew that she was working late with David and David was kept out of the picture with the sleeping pills. She would like to have confided in David but she didn't want to risk losing him. This, she thought, was just between her and Albert Stern. The door swung open and David walked into the bathroom. He wrapped his arms around her from behind and spoke gently to her reflection in the mirror.

"We had better go."

"Yes," she said, then turned and pulled him close, her cheek resting on his chest. David stroked her long black hair.

"Frank's bound to find out if we stay this late." He spoke quietly.

Jackie talked against his body. "He doesn't suspect anything..I describe you as boring and pompous to Frank, it makes him laugh when I say I'm not surprised you don't have a girlfriend, he even tries to defend you!"

She pulled back, looked up at him and grinned.

"He thinks that I think you're a bit of a prat!"

"Bloody cheek." David feigned annoyance. " But how do we explain working this late?"

"Easy," she said, "we've been out doing a survey at Bulmer Cot

16

tage. Frank knows how busy I am during the day and insists that I have an escort if I go into the countryside at night. I don't know what he's worried about but he'd rather have a prat like you to defend me than have me go out on my own."

Jackie laughed, and darted off into the bedroom. David chased her playfully.

"You!" He grabbed her towel and Jackie squealed as he tried to unravel it from her waist.

They realised that they were making a lot of noise.

"Stop it," Jackie cautioned David with her eyes.

"We had best be going.."

They dressed quickly and left the building by the back door. Jackie had deliberately deterred customers from the rented cottage because it had been ideal as a love nest for David and herself. The cottage was quiet and private, the nearest neighbour being old Mrs Cummings and she kept herself to herself. Albert Stern had ruined it of course, but that could not have been anticipated.

They slipped out of the backdoor, through the back gate, and across a dark courtyard to the barn where David hid his car. David drove a careful route to the office and stopped outside. Jackie looked at him briefly, squeezed his hand and got out. As he drove home David vowed not to take anymore risks with Jackie. He would be more careful, he couldn't stop now, he had fallen in love. He still felt strangely groggy.

Bernie Small ran out of Albert Stern's house. He made unsteady progress across the lawn, the fresh air made him giddy as it fuelled the alcohol in his system. Things hadn't gone at all well in Stern's house, Stern owed Bernie almost two thousand pounds in gambling debts and Bernie needed the money. He should never have allowed the debt to accumulate but Stern's suave manner and assurances had prevented him from pushing the issue. Bernie always had a grudging respect for class anyway and Stern's presence at his card school had given it an air of respectability. Also Stern was not a bad poker player. Bernie rather enjoyed it when everyone else had stacked their hands leaving he and Stern to brave it out across the table. The stakes had become higher as Stern tried to recover his debts. Bernie loved that part.

"Sure you're good for that Albert?" He would say provocatively as

Stern raised the stakes.

Stern would look across at Small, tilt back his head and brush his moustache with his forefinger.

"I think we can manage Mr Small."

'Manage my arse,' thought Bernie. He had reached the road and paused trying to think which way to turn. He held onto the gate, swaying, then set off towards the town.

Perhaps he shouldn't have gone there drunk, but Stern had made him see red with his constant stalling.

"My dear Bernie," he had said, "you'll get your money, it's just a little hard to access it right now."

Small had grabbed Stern by the lapels.

"Call yourself a gentleman," he had said.

But Stern's seventy year old frame wasn't used to such treatment and perhaps Bernie had been rougher than he intended; either way Stern lost his footing, and fell, striking his head on the corner of a chair. Bernie, not thinking straight through a dozen or so whiskies, watched with alarm as Stern's eyes rolled to the top of his head. Bernie looked at the motionless figure for a moment and then fled in panic. He did not even noticing the small grey Volvo, parked in the dark shadows under the Chestnut trees, fifteen yards to his right.

Mrs Cummings saw him leave. The nightly vigil of gazing from the window was proving more eventful than usual. It did little to lift her continuous depression, but it did make her evening very interesting; unlike Bernie Small, Mrs Cummings *had* noticed the grey Volvo..

Lenny James sat in the Volvo. His eighteen stone spread generously over the front seat. Around him had amassed an untidy pile of chocolate wrappers. Lenny's heavy asthmatic breathing misted up the windscreen and he wiped it with the back of his hand to try to see out.

Lenny James had seen better days. In his youth he had been a professional boxer and with a certain amount of success. There was even talk at one stage of Lenny having a shot at the British title. Unfortunately, in the early sixties, Lenny fell upon hard times and into bad company. He began to make a living as a 'minder' and was sometimes recruited to bring his weight to bear upon uncooperative clients who were not responding favourably to the generous offer of 'protection' which his employers had made. At one time Lenny was considered a 'man to know' in the doubtful scene of the gangland East End of London. A long spell in prison and even harder times had eventually brought about Lenny's downfall. Now, in poor health, he just did odd jobs for his old friends. This one was a right pain though.. Lenny unwrapped another bar of chocolate..

Debbie recovered her composure. Seeing Mr Finch running clumsily through the woods had alarmed her. What on earth had he been up to covered in what looked like boot polish? She felt embarrassed being caught in the woods like that, before long the whole town would know. As it was they were convinced that she was having a 'thing' with Mr Stern. 'If only they knew,' she thought. Her companion was Ian Green, a young farmer from Ixdon. He pulled her towards him. Debbie pushed him away.

"What was he doing?" she asked, looking nervously into the woods where Ronald had disappeared. The trees, half lit by the nearby houses, looked ominous and eerie. Ian was not concerned. He had other things on his mind.

"I don't know," he said, "this town is full of weird people, come here."

Ian pulled gently on her arm; Debbie was irritated. She pushed him away again. This was the third time she had gone out with Ian and his attitude tonight was annoying her.

"No! Leave me alone. Look, that was Mr Finch; he had just come from Mr Stern's place hadn't he? What *was* he doing, his face all black like that?"

"I don't know." Ian shrugged, "perhaps he fell in a ditch, come on Debbie, give us a kiss."

Debbie was in no mood for Ian's affections. She had a troubled meeting with Albert Stern earlier and was puzzled at Finch's antics. She turned and walked around Stern's grounds back to the main road. Bernie Small was staggering up the street weaving a mean course towards the town centre, across the road Debbie could see the figure of Mrs Cummings in the upstairs window, silhouetted by the moonlight reflecting off her pale bedroom walls. The grey Volvo in the darkening inky night was now invisible under the large rustling chestnut trees.

Forty miles away in the centre of Norwich, 'Alfredo's', a recently opened Italian 'theme' cafe, was filled with chattering couples sitting crammed at small pine tables. On the tables red candles flickered brightly in wicker-clad Chianti bottles. The candlelight reflected in the large restaurant windows, which were tastelessly draped with heavy red curtain material. The purpose of the heavy curtains was to lend warmth to the room, but they also served to deaden the intrusive cacophony of cutlery and glasses that would otherwise have spoilt the cosy atmosphere within the tiny restaurant. Unobtrusively, by one of these curtained windows, sat Nick King, with his long term, or as she would describe it, long suffering girlfriend, Amanda.

Norwich, apart from being a county town, was arguably the most exciting city in East-Anglia and Nick had recently started work there as a journalist with The Norwich Standard, the main city newspaper. He was very happy with the position, having spent two years with a small town free press reporting on dull provincial issues. Now, he felt, he was making progress towards serious journalism. The Norwich Standard had a respectable circulation and perhaps, Nick thought, if he played his cards right, he was just a short step from a job with a national newspaper. That day his optimism and ambition had been dealt a crushing blow. Derek Bryant, The Norwich Standard editor, had given Nick a mundane story to report on. He had to go to Melbury to cover an aspect of the forthcoming 'Beekeeper Show.' Nick felt so disappointed that Amanda had insisted on taking him out to Alfredo's restaurant for dinner.

Nick sipped a glass of red wine appreciatively and looked closely at the label on the wine bottle in front of him.

"You know," he said, tilting the bottle back slightly, "I don't think they realise how good this Chianti Classico is; 1994 is supposed to have been a great year in Tuscany. It's worth coming here just for this, especially at ten pounds a bottle."

Amanda Jennings looked curiously across the table; she fiddled with the stained Chianti wine cork, turning it nervously in her fingers. She knew she was about to embark upon a controversial subject and she also knew that it usually ended up with an argument. But as

Nick seemed to have cheered up a bit she was going to go there anyway.

"N-i-c-k," Amanda's tone suggested a subject of some gravity. Nick continued his inspection of the wine label.

"Hmm?"

"Do you think we will ever be together?"

Nick looked up from the wine bottle, puzzled.

"We are together."

"No, I mean *really* together."

"We are really together."

"You know what I mean, I mean *living* together."

Here we go, thought Nick; marriage; commitment; babies.

"How do I know what's going to happen." He answered shrugging. "Que sera sera."

Nick hated this: the evening, he knew from experience, was now ruined. Amanda was now going to go on about 'being together' all night. He didn't know how he put up with it really; he supposed he was just a good bloke.

"You're a man aren't you?" said Amanda, this in her mind, being a perfectly good reason for Nick 'knowing things'. The wine cork, finally obeying the laws of physics, flicked out of her fingers and onto the wooden floor. She glanced down as the cork spun under the table next to them.

"Besides," she continued, "life is not, 'what will be will be', we are masters of our own destiny."

"Look," said Nick patiently, he placed his palms flat on the table. "Let's not spoil the evening talking about this again. lets talk about something else." He reached for one of the dry Italian bread sticks that were lying in a basket on the table and absently dipped it in his wine.

"I don't want to talk about something else, you always try to change the subject."

"Let's talk about my thrilling assignment in Melbury," said Nick with some sarcasm. He broke the breadstick in half, showering crumbs on the tablecloth in front of him. "I can't believe it, they have a riot here in Norwich and I'm sent to cover a stupid story about rivalry at a flower show."

"I thought it was called the Beekeeper Show?" Amanda looked

disapprovingly at the mess on the table.

"Apparently it's called The Beekeeper Show for some unknown, disappeared in the annals of history, reason, but it's really an horticultural show. Apparently two old men in Melbury are at war over who wins it every year, anyway my editor seems to think it's a good 'human interest story,' so I've got to spend a couple of days down there. It shows you with what high esteem The Norwich Standard holds me in. I mean I used to do fetes and flower shows with the free press, now, I when I think I might get some decent assignments, they send me to cover a blasted horticultural show!" Nick snorted in disgust and took a large frustrated gulp from his wine glass.

Amanda could see that Nick was still fed up. She tried to cheer him up.

"Well you've only just started with The Standard. Besides," she said optimistically, "I can come with you, we can make it a sort of holiday. Melbury is supposed to be a really pretty town."

"Well you can't."

"Why not?"

'Because you're a pain in the ass that's why,' thought Nick.

"Because there is no way that the newspaper will pay for a double room that's why."

Nick opted for a more diplomatic answer.

A young waitress appeared at Nick's side, she looked at the breadstick scattered over the tablecloth.

"How is your meal sir?"

Nick looked up at a waitress, trying to work out if she was trying to be sarcastic. He decided she wasn't.

"We haven't actually had a meal yet, we are still waiting to order."

The waitress looked embarrassed, the hint of reprimand in her voice disappeared.

"Oh, I'm very sorry sir, we are terribly busy tonight."

"Another bottle of the Classico might ease the pain," Nick smiled at the girl disarmingly.

The waitress seemed relieved.

"I'll see what I can do sir. This evening's specials are on the blackboard by the door." She turned on her heel and hurried off, dodging around the tables towards the kitchen.

"We don't need a double room. We can cuddle up in a single bed.

It will be romantic."

"Pardon?" Nick looked blankly at Amanda, he picked absently at the red candle wax that had run down and solidified in lumps on the side of the Chianti bottle in front of them. "Oh, oh yes, Melbury. No you don't understand I'm going there to work, it's not a holiday."

Amanda's lips quivered in disappointment, "I could help you." Nick looked at her: she was quite irresistible, with boyish cropped auburn hair and perfect little features she looked like a French film star from the sixties, perhaps the heroine to Belmondo. All she needed was the blue striped T-shirt. She got on his nerves of course, but he guessed he still loved her, in a sort of way anyway.

"I'll be very discreet," insisted Amanda, "and I might be useful."

"It's out of the question," said Nick firmly, "I know you normally get your way, but this time I'm putting my foot down."

Chapter 3

The next morning Nick and Amanda set off towards Melbury, Amanda, sitting contentedly in Nick's rather tired Volkswagen, was enjoying the East Anglian scenery.

"Isn't it lovely," she said, "look at the poppies in that cornfield, there must be a thousand of them."

Nick was a little annoyed with himself for giving way to her.

"Now see here," he said sternly, "you can come around with me in Melbury but pretend that you're my assistant, don't ask any questions. Ok?"

Amanda looked up at him and smiled.

"I like us going away together," she said happily and, despite the limitations of the Volkswagen, she pulled herself up on the seat, leaned across and kissed Nick firmly on the cheek.

Nick gave an exasperated sigh. 'I'll just have to hope for the best he thought.' He had to admit though, it was quite nice having Amanda with him. Just then his mobile telephone rang. It was Derek Bryant, the editor of The Norwich Standard.

Ronald Finch lay in bed late the next morning thinking about his previous night's activities. He felt a mixture of remorse and excitement; the excitement was partly because he was beginning to feel rather brave about his adventure and partly because he knew at last, that this year, he would beat Stern at the Beekeeper Show. At eleven-o'clock he wandered downstairs. Mrs Finch was already bustling back from town, her Thursday morning shopping curtailed early.

Ronald made his way to the kitchen. The night's exercise had given him an appetite so he prepared a breakfast of eggs, bacon and hot buttered toast. Then he remembered the strong Kenyan coffee that was part of the Christmas hamper they had won in last years raffle. He found the percolator at the back of a cupboard, filled it clumsily and then ravenously devoured the food as the percolator spluttered noisily in the background. Finally, satisfied, he poured some coffee and sat back in the pine farmhouse chair to study his weekly gardening magazine.

Mrs Finch burst through the back door, startling her husband by her unusually expeditious entrance.

"Ronald, *Ronald* what have you done!"

Mrs Finch wrung her hands, Ronald looked at her, puzzled, he wasn't thinking very quickly this morning. He looked at the mess he'd made preparing his breakfast.

"Oh, I'm sorry dear, I'll clear it up in a moment."

"No no! What did you do last night? It's all round town!"

His wife was clearly upset; surely Stern's bad luck could not be public knowledge already. The old boy must have been totally reliant on that plant to win the show if he's already put the word out. Perhaps he even suspected sabotage. Either way there was no hiding it from Dorothy. Finch put his coffee on the pine table and tried to explain.

"I didn't intend to do it really, I just got there and my hand.."

Mrs Finch interrupted him by wailing and combined shaking her hands with a curious jerking movement of her body. Even to Finch her dismay seemed excessive.

"Nobody knows I did it," reasoned Ronald bleakly.

"It could easily have been done by a beetle."

"A beetle!.. A BEETLE!" Mrs Finch began to weep holding her hands against her face.

"You are mad!" The words came stifled from behind her hands, "I knew you didn't like Mr Stern but I didn't know you hated him that much."

Ronald was beginning to think it was getting out of hand; he decided to sound upbeat.

"At least I'll win the Beekeeper Show this year," he said cheerfully.

His wife looked at him strangely, as if seeing a new man.

"MAD!" she cried, "What shall we do? Oh God!"

Mrs Finch was not prone to profanity, Finch put a comforting arm around her shoulder, she shook him away.

"Get your hands off me you *murderer*!"

25

Now Ronald Finch had always had the greatest respect for pom pom dahlias and ruining one deliberately was undoubtedly a sacrilege; had he not tried to perfect them himself for nearly thirty years? Nevertheless, he would not have described the desecration of one in such emotive terms.

"It's not that bad dear," he consoled her, "look on the bright side," Finch shrugged his shoulders and spread his hands expansively, "this year there's *no* competition!"

He allowed himself a chuckle despite himself. Mrs Finch fled the kitchen and ran upstairs with a shriek.

Melbury was in turmoil. Since its weaving days the town had not seen such activity. People blocked the pavement in small agitated groups and the bar at the Bell was bursting at the seams. The news of the death of Mr Stern had broken at ten o' clock. Mrs Waterer, his cleaning lady, had found him. She had entered Stern's kitchen at nine o' clock and collected together some cleaning materials from the cupboard below the sink. Normally at this time of day Mr Stern would be sitting in the kitchen dressed in his silk dressing gown and reading the morning paper. She had gone to see if he was in the lounge and as she turned into the hall the sight that greeted her was now the talk of Melbury. Stern was lying in a pool of blood that seeped across the cream hall carpet, he was on his side, half in the hall and half in the lounge, his eyes staring vacantly into space. One arm was inclined at an impossible angle and his mouth gaped under his tangled moustache. A large kitchen knife protruded from his side. Mrs Waterer had not screamed. She had stood motionless for seconds allowing the reality of what she was seeing to sink in, then, her hands shaking, she had gone to the hall telephone.

Larcum pumped the beer at the Bell and moved between animated conversations at the bar. "Debbie said she saw 'im running from the house at half past eleven," said Ivan Hillsdon, the town blacksmith. "Finch has always hated old Stern on account of his winning at the Beekeeper Show every year."

"He didn't like him for a lot of other reasons 'n all" Jenny Larcombe said darkly, she had closed down her haberdashers shop to keep up with the story.

26

"Yeah but 'ee wouldn't murder 'im," Roy Barnes took a magisterial stance, his strong Suffolk tones adding authenticity to his point. "that old duffer wouldn't harm a fly.. unless it were a greenfly that is." He cackled an unhealthy woodbine laugh. Old Mrs Baker, known throughout Melbury for her unfortunate malapropisms, clutched her sherry.

"People is strange you know," she said ominously. "Years of losing that show probably made 'im crack. He was strong though, look at them trees 'ee pulled up last year." Little slipped attention in Melbury. "Watch mind," she added, nodding grimly. "The long testicles of the law will catch up with 'im."

"Tentacles dear," said Jenny Larcombe patiently. "Anyway you've got it completely wrong as usual; It's the long arm of the law, not long tentacles."

"Well I don't care, whatever," said Mrs Baker, undaunted. "They've got Ronald Finch hot stick and wanker."

Roy Barnes roared with laughter and slapped his leg.

"Hook line and sinker," said Jenny, looking sternly at the old lady. "Really Mrs Baker, you're getting worse. We're going to have to do something."

"She's all right," said Roy jovially. "Leave her be, anyway, she's right, old Finch has had it."

Larcum appeared over the bar, "another sherry Mrs Baker?"

"She's had enough," said Jenny. "She's hardly making any sense now. Gawd knows what she'll come out with if she has any more." Throughout the bar the conversation continued to revolve around the murder. The general consensus was that Finch had gone over the edge and had done for Mr Stern.

The police appeared at Mr Finch's house a little after lunchtime. Inspector John Downs looked every part the efficient detective, albeit from the 1950's movies which he had loved as a boy and which had inspired him to join the police force. He wore a light brown suit and a brown racing trilby. At his side stood the stalwart Sergeant Ellis, a local man used to handling late night drunks and shoplifters, he was a little in awe of Inspector Downs, who, to Sergeant Ellis, had all the attributes of the policeman he aspired to be. What Sergeant Ellis did not realize was, that despite his authoritarian manner and self-conviction, Inspector Downs was, in fact, rather stupid. Downs, contrary to all police training, formed opinions and conclusions from very limited facts, relying on what he called 'nouse' and a 'hunch.' This ability to perceive answers with very limited information explained his presence in Melbury. Already in his career he and his hunch had arrested an off duty policeman and a bishop, both of whom were about their lawful business. Inspector Down's superiors decided that although Downs was undoubtedly a dedicated officer, he might do less harm in rural Suffolk. Theoretically the population of Melbury and the surrounding area could have qualified for a Superintendent as their chief policeman, but the lack of crime and general slow pace of the neighbourhood convinced Chief Superintendent Ross, the Norwich Police Chief, that an inspector would suffice and furthermore that the post was perfect for John Downs.

In fact Downs experience prior to being sent to Norwich was considerable. Despite his occasional errors he could have qualified for work on major incidents, even as part of a murder squad, should one be required. Thus, Chief Superintendent Ross, having scrutinized Inspector Down's career file, felt rather pleased that he had managed to send him to Melbury.

"Of course the position warrants a Superintendent," he had told Downs airily, "but with your experience I feel confident that you can cope."

Despite his Chief's flattering speech, Inspector Downs realized that in Melbury he was out of the main career stream of the police force. Now though, with a murder on his patch, he had the chance to show what he was worth. He already had enough information to be sure that Finch had murdered Stern, but he would play it carefully. After all he had been pretty convinced about that bishop holding up the building society, only he had missed some fairly revealing facts; namely that the suspect was in fact, The Bishop of Wessex who had, at the time of the crime, been celebrating a church service in front of a congregation of about two hundred people. He had released the bishop straight away of course and as he explained to his superior officer at the time, he was completely unaware that the car used in the crime had been stolen from the bishop's house that morning. Bad luck really. Anyway, this time, it would be different.

Sergeant Ellis knocked at the old cottage door; Ronald Finch appeared and looked blankly from Sergeant Ellis's uniform to the solemn face above the brown suit.

"Mr Ronald Finch," the face spoke. Inspector Downs was enjoying the moment.

"Yes," Finch still looked blank.

"My name is Inspector John Downs of the Melbury Police, I would like you to accompany me to the police station to answer questions regarding certain events that happened last night. You need not say anything but any thing you do say will be written down and may be used in evidence against you." Downs kept it deliberately vague; he smarted from the bishop affair, this time he wanted a confession, preferably before provincial forces got involved.

Sergeant Ellis looked concerned. He hesitated, but finally spoke, or rather he hissed under his breath.

"Don't forget the lawyer sir."

Downs looked blankly at Ellis, then realized what he meant.

"Ahem, Oh yes, and you have the right to a lawyer and if you do not have one, a lawyer can be provided." Down's was annoyed with himself; thus far in his career he had yet to get the wording of a caution right.

Ronald's heart sank. This was all too much. His reputation in the neighbourhood must be preserved at all costs; he could not bear the shame of Melbury knowing that he had cheated to win the Beekeeper Show. As is often the case with folk who consider something important, they assume that subject has the same precedence with everyone. For Ronald Finch, winning at the annual Beekeeper Show was his equivalent to a New Year honour, the finest accolade; a success that would enable him to hold his head high in Melbury. It did not occur to Ronald's obsessed mind that the sabotage of a pom-pom dahlia was not of sufficient consequence to occupy police attention: Finch spoke nervously.

"Is it to do with what happened at Albert Stern's? My wife told me about it."

"It is," Downs was guarded, could this lead to an admission? Finch continued.

"It sounds like the work of a beetle to me." Ronald wished that he had never gone over to Stern's house.

"I beg your Pardon?"

"It sounds like a beetle did it, I'm an expert in these things."

Downs turned to Sergeant Ellis who was busy scribbling on a small pad.

"What did he say?"

"He says he thinks a beetle did it sir."

Ellis turned his eyes, the rumour that Finch had gone mad and murdered Stern was the talk of the town but he had not realized quite how insane the old boy had become. Inspector Downs was taken aback, nevertheless, drawing on previous experience he was determined that Finch should incriminate himself. Downs spoke quietly but carefully.

"How, exactly," he paused for effect, "how exactly did a beetle do it sir?"

Finch looked at Downs fearfully.

"It ..it just sounds like the sort of thing a beetle would do," he said lamely. Downs decided that the line of conversation was too good to miss, Sergeant Ellis scribbled furiously.

"Have you ever seen a beetle with a carving knife sir?"
Sergeant Ellis clenched his jaw but he could not prevent a slight guffaw escaping. He looked guiltily at Inspector Downs who scowled back.

Finch seemed puzzled; Inspector Downs obviously knew nothing about horticulture or chafer beetles.

"No, chafer beetles just use their jaws, they can do immense damage."

Downs looked ominously at the quaking Finch. "*This* beetle, it appears, used a large stainless steel carving knife!" His voice rose at the end of the sentence, Finch was totally confused and intimidated, he began to bluster.

"I-It can look that way..I-I mean their jaws sort of zig-zag, it could look like a carving knife.." Finch tailed off and looked apprehensively at the policemen. Inspector Downs could see that he that he was not going to get far on the doorstep. This, he thought, would need his finest interrogation technique. Downs instructed Sergeant Ellis to handcuff Finch and lead him to the waiting police car. He wasn't going to take any chances with this maniac.

Mrs Finch watched from the bedroom window as the two policemen led Ronald up the path. He looked defeated. His normally proud shoulders sagged. She felt a sudden surge of guilt that she was not standing by him. Even if he had done something awful she *was* his wife. Unsure of what action to take, Dorothy Finch did what she always did in circumstances of stress; she went to the church to pray.

Jackie White sat at her desk in the 'Francis White Realty' Melbury office. Outside the town enjoyed another glorious day in the unbroken hot summer. Jackie did not notice the weather. She lit her fourth Gauloise of the morning and tried to look engrossed in the survey of Bulmer Cottage. In fact, in her mind, she was picking through the events of the previous night; replaying the evening to herself as if she were reviewing a film. Jackie mentally marked events as they occurred: David was asleep under the effects of the temazapan. She dressed, touched up her make up, then slipped out through the rear cottage door and across the dimly lit road. Stern let her in via his own back door, ushered her into the lounge and in a suave manner, offered her a drink. She accepted a gin and tonic. He proffered a cigarette from a carved walnut box; "I prefer my own" she said, taking a cigarette from her case, allowing Stern to light it. She inhaled deeply then blew a blue haze across the room. She was nervous.

"It's no good playing the gentleman whilst you're trying to blackmail me." Jackie inhaled again from the cigarette and fixed Stern with an injured gaze, her blue eyes betraying inner turmoil. Stern turned to her gesturing with a crystal glass half full of whiskey, the ice rattled against the glass as he spoke.

"My dear, my dear," his tones were conciliatory and soothing.

"I am not blackmailing you, I am simply asking for your help. I dropped you the note because I have a few debts and I can't access any more cash. You wouldn't believe the financial demands being made on me right now; people these days simply have no patience." Jackie drew on her cigarette again, and then after looking pensively but unfocused at the floor, returned her fixed gaze to Stern.

"If I interpret your letter correctly you want two thousand pounds just to keep your mouth shut." Stern winced, hunched his shoulders and gestured magnanimously with his hands.

"Really Jackie, I am simply asking for assistance with my finances. Naturally I will pay you back when I can. I only mentioned that I was aware of your little liaison with young Robinson because I thought it might encourage you to help me, both of us sharing the secret sort of thing." Stern sipped his drink and his eyes twinkled mischievously at his guest.

"Are you aware," said Jackie stubbing her cigarette out in a glass ashtray, "of what my husband might do if he found out?"

Stern grimaced. "I know that Frank is.. shall we say a rough diamond, but come come Jackie, I'm not going to tell anyone! I'm sure you won't mind helping me out. I mean I would normally go to the bank but they don't seem very enamoured with me right now."

Jackie stared pensively into her drink. "How do I know you won't ask for more in the future?" She asked. Stern seemed hurt. "My dear Jackie you have my word as a retired British officer." Stern raised himself straight as if the point were incontrovertible.

Jackie looked at the lean old figure. He was clearly an unscrupulous rogue, but strangely she felt a little sorry for the old man. Despite his bravado he must be in dire straits to pull a stunt like this. Also there was something in his eyes that made her think that thirty or forty years earlier this old man was probably a lot of fun to be with. Fortunately, by virtue of her husband's success she had a good deal of money and other matters on her mind. Jackie looked at her watch and came to a decision.

"Quite frankly Mr Stern I have enough problems at the moment. I am quite disgusted with you, however I will lend you the money. I can assure you though, that if this becomes full scale blackmail I have no intention of participating." She looked angrily at the old man.

Stern held up his hand in mock defence. "I have had enough of the wrath of women in my life; your secret is safe with me I assure you. I feel a little embarrassed asking you for the favour as it is." Jackie looked sceptically at Stern; she doubted that he had ever been embarrassed in his life. Even in this situation confidence oozed through Stern's supposed humility. She put down her drink and started towards the kitchen, as she approached the back door Stern coughed politely. Jackie turned and gave him a contemptuous look. "Come to my office on Tuesday at about twelve thirty, I should be alone. If not ask for an evaluation or something." Then, turning, she ran out into the night.

Across the office a telephone began to ring. The sound permeated

Jackie's mind and brought her back to the present. Ethel, the branch secretary, picked up the receiver and Jackie returned to the problem which had occupied her morning: the police could probably connect the gin and tonic glass and the cigarette stub with a woman, however there was no reason why they should necessarily single *her* out. She had had no previous dealings with Stern. Of course she knew who he was, she had heard all about that silly rivalry between Stern and Finch at the show. Who hadn't in Melbury? It was a standing joke, but apart from knowing who he was, there was no link between her and the dead man: unless someone saw her going into or out of Stern's house of course. Jackie's heart began to thump as she thought again of the implications: she was being blackmailed! She had a motive for killing Stern! The letter! She began to panic as she rummaged in her bag for Stern's note. It was there; but was there a copy at Stern's house? Perhaps he kept records? She tried to calm herself. She had an alibi with David of course, but the whole purpose of the sleeping pills had been to keep David, literally, in the dark. The jangling bell of the front door brought her back to the real world for a second time. David appeared excited as he burst through the door.

"Have you heard the news?"

Ethel and Jackie looked at him. They had heard the news hours ago.

"Old Stern's been murdered! Stabbed with his own carving knife.." He looked around, disappointed at the lack of reaction to his words.

"We know," said Jackie projecting outward calm. "Where have you been? Everyone knew hours ago."

"Oh: I was out at Boulmer Cottage.."

"Good," said Jackie, "I've just been reading the survey of Boulmer Cottage. I want to go and look at the place again. Are you free now?" David caught the sense of urgency in Jackie's eyes. He looked at his watch. "Well, yes, I have a bit of time," Jackie picked up her handbag pushed her chair back and walked around the desk.

"I shan't be long Ethel, are you ok for a while?"

"No problem Mrs White, go out and enjoy the sunshine."

Ethel watched the pair leave. Something stirred in her female intuition. Mrs White was certainly not herself this morning, still, she thought, everyone in Melbury was upset about the murder. It was normally such a quiet town. Either way though, there was something

33

funny about those two.. Ethel dismissed the notion and decided to take advantage of the situation. She put on the kettle for a tea break and tried to think whom to telephone for a chat.

Bernie Small awoke at ten o' clock with a sandpaper dry mouth, a pounding head and no immediate memory of the night before. He looked at the alarm clock, groaned and delicately rolled out of bed, steadying himself for a moment on the gently sloping floorboards of the bedroom. His house, like most of the old properties in Melbury, was built without any foundations and was suffering from a few hundred years of subsidence. Bernie groped in the cupboard for some suitable clothes and then plodded wearily to the bathroom. Ten minutes later, vaguely refreshed, he emerged and made his way downstairs to the kitchen. Bernie's wife looked on sourly as her husband absently began to fill the kettle.

"This is a fine time to start the day," began Mrs Small.

"Oh great," groaned Bernie, holding a hand to his throbbing head. "Just what I need! You know what I thought to myself when I woke up this morning? I thought what you need to start the day Bernie, is a good nagging. After all you feel like death, you're practically bankrupt, you've got a hangover, business is goin' down the tubes, you're being sued by an ex-employee: a good nagging will do you good."

"All right, you've made your point," said Mrs Small, "but don't expect sympathy. If we're so hard up how come you can spend all night at the Bell; anyway you've missed all the excitement, there's been a murder in town last night."

Bernie picked up a teabag. "A murder, what are you talking about, what kind of murder?"

"Old Mr Stern was done in last night.. In his own home. Mrs Waterer found him this morning."

Small froze, teabag in hand. He suddenly remembered where he had been last night. He remembered Stern's fall and the way that the old man's eyes had rolled when his head had struck the chair. Bernie's wife was a little surprised at her husband's reaction.

"What's the matter with you?" She said. "The colour's gone right out of you. You'd better sit down."

Mrs Small pulled up a chair, Small slowly lowered himself into it, put his elbows on the table and raised a shaking hand to his forehead.

"Oh my gawd," he muttered.

Mrs Small was quite impressed at the effect her news had on her husband; normally he didn't listen to a word she said.

"Yes the whole town is buzzing, they reckon Mr Finch.."

"Hold on, shut up I'm trying to think!"

"Suit yourself, and don't expect any sympathy from me just 'cos you've been drinking all night."

Mrs Small picked up some dry washing and walked from the kitchen towards the stairs, muttering under her breath about how her parents were right about Bernie and how she should have married Lionel, even if he did have spots.

The more Small thought, the more he began to panic: his fingerprints were all over Stern's lounge.. oh gawd.. he hadn't meant to kill the old boy. Bernie looked at his watch, it was just gone eleven o' clock, he checked that his wallet was still in his trousers from the previous night, stood up and walked unsteadily to the front door. He wasn't quite sure what he would do, but he would start where he always did when business was bad or when his horse did not come in: Bernie headed for the Bell Hotel.

Father Simpson was alone with his thoughts in the vestry of Saint Theresa's Church. He was content with his own company and hummed tunefully to himself as he arranged his cassock on a hanger and then lightly polished the silver chalice. A smell of incense, a remnant of that morning's church service, lingered in the warm dry air, mixing pleasantly with the musty scent of the chapel interior. Gradually the priest became aware of a sound from inside the church invading his thoughts. He walked through the vestry, opened the door slightly and looked for the source of the noise. Mrs Finch was kneeling on the back row of pews, sobbing gently into her hands. Father Simpson, anxious not to clumsily invade someone's grief, walked diplomatically into the church and began to arrange some hymn books by the back door. Mrs Finch continued her sobbing unabated. Father Simpson approached her and put his hand gently on her shoulder.

"Dorothy," he said quietly, "what's the matter? Can I be of help?"

Mrs Finch looked up; her eyes were red and unhappy.

"Oh Father! .. That silly old man, I can't believe what has happened."

She clipped open her large handbag and rummaged inside to find a handkerchief, wiping her face before drawing a deep shaky breath. "Come indoors with me Dorothy," said the priest. "Come and tell me all about it."

The small doctor's surgery on Church Street was quiet that morning. Most of the townsfolk were more interested in the news of the murder than in dealing with their ailments. 'Just as well,' thought Madeleine Hart, 'Maddie' had dutifully arrived at her work as Doctor Vandersteen's receptionist to find a note from the doctor lying on her desk:

'Maddie,
I have suffered from a poor night's sleep. Please do not disturb me until midday.'

Maddie sighed. She had thought that being a doctor's receptionist would be an easy job, but David Vandersteen had been a difficult man to work for. He was undoubtedly a brilliant doctor, but since the death of his wife last year Vandersteen had experienced bouts of disinterest in his profession. On some days he would be fine, but on others his behaviour could be erratic and even hostile. People whom he considered malingerers and time wasters received very short shrift and were practically thrown out of his surgery, much to the alarm of waiting patients. On the other hand he dealt with some of his cases with great sensitivity; his own bereavement having made him particularly adept at counselling people who were having problems in their lives. The loss of Doctor Vandersteen's wife had been a great shock to him; they had been a devoted couple and a childless marriage had drawn them even closer to each other. Now, living alone, he had become rather eccentric and unpredictable. He had also become prone to sporadic attacks of migraine, which apart from disrupting appointments caused him to be bad tempered with anyone in his vicinity at the time.

Maddie dutifully rearranged the morning's surgery to start after lunch. Some patients protested but most were used to Doctor Vandersteen's ways, and despite them, still preferred him to alternative doctors in the area.

Maddie looked at her watch. It was twelve fifteen; she glanced at the door dividing the reception area from the doctor's house. She had better go and see if he was ready for the afternoon's work, she thought. She had heard no sign of movement from the house thus far that morning; usually she could hear something. 'Better risk his wrath and wake him,' she decided bravely. Maddie opened the adjoining door and wandered into the doctor's sitting room: the room was empty.

Maddie called out to make her presence less intrusive.

"Doctor Vandersteen!"

The house remained silent. She tried again.

"Doctor Vandersteen!"

He was clearly not awake yet. As Maddie made her way towards the stairs she noticed that the door connecting the living room to the consulting room was half open. Maddie turned back to look in. The doctor's desk lamp was on. Maddie walked across to the desk. As she was about to switch the lamp off she noticed a piece of foolscap paper, lying by Doctor Vandersteen's writing pad, a note was written in eye-catching bold capitals:

I cannot bear the loneliness anymore
I want to be with my wife

Maddie looked perplexed, then the significance of the note struck her. She felt her heart beating in panic as she ran back through the lounge and towards the stairs. She called out again.

"Doctor Vandersteen, where are you!"

Maddie reached the top of the stairs and hesitated. For some reason she looked in the bathroom. It was empty.

The doctor's bedroom was on the left she thought. The door was slightly ajar. Maddie pushed the door open. Doctor Vandersteen was lying on top of the bed fully clothed, the bedspread was covered in blood, as was the floor to both sides of the bed. Maddie looked horrified at the spectacle. She stepped closer to the doctor. He was clearly dead, both his wrists had been cut; a plastic sharp surgical knife lay in the pool of blood near his right hand. Maddie cupped her face in her hands, gave a strangled cry, turned and fled from the room.

Chapter 4

Inspector Downs looked curiously at the figure sitting opposite him. Ronald Finch was examining his hands nervously.

"Are you sure that you don't want a lawyer present Mr Finch?" Asked Downs. He glanced at a tape-recorder, which was whirring noisily on the table.

Ronald wanted as little fuss as possible. "No.. No really, it's alright."

Downs was fortunate to be conducting the investigation. He had just been on the telephone to Norwich. Chief Superintendent Ross, as it happened, was snowed under. The 'trouble with some football supporters' had become a full-scale riot in the Norwich town-centre. The Norwich 'Canaries' had beaten Millwall two-nil, and the Millwall 'mile end mob' had extracted their revenge by going berserk in the high street. Downs could hear the bedlam in the Norwich Police Station as Ross yelled at him down the telephone.

"Look here Downs, I've got a station full of hooligans, press, politicians, tell you the truth I'm not sure which is worse, either way you will have to start the preliminaries. Are you sure that it's a simple matter?"

"Absolutely sir, this is cut and dried. We've got witnesses, motive, everything. I mean the suspect has practically confessed!"

"Well I can't afford the men to set up a murder squad in Melbury.."

Chief Superintendent Ross paused as there was a loud scream followed by an equally loud crashing sound outside his office; Downs pulled the telephone slightly away from his ear and winced at the noise. Ross continued:

" Be lucky if we get out of this alive; it's like a bloody battlefield here."

Another crash punctuated the conversation.

"Yes sir," said Downs,   "I know that you are stretched up in Norwich." He held the phone away from his ear again as Ross shouted instructions above the pandemonium in the background.

"Yes sir," replied Downs, "I promise I won't screw it up. It's all under control, forensic chaps on their way? Marvellous, yes; absolutely; leave it to me, I can do everything else."

Bloody cheek! Screw it up indeed! Nobody trusted him just because of one little mistake. Mind you, he thought, perhaps the Chief Constable thought that arresting a bishop was a big mistake.

Downs flushed as he thought of it. He returned his attention to Ronald Finch who was still trying to think of an excuse for ruining what was probably the world's finest pom pom dahlia.

"Are you aware Mr Finch, as to why you are here?"

"Yes; well yes, I think so."

Downs continued. "This is a murder investigation."

Finch still felt that the sabotage of a pom pom dahlia, heinous though it was, should not be expressed in such emotive terms, but people were strange.

"I think murder is a bit strong," said Finch, "pom pom dahlias are notorious for beetle damage."

'Beetles again,' thought Downs, 'and now dahlias; this chap is stark raving crackers.'

Downs was beginning to wonder if he was safe in the same room as Finch. He looked across the small interview room at Sergeant Ellis, who was standing impassively by the door. 'I suppose it will be alright,' he thought. He addressed Ronald Finch again.

"Perhaps, sir, we could start with your movements, from say, nine o clock last night?"

Downs began the interview in earnest.

Finch tried to stay calm, "I.. er I was at home with my wife Dorothy, ..er, she was baking some cakes for the show."

"All night?" asked Downs, "You were in all night?"

Finch hesitated; he didn't like to lie, but his reputation..

"Well I may have gone out for a walk: you know, for some fresh air."

"With your face blackened and wearing a blue boiler suit perhaps?" Downs raised his left eyebrow inquisitively.

Finch was alarmed. The barmaid in the woods! He'd forgotten

about Debbie!

"Running through the woods from Mr Stern's house even." Continued Downs, he was enjoying this. These moments were rare in the career of a police officer.

A rap on the door interrupted the proceedings. Downs scowled, annoyed at the disruption.

"What do you want?" He called.

The bald head of the desk sergeant peered around the door. "Sorry to interrupt sir, forensic have arrived from Norwich."

"Send them to Stern's house," said Downs irritated. "Use your initiative Sergeant Price, this is a murder investigation!"

The head disappeared, closing the door.

'Forensic? Murder? That word again?' Finch was becoming worried. There was something going on here that he didn't understand. He began to query the situation.

"Exactly what.."

"I'll ask the questions here Mr Finch," said Downs officiously.

"But.."

"Let's get down to it Mr Finch," Downs decided it was time to force the confession.

"Did you or did you not, on the night of Wednesday the twenty first of August.."

Sergeant Ellis interrupted. "Sorry sir, the twentieth."

Downs looked up annoyed.

"What?"

"Today is the twenty first, yesterday was the twentieth."

Down's fixed Sergeant Ellis with an icy gaze.

"Are you trying to tell me that I don't know what day it is Sergeant Ellis?"

Ellis was about to reply when Ronald Finch joined in.

"The sergeant is right inspector, The Beekeeper Show is in ten days time on the thirty first, so today must be the twenty first."

"I'll get a calendar," said Ellis helpfully and rushed out of the room.

"No. Wait a minute! *Sergeant Ellis come back in here*," yelled Downs, then, realizing that this was undignified, he looked at Ronald Finch and began to rap his fingers on the desk humming quietly to hide his embarrassment.

Sergeant Ellis burst back through the door clutching a calendar.

"Yesterday was the twentieth sir, look.."

"Never mind! Never mind! Shut the door! Now." Downs composed himself.

"Mr Ronald Finch, did you or did you not, on the night of," he glanced menacingly at Sergeant Ellis, "Wednesday the twentieth of August.."

Downs thrust his face forward, "last night, murder Mr Albert Stern, of Jasmine Cottage, Melbury, with a large, stainless steel, carving knife!"

Downs flopped back in his chair. He had thought this was going to be easy.

Ronald looked at Downs, shocked. After a pause he spoke:

"Murdered! Albert Stern is dead! No, he can't be. I saw him yesterday!"

"You certainly did," said Downs grinning sarcastically. "You saw him just before you stuck *a bloody great knife in him*!" He really must stop raising his voice, he thought.

Ronald Finch began to feel faint. The room was beginning to spin.

"Do you think," he asked weakly, "do you think that I could have a cup of tea?"

Father Simpson stood up from his chair and walked across to the window. He looked for a moment at the tower of the town church. He was shocked by both the murder and by Dorothy Finch's story. He spoke quietly with his back to the room.

"Do you really believe that Ronald did this?" He asked.

"Well, he went over to Mr Stern's house last night and he came back saying he couldn't believe what he had done." said Dorothy, she had calmed down now. She knew that she had to be strong.

"What was his mental state like? I mean did he seem as if he had murder on his mind?"

Father Simpson turned around and walked back to sit next to Dorothy.

"Well no," Dorothy's lower lip quivered slightly, she breathed in deeply. "I mean he always gets a bit funny at this time of year, just before the show, but he's not violent, he's a good man."

"That's right," agreed Father Simpson, "I know Ronald and I don't believe that he could have killed Albert Stern, despite the apparent evidence. I think that the best thing we can do is to go across to the police station. First though let's say a prayer." Father Simpson held Dorothy's frail hands in his loosely joined palms and bowed his head.

"Oh Lord, grant us all the strength to endure coming trials, let justice and truth prevail and grant peace for the soul of our fellow parishioner, Albert Stern."

"Amen," said Dorothy. Suddenly she felt stronger, she looked up at Father Simpson and smiled faintly.

"I'm ready," she said, picking up her handbag. "Let's go."

As they reached the door to leave the telephone rang in the hall. Father Simpson answered it: it was clearly bad news; the priest shook his head continuously, after a brief farewell he turned to Dorothy.

"That was the Vicar," he said quietly, "It's Doctor Vandersteen on Church Street. Apparently he killed himself last night."

Jackie White sat in silence as David drove his company Vauxhall slowly along the winding lane leading towards Boulmer Cottage. David broke the silence.

"Alright, so what's this about Jackie? You don't want to see Boulmer Cottage again."

Jackie reached in her bag for a cigarette and fumbled with the car lighter.

"You can't smoke in the car," said David.

Jackie lit the cigarette and inhaled deeply before speaking.

"We're in trouble David."

David looked across at her, alarmed.

"What? You mean Frank's found out about us!" He looked back at the road, just in time to negotiate a corner.

"No, I mean I was over at Albert Stern's house last night."

David pulled onto the verge and stopped the car perilously close to a ditch. He turned in his seat and looked bewildered at his passenger.

"What are you talking about Jackie? You were with me last night."

Jackie gave a resigned sigh and started to explain.

"Stern was blackmailing me. Somehow or other he must have seen us both and put two and two together: either way he wanted two thousand pounds from me to buy his silence."

David leaned back in his seat and stared out of the windscreen at the distant poplar trees.

"The old bastard!"

Jackie continued.

"Anyway, I didn't want you involved, I thought you'd probably break off the relationship if you found out. You probably will anyway when you hear the rest. I decided to go and see Stern and the best time was when you were asleep. You know how we sometimes doze off after.."

She hesitated; David looked slightly embarrassed, Jackie rubbed the back of his hand and continued.

"Well anyway Frank thought that I was working late and it all seemed very convenient so I put a sleeping pill in your wine to make sure that you fell asleep. Actually I put two in."

David looked at Jackie incredulously. "You put sleeping pills in my wine?"

Jackie ignored him. "Then I went over the road to Stern's place and agreed, in the end, to pay him. It seemed the simplest way. To be honest I felt a bit sorry for him."

David looked shocked again. This was unbelievable. "You paid a blackmailer!"

Jackie looked impatiently at David. "No, I didn't pay him because he's been murdered hasn't he? I was going to pay him on Tuesday."

David sat in silence for a moment, then he stepped out of the car and stood by the field, looking across the ripe unharvested wheat that rippled in the light warm breeze. Poppies and pale blue corn-flowers broke up the swaying monotone of gold.

"You should have told me," he said, "I would have stuck with you."

Jackie stepped out of the car and leaned arms folded against the door. She looked at David and felt a little ashamed and foolish.

"I know."

"You must go to the police," said David. "You might be able to help them."

Jackie looked at David incredulously. "Are you mad? I was being blackmailed. They will think I did it. That is why we are in trouble. My fingerprints are all over a glass at Stern's house, it is probably covered in lipstick, then there is a cigarette end, perhaps two. Who else in town smokes French cigarettes? If the police start making a few enquiries and fingerprint a few people they could easily find me.

Then what? At best Frank finds out what has been going on, at worst I'm suspected of murder..you know: motive, circumstantial evidence. It's enough."

"Whew!" David exhaled dramatically and brushed back his hair with his fingers. "You've got a point!"

"Look." said Jackie, "we've been long enough, lets go back and think what to do on the way."

They drove in silence for a while, deep in thought. Then as the Melbury church tower appeared in the distance, Jackie spoke.

"David, right now they are pretty sure that Ronald Finch killed Stern, they think he flipped over losing at that Beekeeper Show every year and murdered him."

David slowed down as they were quickly approaching the town.

"So they don't suspect anyone else anyway, perhaps we are making too much of it. Is that what you mean?" said David helpfully.

"No David. That is not what I mean." Jackie adopted a patronizing tone. "What I mean is they are not looking for someone else right now, so maybe the police have not worried about the cigarette ends and the gin glass."

"You mean that the evidence may still be in Stern's house." said David.

"Exactly."

The couple thought about this as David turned over the stone bridge and into the high street. He stopped outside White's Realty, put on the hand brake and turned off the engine.

He turned to Jackie. "I suppose then," he said slowly, "we'd better go and get it."

Nick King switched off his mobile telephone and glancing at the display put it back on the dashboard of the Volkswagen. Amanda had been listening in disbelief to the conversation:

"Yes Mr Bryant, I am well on the way to Melbury; someone's been murdered you say! Yes I'm with it.. Yes it probably is domestic but I'll root around and see what the story is."

"What was all that about?" asked Amanda, incredulously.

Nick could hardly contain his excitement.

"Never mind the flower show, we are now on our way to report on a murder. An old man was found stabbed to death in his front room this morning. How about that! Destiny or what!"

Amanda scowled, "You know what my views on destiny are."

Nick turned off the main road onto the smaller lanes that led to the towns in the Bey Valley.

"This is a different kind of destiny," he explained. "You can't arrange for someone to be killed for a journalistic opportunity. This is fate."

Amanda looked concerned. "It sounds awful, I don't think you should be so pleased about someone losing their life."

Nick squeezed Amanda's hand and glanced at her approvingly. "You're right Amanda, I'm not pleased someone is dead, but this is an opportunity for me. I didn't make it happen, I just happen to be here. Don't shoot me, I'm just going to be the messenger.. and a damned good one at that!"

Ronald Finch sipped his cup of tea and looked nervously at Sergeant Ellis who sat impassively by the door of the interview room. Inspector Downs had been summoned urgently by Price, the Desk Sergeant and was now finding the cause of yet another interruption.

"It's a Miss Hart sir, she has just called from Doctor Vandersteen's surgery. Apparently the doctor has committed suicide, she was very upset so I have sent Constable Jones straight over."

Inspector Downs raised his eyebrows in surprise.

"Suicide? When did this happen sergeant? This morning?"

"Apparently not sir, Miss Hart only discovered the body at midday, the doctor had left a note not to be disturbed, there is also a suicide note with the body. Apparently he slashed his wrists."

The inspector shook his head in disbelief.

"What's the matter with this town? Nothing happens here for months and then everyone starts dying! Slashed his wrists you say?"

Inspector Downs shook his head again.

"Very well sergeant, send for an ambulance and for Doctor Rotton from Chapel Street. I'll meet the doctor there."

At Doctor Vandersteen's surgery the inspector, Doctor Rotton and the police constable surveyed the grim scene and awaited the arrival of an ambulance.

"Poor chap," said Doctor Rotton sadly, "he has been very depressed since his wife died but I never thought it would come to this."

"I suppose there is no doubt that it is suicide is there Doctor Rotton?" Asked the inspector. "I mean nothing has been broken into by the look of it, there doesn't seem any reason to suspect foul play?"

Doctor Rotton looked at the body and shook his head.

"No. Though I must say I would have thought that a medical man would have found a less painful and messy way of ending it all but people do strange things when they are depressed. There will have to be a post-mortem of course, but I think we can safely say the doctor here killed himself."

Inspector Downs looked relieved.

"Yes," he agreed. He looked around the room absently, "he's made a dreadful mess of the carpet."

Down's caught the doctor giving him an odd look; he cleared his throat.

"Yes, ah well er very well doctor, If I could leave the paperwork to you, the death certificate etceteras, I will just have a quick word with Miss Hart and then I'll get back to the station. There is a small matter of a murder to deal with."

"Oh yes," agreed Doctor Rotton, "that other matter, terrible, terrible! Poor Mr Stern!"

Inspector Downs left Doctor Rotton muttering to himself and walked to the reception area where Madeleine Hart sat patiently, looking pale and unhappy. She jumped to her feet when the inspector walked in.

"Ah, Miss Hart, please sit down, I know this has been very harrowing for you but I must ask a couple of questions before you go."

Maddie sat down and clasped her hands on her lap.

"Of course inspector please carry on."

Inspector Downs stroked his moustache with his right hand and stood by the reception desk. He found Maddie rather distracting. He normally did not have time for the opposite sex but Maddie was extremely beautiful with shining dark hair and feminine curves that could not escape unnoticed. The inspector found that his gaze kept straying to Maddie's bosoms, which were hidden, provocatively to Down's point of view, under a fairly conservative summer dress. Downs dealt with the situation by addressing the wall opposite whilst talking to her.

" Miss Hart how was Doctor Vandersteen's, er, shall we say 'manner' recently, I mean did you get the impression that he was suicidal?"

Maddie clasped and unclasped her hands nervously.

"Well yes, I mean no, I mean I didn't think that he would kill himself..Oh dear.."

Maddie held her face in her hands and sobbed unhappily.

"Oh poor Doctor Vandersteen, I should have thought.."

Inspector Downs walked over and nervously patted Maddie's shoulder. He was moved to see her so upset.

"There there Miss Hart, it has been a great shock, there was nothing you could have done. I suggest that you go home and we can talk later if necessary. We can deal with everything here, an ambulance will be arriving shortly."

Maddie looked up at the inspector.

"I can't go home inspector. I have to call all Doctor Vandersteen's appointments, and then someone has to speak to his family and relatives. I think he has a sister somewhere. Oh dear what a mess, I never realized he was so depressed."

Maddie began to weep again. The inspector sat down next to her.

"Miss Hart," he began sympathetically, "cancel the appointments then please go home. If you show Constable Jones how to contact any relatives, he can take care of that. Go home today, I'll talk to you tomorrow and you can sort out any administration that is needed."

Maddie took Inspector Down's advice and having telephoned the morning's patients she collected her handbag and set off home. After an ambulance had taken Doctor Vandersteen's body away the inspector drove the short journey back to the police station. He thought about Ronald Finch; he'd make him confess! The suicide was awful of course, then he thought about Madeleine Hart. It would be nice to talk to her again. She was very attractive..

Nick parked his car behind the Bell hotel and clutching their bags he and Amanda found their way through the front door to the cluttered hotel reception desk. The reception was unmanned but the lounge sounded busy so Nick walked in and stood patiently at the end of the bar. By the window a small group of people, seated around a small oak table, seemed in fine spirits. The gathering were obviously having morning coffee although the conspicuous presence of sherry and brandy glasses accounted for the boisterous conversation. This, thought Nick, was obviously a town meeting place and judging by their conversation, these people were in regular attendance. He made a mental note that such gossip parlour might be a useful source of information.

Jenny Larcombe was talking:

"Oh yes, mark my words, that Inspector Downs'll get a confession out of 'im."

Roy Barnes laughed. "That idiot! 'Ee couldn't get a confession from a canary! You watch 'im cock it up! I'm surprised 'ee 'asn't arrested Father Simpson with 'is record of arrestin' the clergy!"

The assembled group laughed, they had all heard about the bishop. Mrs Baker leaned forward, her sherry glass shaking perilously in her hand.

"Old Finch will copulate soon enough, you watch."

Roy looked perplexed.

"She means capitulate," said Jenny, who seemed to have the knack of understanding Mrs Baker. "At least I think so. I don't know why but everything she mixes up is rude. I'm sure she does it on purpose." She glared at Mrs Baker who scowled back unrepentantly.

Larcum sitting amongst the group noticed Nick; he stood up and spoke cheerfully.

"What can I do for you young man?"

"I'm Mr King from The Norwich Standard, I believe I have a room booked?"

"Ah yes," said Larcum, "my wife deals with bookings, If you go to reception she'll be through in a moment."

"Right-ho" said Nick, heading out of the room.

Larcum put his head through the kitchen door at the back of the bar.

"*Fran! Fran!* Customer at reception."

"*No need to yell!*" yelled Fran.

Larcum walked back to the table.

"She's an angel that wife of mine," he said proudly.

"You're lucky," chuckled Roy Barnes, "my wife's still alive," his yellowing woodbine stuck to his lower lip as he spoke.

"If you ask me you're lucky to have a wife!" Said Jenny Larcombe; "I wouldn't live with you!"

The group laughed. "Just think," said Roy wistfully, "If I'd strangled my missus on the honeymoon, I'd have been out by now."
Jenny rose to cuff him around the ear and Roy cowered in mock fear. Mrs Baker was feeling left out:

"My sons wife went hysterectomy when they split up," she nodded emphatically. "Said he kept pestering her."

Roy looked puzzled as usual.

"She means ex-directory," said Jenny, glaring again at Mrs Baker. "I don't know why you always mix things up in such a disgusting way Mrs Baker, I think you just like annoying me. Why even the space- shuttle became the something cock."

"Shuttle-cock," corrected Roy Barnes, "she called it the shuttle-cock."

"I know what I mean!" Said Mrs Baker defiantly, "I just get things a bit wrong sometimes that's all."

"Anyway," said Roy, feeling that Mrs Baker needed some support, "when she asked for that 'metropolitan' ice-cream she wasn't being rude."

"It was rude if you happened to be Neapolitan," pointed out Larcum from the bar.

Roy stood up, "I think for that comment Larcum," he walked across to the bar and winked at the assembled group, "you should stand Mrs Baker another sherry on the house."

At the reception desk Nick was confronted by a stone-faced landlady.

Fran Todd looked from Nick to Amanda and then back to Nick.

"The booking was for a single room," said Fran looking theatrically at Amanda's bare left hand. Amanda, embarrassed, moved her hand out of sight.

"Please Mrs Todd," said Amanda, "we never get the chance to go away together, this is such a treat."

Fran looked at Amanda's wide innocent eyes for a moment and then relented.

"Well..very well but it is only a single bed."

"We don't mind," said Amanda looking happily at Nick, it was Nick's turn to look embarrassed.

They signed the guest book and following Fran's directions,

climbed a dark stairway leading to the back of the hotel. After struggling with the key for a moment, Nick finally opened an oak door.
Amanda clapped her hands in delight.

"It's beautiful," she exclaimed. The room certainly had its charms,
with dark wooden walls, hanging tapestries and an Elizabethan fireplace. Nick put their cases by the bed.

"I was impressed by your performance downstairs," he said. "Your
charm could be quite useful in the next couple of days."

"It was nothing," said Amanda in mock modesty. "We girls have
our ways you know."

She sidled up to Nick and began undoing his shirt buttons.

"Stop it!" said Nick moving away, "I've got some serious work to
do.. and I think I might start my enquiries in that gossip parlour
downstairs.."

Downstairs the Bell customers had fallen silent digesting the lat-
est news. Word had reached them of Doctor Vandersteen's death.

Jenny Larcombe was the first to speak.

"The town is cursed I tell you, two strange deaths in one night! It
'aint natural!"

"Doctor Vandersteen!" said Roy Barnes incredulously; "who would
have thought it?"

Mrs Baker, who by now *had* drunk far too much sherry, joined in:
"that's all we need now!" She said, wobbling slightly, " a Karma-
Sutra doctor!"

"Kamikaze," corrected Jenny, automatically, "anyway I tell you,"
she added darkly, "there are unnatural forces at work in Melbury
right now."

Ivan Hillsdon had had enough.

"Oh shut up Jenny! It's an unfortunate coincidence that's all. Everyone knows that Vandersteen had been miserable since his wife died,
there is nothing unnatural about it."

Jenny eyed the blacksmith malevolently.

"Oh yes? You wait and see, I'll bet there is more than coincidence
to all this; you mark my words.."

Inspector Downs looked impassively at Ronald Finch. Back in the
police station he had resumed the interview but he seemed to be getting no nearer to a confession.

"So let's get this right," Downs said wearily, "you went to Stern's house covered in boot polish to look at Mr Stern's greenhouse, and you thought that you had been arrested for sabotaging a dahlia."

"Yes! That's it," said Mr Finch who had just about recovered from the shock of the news of Stern's murder. "Can I go now, my wife, Dorothy, she'll be worried about me."

Downs leapt out of his chair and snapped off the tape-recorder.

"No you can't bloody well go! Not until you admit that you murdered Albert Stern. You don't fool me with this feigned madness, it's a cunning ploy, you are really a ruthless scheming killer and the public is not safe until you are locked up!"

Mr Finch quaked at this onslaught.

"L..Look I think I'd better have a solicitor here a..and I want to see my wife, and I'm hungry."

Downs exasperated looked over at Sergeant Ellis. "Take the suspect away Sergeant Ellis. See that he gets fed and fix him a solicitor." Downs turned to look menacingly at Mr Finch. "We will resume this conversation later."

Father Simpson and Mrs Finch arrived at the police station and presented themselves at the front desk. The desk sergeant was immersed in a comic and started when Father Simpson coughed politely.

"Oh-sorry father.. Mrs Finch. It's been a long day."

"We've come to see Ronald Finch," said Father Simpson quietly.

"I'll just check and see if it's all right Father Simpson."

The desk sergeant began to play with the squawk box under his counter, a loud screeching could be heard at the end of the corridor.

Inspector Downs was yelling again as he marched up the corridor to the front desk.

"Turn that infernal thing off you idiot! I've told you.."

The inspector spotted the couple standing by the front desk. Downs greeted the priest cheerfully.

"Father Simpson! What a pleasure. What brings you to my establishment on such a fine day?"

"This is Mrs Finch," said the priest. "We have both come to talk her husband."

The inspector gestured courteously down the corridor. "Come into my office; you might have more success at getting a confession than I father!" He grinned tactlessly, then realizing his faux-pas, Downs grimaced.

"Yes-well," he looked at the priest ruefully, "I'm sorry, it's been a stressful morning as you can imagine. You heard about Doctor Vandersteen I suppose?"

"Yes, terrible news," said Father Simpson as they followed the inspector back down the corridor. "The Vicar telephoned me, if I can be of assistance please let me know. Right now though, if it is acceptable to you, we just want to talk to Ronald and see that he is all right."

"Well I don't know about that father," Downs gestured them both to the austere office chairs. "The questioning is at a very critical stage: I mean with all due respect to Mrs Finch here we've got enough circumstantial evidence to hang, er I mean convict Mr Finch already; I don't think a confession is very far away. We are just awaiting the arrival of a solicitor before continuing."

Downs leaned back in his chair and wiped the front of his moustache with his forefingers.

"Please let us see him inspector," said Mrs Finch leaning forward urgently, he must be very unhappy. I'm worried about him."

"He's not half as unhappy as poor old Albert Stern I can tell you!" Said the inspector. "Oh no! That's for sure and I can tell you that your husband trying to make out that he's stark raving potty wont work either. Beetles! Dahlias! I've never heard such rubbish!"

The desk sergeant's baldpate appeared round the door again.

"I'm sorry to bother you sir, it's Norwich on the phone."

Downs sighed and wiped his brow with his right hand.

"Oh gawd," he looked uncomfortably at the clergyman again. "Alright put them through, and take Father Simpson and Mrs Finch to Mr Finch; fifteen minutes and no more mind."

The couple were ushered out of the office and up the corridor. As they went they could hear Inspector Downs talking on the telephone.

"Oh yes sir, no problem whatsoever, forensic are there right now and I think we'll have a full confession by the end of the day; absolutely sir, no sir, don't worry I'll get it right; yes a most unfortunate suicide; no, there's no doubt about it; yes sir, I assure you it is all definitely under control."

Chapter 5

The two forensic officers drove their van slowly along the road and over the stone bridge. Fred Brown had been working in 'forensic' for two years and the sometimes-gruesome business had made him efficiently detached at his trade. Bill Simpkins was relatively new to forensic but was a skilled and incisive policeman, having spent some hectic years on the force in the East End of London. His wife had insisted upon him volunteering for 'forensic' training when the Metropolitan Police had decided that there should be a more direct link between criminal and forensic investigation. The new police chief had a bee in his bonnet about the two forms of crime detection drifting apart. Bill, still officially a Police Sergeant, was one of two 'serving' policemen in Norfolk used in a 'forensic training' trial. The experiment did not require them to have a deep scientific knowledge of the subject, but they were obliged to have a better than average understanding of what forensic science could do. Other police forces in the country had either civilian forensic investigators or a mixture of the two, civilian and uniformed. Bill the larger of the two men was driving the van. Fred was tucking into a sandwich.

"What do you think of it so far Fred, the silly bugger let them move the body straight off! No photographs, nothing! We've even got to go to hospital to see the murder weapon!"

"I know Bill," Fred scattered crumbs over the van as he spoke. "Downs is making a hash of it, fortunately he's probably got the right man; at least he's had the house guarded so the evidence should be uncontaminated; here it is.."

Bill stopped the van by a white fence and the two men surveyed the house.

"Jasmine Cottage," said Bill, "and very nice too. Lets leave the van here Fred, we'll check the drive as well."

Jasmine Cottage certainly did look 'very nice'. The front garden was a sea of roses and summer perennials, a mature green vine twisted up the front of the house and the musky scent of honeysuckle greeted the two officers as they opened the gate and walked over the mexican daises which spilled onto the path. A young policeman, PC Dobbs, opened the front door.

"Am I pleased to see you!" said the relieved young man. "This place is giving me the creeps. There's blood all over the place."

"We like a bit of blood." said Fred darkly. "It's all good forensic bread and butter to us." The young policeman glanced apprehensively at the half-consumed sandwich Fred was holding. The two officers stepped over the threshold and looked around the hallway. Fred spoke again.

"Go for a walk or something son; we'll be a while here. Just point us at the kettle.."

The bar of the Bell Hotel was filling with lunchtime custom. In the corner Bernie Small was muttering to himself and starting his fourth scotch.

"What's eating him?" asked Ivan Hillsdon, tilting his head in Small's direction.

Larcum looked across at Bernie. "I'm not sure, he came in about an hour ago and he's been drinking and mumbling to himself ever since. I can't get any sense from him. Could be he's worried about being sued by young Solomon Weinstein over that dismissal thing."

"A lot of people are acting a bit strange since old Stern's murder," said Jenny Larcombe, looking meaningfully around the bar. "Take that young Robinson for instance, don't usually see him in here drinking at lunchtime."

Sure enough David Robinson sat moodily at the end of the bar, staring at a half-pint of bitter in front of him.

"Young Debbie is actin' strange too," continued Jenny.
Debbie, serving at the other end of the bar, was looking pale and strained.

"Leave her be," said Larcum, "it's been a big shock to all of us, Debbie was always talking to old Stern; they were friends."

"More than friends some say," added Jenny meaningfully.

Nick King sat at a nearby table with Amanda.

"Did you hear that," whispered Nick, "Debbie was the one who saw Finch in the woods. I'd better have a word with her."

"Why don't I talk to her," said Amanda, "she might open up more to a woman."

PC Dobbs came into the bar and pushed his way to the front of the crowd.

"I need a drink," he exclaimed. "I've just spent all morning in old Stern's place. Gave me the jitters being in that house!"

Larcum poured the constable a large whiskey.

"Here son, this is on the house; you've earned it."

Unnoticed to the assembled customers, David Robinson slipped quietly out the door.

Ronald Finch looked a forlorn figure as Father Simpson and Dorothy entered the makeshift interrogation room. Sergeant Ellis was by the door and looked questioningly at the desk sergeant.

"It's ok Sergeant Ellis, the inspector said they could have fifteen minutes."

"Oh, right," said Ellis, "we'll leave you to it then father," he nodded respectfully to Dorothy, "Mrs Finch, come on Bert let's get a quick cup of tea."

Father Simpson sat down opposite Ronald; Dorothy walked around the table and gave her husband a comforting and emotional hug. The afternoon sun cast criss-cross shadows from the window frame onto the dull yellow police station walls, as if to emphasise Ronald's detention.

Ronald began to speak excitedly.

"They think I killed Albert Stern! I didn't even know he was dead until a few minutes ago." He turned to his wife. "I didn't do it Dot'! I only went to see what Stern was putting in the Beekeeper Show this year! This is just a mix-up!"

Dorothy rubbed Ronald's forearm comfortingly.

"I know dear, we all know."

"The question is," Father Simpson spoke with gravity, "who did do it? Inspector Downs has so much evidence against you Ronald that if we don't come up with another suspect soon he will press charges."

"What for murder?" said Ronald alarmed, he put his hand to his forehead, "Oh dear! Oh dear!"

"What do we do?" asked Dorothy, "who would want to murder a harmless old man like Albert Stern?"

"We shall have to find out," said Father Simpson, thinking suddenly, that local information web that his calling gave him access to, may at last prove to be useful. He turned again to Finch.

"Ronald, tell me everything that happened the night you went over to Stern's house."

Ronald gave a detailed account. When he came to talk about the sabotage of the dahlia Ronald flushed with shame.

"I..I didn't go to cause any damage father, honestly, I was well..I.."

"I understand Ronald," Father Simpson was reassuring, "we are all just human. Even gardeners," he added with a slight smile, "but tell me, did you hear anything when you were at the back of Stern's house? Anything to suggest that all was not well?"

Ronald sat and thought for a moment, then his face lit up.

"Yes! Yes! There was a crashing noise from the house, like someone had dropped something. That's when I left the greenhouse and ran back through the woods."

"That is when you met young Debbie, the new barmaid at the Bell?"

"Yes she was with that farmer fellow from Ixdon."

"What time was this?"

Finch paused, "No; I can't remember, about ten o' clock I think.."

"He got home at half past ten," said Dorothy assertively. "I know that because he ruined the start of that new costume drama on TV."

"I see," mused Father Simpson. "Well I think that I'll make some enquiries..I'm sure this town can't keep its secrets for too long.. I'll start by having a word with young Debbie.."

Simpkins and Brown were deeply engrossed in their afternoon's business at Albert Stern's house.

"Are you sure this place has been guarded Bill?" Asked Fred, as he dusted powder onto the mahogany bureau. "So far I reckon I've found six sets of fresh prints, not including the ones on the sills outside."

Simpkins was on his knees examining a wooden chair by the hearth.

"I don't know, that young lad seemed conscientious enough, he looked as if there were a dozen places he would rather be. Poor sod was frightened to death."

Using a small pair of tweezers Simpkins delicately picked at some hair and blood on the chair's arm and put it in a small plastic bag. Brown opened the oak bureau and began examining the contents; an old fashioned fountain pen lay next to a pad of high quality writing paper, in the left-hand recess sat several official looking typed documents and some household bills. Underneath these Stern had filed small bundles of paper, neatly tied with ribbon.

"Our Albert was a tidy fellow," commented Brown, selecting a bundle and gently tugging on its ribbon.

"Ex-service you see," explained Simpkins, standing upright and carefully sealing the plastic bag. "Military people are always well organized."

Simpkins glanced at Brown who was still engrossed in the documents from the bureau.

"Come on Fred, I don't suppose there is anything of interest in there; concentrate on looking for more prints." He tilted his head towards the fireplace next to him; "try those drink glasses on the mantelpiece, then we can look at the ashtray." A wicker basket by the hearth caught the policeman's attention. "Waste-bins can be interesting too."

Simpkins crouched down again, looking closely at the floor. Some scuffs in the deep pile carpet were puzzling him. He sat on his heels and stroked his chin. Brown, ignoring his colleagues suggestions, spread the bundle of papers on the bureau desk and began sifting through them.

"Looks like he kept records of everything; wish my wife were more like that. Look at this." Brown held up a crumpled piece of paper embossed with a crest and the words: '*The Cavalry Club, Mayfair.*' Under the date was a detailed list of various gambling activities from roulette to poker, at the bottom of the list was a figure highlighted in red. Brown scratched his head.

"Phew! Six hundred and fifty quid; bit of a gambler our Albert eh!"

Simpkins looked up exasperated.

"Come on Fred, that's not our territory, take a look at those glasses, we haven't got all day."

Brown was studying another document. He looked at Simpkins.

"Take a look at this."

Simpkins was about to reprimand his colleague again but the look in Fred's eyes was enough to make him pull his ungainly figure to its feet and walk over to the bureau. Simpkins took the paper. It bore the title: *'Criminal Record of Francis J White.'* He studied the document, which appeared to carefully detail all of Frank White's past misdemeanours as judged by the Old Bailey and other lesser London courts.

Simpkins raised his eyebrows in surprise.

"Is this who I think it is?"

"I reckon so," said Brown, "Frank White of 'White's Realty,' it doesn't surprise me; he comes over as a real hard case."

Simpkins read the document carefully.

"Where do you think old Stern got all this from?"

Brown shrugged. "I suppose it's easy enough if you know the right people and Albert Stern seems like the sort who would know the right people."

Simpkins continued to peruse the list of offences.

"Look at this: *1969 Seven years, Manslaughter of Derek Hatfield, Jamaica Club, Bethnal Green.*" Simpkins furrowed his brow. "This is really hot stuff; can you imagine the local scandal if this came out."

"I wouldn't think Frank would be too pleased." Agreed Brown.

"You are absolutely right Fred," said Simpkins thoughtfully. "There could be more to this than meets eye. Why do you think Albert Stern kept this information?"

Fred looked inquisitively at his partner.

"Go on."

Simpkins considered the list again: "Look we've just seen that Stern was running up gambling debts, look around you, he wasn't a rich man. What do you think he was doing with a detailed breakdown of the criminal record of a rich local businessman."

Realization dawned on Brown's face. "Well blow me, blackmail! You mean you think that Stern was.."

"I wouldn't be surprised," said Simpkins. "Let's get this down to the station, it could well put a new perspective on things. It's only circumstantial but I'll wager Stern was blackmailing Frank White. Leave the other stuff here for now; we'll come back later. In my experience, blackmail is as good a motive for murder as any I know. Get rid of the blackmailer and.." Simpkins snapped his fingers, "bang!

Your problem's solved."

"I'll call for someone to watch the house," said Brown, walking towards a black telephone.

"Wait," Simpkins stopped Brown in his tracks, "we haven't checked the telephone for prints yet, we can call from the mobile in the vehicle."

The two men walked down the drive and climbed into the van. Brown picked up the mobile telephone and called Melbury Police Station.

"Hello Sarg' it's forensic here at the house, we're bringing something in for Inspector Downs, can you send a lad to keep an eye on the place; yes; thanks; cheers."

Brown flipped the mobile telephone closed and they sat back in the soporific warmth of the van to wait for their relief. Simpkins relaxed into the seat and looked across at the house with half closed eyes. Brown surveyed at a standard rose growing in the centre of the front lawn. Small pink flowers spilled out in profusion over a wooden support. He made a mental note to find out the name of the plant, one like it would look very good on his own lawn. Brown was just about to say so when, to his alarm, Simpkins suddenly jerked upright and grasped his colleague's arm.

"Watch it Bill, you made me jump, what's up?"

"The house!" Hissed Simpkins, "look through the windows on the left!"

Brown peered at the house. Inside the living room, highlighted by the French windows, the dark silhouette of a figure could be seen moving stealthily about.

After leaving the 'Bell' David Robinson turned right and set off towards Albert Stern's house. He may be wrong, he thought, but if that policeman had left the house unattended this was the ideal time to retrieve the evidence that linked Jackie to Stern. He was annoyed that Jackie had not confided in him, but slightly flattered that she valued their relationship highly enough to protect him from the facts. Did she really think that he would leave her because she was being blackmailed? There was too much passion between them for that.

David turned down a dusty footpath a few hundred yards short of the house and slipped into the woods that ran behind all the houses in that road. He made his way through the woods and stopped behind Jasmine Cottage. Looking through Albert Stern's neat back garden he could see that the drive at the front was empty. He gingerly stepped over the fence bordering the property and carefully made his way across the lawn past the greenhouse and up to the rear of the house. David listened intently by the back door and, apparently satisfied, he crept along the wall and peered through the French windows. The room was empty and furthermore he could clearly see two crystal glasses sitting on the coffee table.

At the back of the kitchen David found the top skylight window wedged ajar. Few homes had all their windows closed this summer, even though it invited the thunder bugs to find their way in and into every nook and cranny in the house. David climbed up onto the outside sill and by stretching hard he managed to reach the catch on the main kitchen window. The old window sprang open and he levered himself into the house, negotiating the draining board and sink on the way. As he landed with a heavy thump on the kitchen floor he froze and listened. There was silence apart from the ambient sound of the countryside coming from the open window. A tractor starting, a dog barking, perhaps some children in the distance, but inside the cool house; silence. Now he was inside David began to feel very nervous; what would his excuse be if he got caught? 'He wasn't going to get caught' he thought. As he made his way through the hall to the living room he passed the bloodstain on the carpet. Albert Stern's violent death became a stark reality as David surveyed the large crimson scar that had seeped across the once cream rug. Once in the main living room David easily found two glasses, one had a trace of lipstick on the rim so he picked it up and put it in a plastic bag that he produced from his pocket. He looked around anxiously for the ashtray. It must be here somewhere he thought, then he spotted it on the mantelpiece next to a brass carriage clock. Sure enough the stub of a lipstick stained cigarette was there amongst other assorted rubbish. 'Just as well they weren't looking,' thought David. He picked up the ashtray and was about to tip the contents into the bag when the sudden sound of someone theatrically clearing their throat made David jump convulsively, he dropped the ashtray and turned around. Sergeant Simpkins was leaning nonchalantly against the hall door architrave.

"Oh my god!" David exclaimed.

"No sir," Simpkins spoke with slow irony, "it's just me and Fred. Norfolk Police Constabulary forensic officers, at your service."

"I see you are quite interested in forensic evidence yourself," observed Fred Brown peering over Simpkins shoulder.

"I'll tell you what Bill," he said, "I have a feeling this case isn't as straightforward as our dear Inspector Downs thinks!"

Inspector Downs sat down once again in front of Ronald Finch. It was late afternoon and the criss-cross image on the yellow wall was growing pale and elongated. Sergeant Ellis turned on the wall light switch. A white overhead light flickered into life with little effect. Ronald looked anxious at Downs and then across to his hastily enlisted solicitor. Mr Rupert Crook, from Crook and Tritton, (locally known as Crook and twist'em,) looked equally anxious. Crook and Tritton were primarily in the business of conveyancing with perhaps the occasional divorce case to spice things up. A criminal representation was a new experience for Rupert Crook. He had been urgently summoned that afternoon from his comfortable offices in Dean Street and, after an equally urgent summary of the situation from Ronald Finch, he sat, apprehensively, in the interrogation room. Inspector Downs switched on the noisy tape-recorder, tapped the microphone and spoke into it:

"Present at this interview Mr Ronald Finch, Mr Rupert Crook his solicitor and Sergeant Ellis of the Melbury Police." Downs turned to address Ronald.

"Now, Ronald Finch, do you admit that on the night of.." Downs looked menacingly at sergeant Ellis, "On the night of the twentieth of August, the night Albert Stern was murdered, you went, disguised, to Jasmine Cottage, the residence of the same Albert Stern?"

"Objection!" Mr Crook's exclamation surprised even himself.

Downs looked incredulously at Crook.

"Objection!.. Objection!.. What do you mean; 'Objection?' What do you think this is!"

Rupert Crook squirmed under his hot pinstripe suit.

"That question, it was a leading question."

"So what?" said Downs, "who says I can't ask a leading question?"

Mr Crook looked uncertain. "Well you can't in court."

Downs rolled his eyes to the top of his head; he began to raise his voice.

"This isn't a courtroom. *It's a bloody interview and I'd like to conduct it without idiotic comments from you!*"

Inspector Downs was not known for his people skills. He looked at Ronald.

"Well?"

Ronald looked confused.

"Well what?"

Downs controlled himself to speak quietly.

"Well answer the question." He almost added 'idiot' but restrained himself.

Ronald opened his mouth to answer when the squawk box on the table burst into life and emitted an ear splitting howl.

Downs leapt up angrily, "God! What now Price!"

He opened the door and yelled down the corridor:

"*Turn that blasted thing off! How many times do I have to tell you!*"

The desk sergeant ran down the corridor.

"I'm sorry sir, force of habit, something important's come up. There's a chap at the desk wants to confess to murdering Albert Stern."

Chapter 6

Father Simpson walked into the bar of the Bell Hotel. Apart from a couple in the corner having afternoon tea, the bar was empty. Larcum looked up from his books and was pleasantly surprised too see the priest.

"Father! How nice to see you, would you like a drink; a small Benedictine perhaps?"

Father Simpson smiled and approached the bar.

"No thanks Larcum, that's very kind of you. Actually I was hoping to have a word with young Debbie."

"I think she's upstairs in her room," said Larcum, "I'll ask Fran to get her."

Father Simpson stopped Larcum in his tracks.

"Don't worry, point me in the right direction, if she doesn't mind I'll chat to her up there."

Larcum shrugged. "Ok, just follow the stairs to the top; Debbie's room is number seven, at the back."

Father Simpson followed Larcum's directions, climbed the dark staircase and tapped gently on a door at the end of the corridor.

After a pause Debbie opened the door. She looked pale and unhappy.

"Hello Debbie, I'm Father William Simpson, I'm a friend of Ronald and Dorothy Finch, would you mind very much if I talked to you for a few moments?"

Debbie looked uncertain.

"I've spoken to the police about it," she said defensively.

"I know," said Father Simpson, "and I don't want to talk about what you saw in the woods. I already know about that."

Debbie looked puzzled.

"Come in," she said, "I'm afraid my room is a bit of a mess."

Debbie moved some clothing and Father Simpson sat down on a small chair. Debbie sat neatly on the edge of the bed, she looked very pretty, even though she was dressed in torn blue jeans and what looked like a man's old green shirt. She thrust her hands between her knees and looked expectantly at the priest.

Father Simpson looked seriously at Debbie. "Contrary to popular opinion, I don't happen to believe that Ronald Finch murdered Albert Stern. I appreciate that there is a lot of circumstantial evidence to the contrary but I have talked to Mr Finch and I'm convinced that he is innocent."

Debbie looked surprised.

"Well he was behaving very strangely in the woods. Anyway if he didn't do it who did?"

Father Simpson sat back with his arms on the chair.

"I don't know, that's why I wanted to talk to you. Is there anything else that you may have seen that night which may be relevant? Did you see anyone else near Mr Stern's house?"

Debbie looked apprehensively at Father Simpson and began to fidget a little as if deciding what to say.

"I suppose it's going to come out eventually," she said unhappily, "I went to see Mr Stern myself that evening."

It was Father Simpson's turn to look surprised. Debbie continued: "you have probably heard some stupid rumours about Mr Stern and I, just because we were often seen talking to each other."

Father Simpson looked apologetic. "I hear most of the talk in Melbury, but I don't heed most of it."

"Well," said Debbie, "there was good reason for Mr Stern and I to appear close, you see Albert Stern was my father."

Father Simpson was used to hearing unusual domestic stories in the confessional, but this was completely unexpected.

"Your father! I didn't even know that Mr Stern had been married."

"He hadn't," Debbie went on, "I was the result of a romantic liaison twenty two years ago. I didn't know who my Father was myself until quite recently, that's why I came to Melbury. My mother finally relented and told me on my twenty first birthday."

"What happened," asked Father Simpson gently, his manner made him an easy confidant for Debbie.

"My father was in the air force when he met my mother. They had been going together for about six or seven months. He found out that my mother was expecting but he was due a posting overseas. He didn't want to get married and apparently after a lot of argument he just left my mother in the lurch. She hated him for it. She didn't want him to have anything to do with me and from what I can gather that suited him fine."

Father Simpson stroked his chin thoughtfully.

"Why did she not wish you to know who your father was? It's healthy to know these things."

Debbie looked agitated; she rocked forward on the bed.

"I badgered my mother for years about it, at least she didn't lie and tell me he was dead or something. She said that she thought of me as a gift from heaven and that my father had let her down badly, that he wasn't worth knowing wherever he was. Eventually she would get so upset when I mentioned the subject that I just avoided it altogether."

"I see," said Father Simpson, "but she told you in the end."

"Yes; out of the blue. She had obviously been thinking about it, and perhaps time made it easier, but on my twenty-first birthday she told me everything. She didn't know where my father lived or even if he was still alive, but I now knew his name. I traced him through the air force; his last base was near Norwich. Someone there told me that he could probably be found via his club in London. They told me he lived here in Melbury."

Father Simpson leaned back in the chair. "So you came here and got the job at the Bell."

He looked at Debbie; he was beginning to see this resourceful young lady in a new light.

"Mr Stern must have got quite a shock when you presented yourself to him."

Debbie stood up and walked to the window.

"He was great! Not at all what I expected. He was delighted; we agreed to keep it quiet, but I was enjoying getting to know him. He was very charming and entertaining but now.."

Her lower lip began to quiver emotionally, "now I feel as if I have lost him twice."

Father Simpson stood up and went to her side by the window; he put a comforting arm on her shoulder. Debbie bit her lip; resentful tears filled her eyes.

"I know he'd done some bad things but he was still my dad. People are so selfish. I hate my mother for not telling me sooner and I hate that man for killing him. I hope they make him pay."

Father Simpson squeezed her shoulder.

"Don't hate your mother, she just did what she thought was right. It was probably hard for her too."

Debbie took a tissue from her jeans pocket and wiped her eyes.

"I suppose so."

"You are very brave Debbie, but I don't think that Mr Finch killed your father. I want to find out who did and you could help."

Debbie looked at the priest.

"I'd like to, but what can I do."

Father Simpson took his arm from Debbie's shoulder.

"Come and sit down again Debbie, I'll take you through it."

Debbie went back to the bed; she sat up by the pillows with her knees pulled up to her chest. Father Simpson went back to the chair.

"The night you went to see Mr Stern. What happened?"

Debbie furrowed her eyebrows quizzically.

"He was strange that night, it was the first time we ever argued. I was supposed to meet a boy I've been seeing from Ixdon.."

"Ian Green, the farmer?"

"Yes, that's it, Ian, anyway I went to see my father first and for the first time I asked him for some money. I don't get much working in the Bell and I thought he might help me out. After all I hadn't cost him anything up until then."

Father Simpson listened closely.

"So what happened?"

Debbie continued. "He went mad, he seemed very stressed, he started shouting and raving, saying that he had no money, that he was in debt, and didn't he have enough problems without me. I said that I had never asked him for anything and that it was about time he did something for me. Thinking about it he was probably embarrassed that he couldn't help me."

"That is probably true," said Father Simpson. "He was a proud man."

Debbie nodded, "anyway, I left telling him he was a mean old man." The tears returned to her eyes, "I feel so bad that I spoke to him like that, especially as I can't speak to him again."

She held her hands to her face and sobbed gently. Father Simpson came to the side of the bed and sat down, his hands on his knees.

"Nobody gets the chance to say a proper good-bye to someone who dies Debbie. They always feel guilty about this or that, about something they said or something they didn't say. Look at it like this, if you and your father quarrelled it was probably the first time that you were behaving like a real family, so in a way you could look upon it as a happy event!"

Debbie looked up and her face brightened. She turned to the priest. "Do you really think so?"

Father Simpson smiled.

"Of course!"

She smiled back and put her left hand on his.

"I'm so glad you came to see me today."

Father Simpson laughed. "It isn't just me, the holy spirit was here as well you know!"

Debbie laughed with him; somehow the priest had made her feel comfortable with herself.

"The holy spirit! Well I'm not very religious, but I think you might convert me!"

Father Simpson was relieved that Debbie seemed happier, but he had other work to do that day.

"You can come to mass on Sunday if you like, but first I need your help."

" I'll try," said Debbie warmly; she squeezed the priest's hand. "What can I do."

Father Simpson looked at Debbie seriously again.

"Debbie, think; was there anything you saw that night that might be helpful in finding your father's killer."

Debbie looked at the ceiling and pursed her lips thoughtfully.

"Oh yes, actually," said Debbie, "I was telling that reporters girlfriend, I don't think it's important but I saw that awful Mr Small staggering up the road drunk outside the house."

"I'll have a word with him, anything else?"

"No. No, I don't think so..well there was something my father said that I didn't understand."

"What was that?"

"Well, when he was ranting on about 'having enough problems,' he said 'first Doctor Vandersteen comes with one thing then you with another'"

Father Simpson started. He looked at Debbie quizzically.

"Doctor Vandersteen, what did he mean?"

Debbie shrugged.

"I don't know exactly but I think he was saying that Doctor Vandersteen had been to see him that night, obviously some sort of problem; probably his arthritis, my father had a lot of trouble with that."

"Are you aware," said Father Simpson slowly, "That Doctor Vandersteen committed suicide last night?"

Debbie looked at the priest in dismay.

"No..no..I don't even know who Doctor Vandersteen is."

She paused; "suicide..! Oh how awful!"

Father Simpson nodded.

"Is there a connection father?"

Father Simpson thought for a minute.

"I don't know; it is strange though.."

They both sat for a moment in silence, then Debbie spoke:

"I know who might have seen something."

Father Simpson looked interested. "Really; who?"

"Across the road from my father's house there's a woman who spends all her time looking out of the window. You know, every village has one."

"Of course," said the priest, "Mrs Cummings."

"Well," said Debbie, "she's a real nosy parker, she will have seen all the comings and goings that night.."

Inspector Downs looked aggrieved as he strode up the corridor towards the unsteady figure of Bernie Small. Bernie, under the bemused gaze of Sergeant Price, was clutching the station front desk for support. Downs had temporarily suspended the interview with Ronald Finch whilst he dealt with this new development. He was beginning to wonder if he would ever finish what at first had seemed to be a simple interrogation. Ronald had been left in the interview room in the company of young Constable Dobbs. The constable was very relieved that he hadn't been sent back to the cottage when forensic had called for a relief.

"So," said Downs, glowering at the swaying garage owner, "you want to confess to murdering Albert Stern?"

Small looked up at the tall police inspector.

"Yesh," Small hiccupped, then belched fumes of whiskey at the assembled company. Down's looked distastefully at the rotund figure.

"Mr Small," he said patiently, we already have Albert Stern's murderer in custody. You are a nuisance. I strongly suggest that you go home and sober up before I throw you in the cells for the night."

Small hiccupped again.

"I did it I tell you! I schmashed his 'ead in!" To emphasise the point Small swung his right hand in a hook, swayed precariously and then glared belligerently at the inspector.

Downs, not for the first time that day, looked exasperated.

"Mr Small, if you don't clear off home, I'll have you arrested, do you understand? We have the murderer, we have plenty of evidence and we don't want a depressed witless drunk messing up our investigation! Comprendez?"

Downs thrust his nose close to Small's face.

"*Now clear off before I lose my cool!*"

"Objection! Er I mean I object!"

Ronald Finch's solicitor had followed the inspector up the corridor and stood just behind his right shoulder watching the proceedings.

Downs took a deep breath and turned to look scathingly over his shoulder at the pinstriped figure.

"What now Mr Crook?"

"He's confessing to a murder, you can't just ignore it. I am obliged, in the interests of my client, to insist that you investigate this matter."

"Yesh," said Small, who then lost his grip on the police desk and slid unceremoniously onto the floor. Downs could see that he wasn't going to win.

"Very well! Sergeant put Mr Small in the cells for the night, I'll talk to him when he's sober."

"Shall I charge him sir?"

Downs fixed Sergeant Price with an angry glare.

"Look, we can't end up with two people in the same police station charged with the same murder can we now and I don't think there is a charge of 'taking the piss out of a police inspector,' use your noddle, just put him in a cell overnight! Oh and tell his wife where he is as well."

As the desk sergeant enlisted help to pick up Bernie Small the front door of the police station burst open and the two forensic officers bustled in. Between them, wearing handcuffs, they held a worried looking young man. Inspector Downs looked with astonishment at David Robinson and the two officers.

"What on earth.."

Simpkins grinned at the inspector. In his left hand he clutched some papers from Albert Stern's desk.

"Inspector Downs!" Simpkins had a note of triumph in his voice. "We have one or two things here that you might be interested in: Mr Brown and I found some very relevant and revealing documents in the deceased's bureau. We also found this gentleman," he turned to David Robinson, "stealing evidence from the scene of the crime, having broken into Mr Stern's cottage. The items in question are in this plastic bag: namely an ashtray, a lipstick stained cigarette, a Gauloise if I'm not mistaken, *and* a similarly lipstick stained glass. We have arrested the gentleman and have brought him here for questioning."

Inspector Downs looked blankly at the forensic officer. Simpkins was clearly anticipating some congratulation on his find. He looked expectantly at the inspector. If he'd had a tail he would have wagged it. The inspector still said nothing. This, he thought, was not happening.

The silence became embarrassing and was finally broken by loud snoring coming from the still supine figure of Bernie Small. The desk sergeant took control of the proceedings.

"Right lads, look lively, take Mr Small to cell two. Mr Brown, please bring your charge this way. Inspector Downs; I'll put this gentleman under guard in our other interview room and come back for your instructions."

The inspector suddenly asserted himself again.

"Yes..Yes very good sergeant, do that, I'll tell you what I want in a moment.."

David Robinson was spirited down the corridor by the forensic officers and the desk sergeant. Bernie Small was manhandled in the opposite direction. Inspector Downs went into his office to think..

Nick King sat in the hotel room tapping at the keys of a second-hand laptop computer. A knock on the hotel room door broke his chain of thought.

"Just a minute."

Nick finished the sentence on the word processor then opened the door. Amanda breezed in past him.

"I don't know why you don't get two keys," she said airily.

"It's simple, they don't have two keys." replied Nick.

Amanda turned to Nick, wrapped her arms around his neck and pressed her slim body against him provocatively. Nick kissed her forehead, then gently pushed her back.

"Look," said Nick excitedly, "I'm just about to send my first copy to The Standard, the locals downstairs are a mine of information, I've got enough talking to them to file a great report.. apparently that poor old chap Stern was murdered because someone called Ronald Finch was jealous at him winning the flower show every year! Can you believe that! What a great story! This is good enough for the 'nationals'!"

"I've been doing some research myself," said Amanda, pouting slightly at Nick's rejection of her advances. "I've been talking to Debbie."

"And?" Queried Nick.

"Well, she told me that she saw Ronald Finch running back from Albert Stern's house at about ten 'o clock. Apparently he was wearing something like boot polish on his face."

"Not very incriminating eh!" Nick smirked.

"That's not all, I pressed her and she remembered seeing the local garage owner, someone called Bernie Small, walking, or rather staggering, up the road from the direction of Mr Stern's house just a few minutes later."

"Ah yes," said Nick, "he was the chap drinking in the corner of the bar. Drinking rather a lot too I reckon; still I must have a chat with him, he might know something. Anything else?"

"Yes," Amanda was enjoying being a part of all this, "Debbie said that a Mrs Cummings was looking out of her window. Apparently she's one of these inquisitive women who spend all their time looking out at other people's business."

"And a blessing to us journalists such people are!" Exclaimed Nick.

"You have done wonderfully Amanda," Nick held her around the waist and gave her an exaggerated kiss on the cheek. Amanda flushed with pleasure.

"There's something else Nick."

"Go on," said Nick, "I'm all ears."

"Well, you are going to laugh, call it female intuition, but I think that Debbie knows something about all this."

"What could she know about a chap being murdered over a flower show!" Nick laughed.

Amanda continued: "It's a bit strange, she seems very upset about Stern being murdered, I mean more upset than everybody else. It's not just shock she seems to be in sort of mourning; she really is very distressed, she is also very defensive, as if she's got something to hide."

"Wow," said Nick, semi-mockingly, "Sherlock Jennings!"

"Believe me," said Amanda seriously, "there is something funny about that girl."

"I believe you," said Nick, "you have done a marvellous job and I'll follow up everything you have said. Meanwhile, Nick put his hands on Amanda's waist and looked her mischievously in the eye, I want to see if we can both fit in that bath across the corridor."

Chapter 7

Frank White drove his beige Bentley over the little stone bridge, past Ronald Finch's house and along the quiet road towards Boulmer Cottage. Frank flicked on the cars CD player and drummed his fingers on the steering wheel as the sound of Pavarotti singing a Puccini aria filled the interior of the limousine. Frank was feeling pleased with himself; here he was, late fifties, fit, rich, with a beautiful intelligent wife and totally in control of his life. He even had time to admire the Melbury countryside, which lapped up the early morning sun. After a couple of miles Frank slowed down and turned right into the Boulmer Cottage drive. His car crunched smoothly over the gravel and was immediately cast into shadow by an old beech tree which grew beside the building. Frank stopped the Bentley in front of a grey Volvo which was discreetly parked behind the tree.

Frank stepped out of the Bentley and squeezed himself into the Volvo beside the large figure in the driver's seat. Lenny James sat staring ahead his breathing erratic and laboured.

Frank looked at Lenny, grinned and slapped him on the back.

"I've got to hand it to you Lenny, that was a real good job."

Lenny continued to stare ahead.

Frank continued: "I mean when I ask you to stop some bastard black-mailer, you certainly stop 'em eh! I mean that old sod: ten grand he was trying to do me for.. I tell you what though if this town found out about that manslaughter rap of mine my business would be ruined. They're a real bunch of pussy bible bashers 'round here! Anyway I didn't mean you to do for old Stern but I can't say I'm sorry; black-mailing bastard eh! You even managed to nail someone else for the rap!" Frank rubbed his hands together gleefully. "What a result!"

Lenny picked up a wilting chocolate from the dashboard.

"Didn't do it," he said laconically.

Frank looked up at him.

"What?"

Lenny popped the molten chocolate in his mouth and mumbled: "I didn't do it. I didn't kill the old bloke."

Frank looked confused.

"What are you on about 'you didn't do it'! Of course you did it! Stop messing about."

"I didn't!" Lenny insisted, "I went in the house and there he was! Dead as a fuckin' doornail, bloody great carving knife stickin' out of 'is side; 'orrible it was, 'is eyes was all staring at me."

Lenny shuddered at the memory.

"I was just goin' to frighten' 'im, I wasn't gonna kill 'im. Blimey he was an old bloke.. I mean I didn't mind gettin' stuck in to some of those nasty geezers in the old days but this was different."

Frank seemed dumbfounded.

"If you didn't kill him," he said, "who the hell did?"

Lenny rummaged in his jacket for another chocolate.

"Search me, far as I can see half the bloody town could 'ave done it. Most of 'em went in and out of the old geezers house that night. I sat there bored to bloody tears watchin' em coming and goin'. Even ran out of chocolate. Tell you what though," Lenny shifted position to search his other pocket, "I reckon your wife's 'avin an affair."

Frank's jaw dropped.

"What!" Frank began to flush, "*What!*" He leaned over and grabbed Lenny by the lapel. "What are you playing at! Didn't do it! Wife having affair! Are you taking the piss!"

Lenny gasped for breath; Frank's face was crimson with anger.

"Go on explain yourself! What do you mean! My wife! Having an affair! This had better be good!" Frank's grip on Lenny's jacket tightened.

Lenny grasped at Frank's hands. "No Frank, me chest hurts, let go.."

Frank released Lenny and calmed himself.

"Ok mate, I'm sorry. Just tell me what's going on, it's all a bit confusing this morning."

Lenny struggled to open the car door.

"I've got to 'ave some air, I feel a bit queer.."

Lenny finally managed to open the door and with considerable effort, extricated himself from the small car. Frank opened his side and getting out he walked around the vehicle just in time to see Lenny drop to the ground with an unceremonious thump and a large cloud of dust. Frank ran around the car and knelt beside the dormant figure.

"Lenny! Lenny! Are you alright!"

Lenny was far from all right and Frank could see it. Lenny in fact was extremely dead and Frank, who had never witnessed a natural death in his life, looked at Lenny with astonishment; this was turning out to be a very bad day..

The Melbury Women's institute was in lunchtime session and planning it's annual summer Fete. The hall where they held their meetings was full of bags of jumble, trestle tables, spinning wheels and all the other paraphernalia which; having spent the year in storage, was being brought out for the event.

Mrs Cummings sat at the head of a rather battered old dining table and chaired the meeting. The other ladies present were chattering excitedly about the recent town events.

"Did you see The Standard this morning?" Said Ethel Turner, Jackie White's secretary.

"The front page is all about the murder. 'Beekeeper Show Murder' they call it. Poor Dorothy, I hope she doesn't read it."

"I say Ronald Finch definitely did it," Jenny Larcombe asserted, indeed her reputation now seemed to depend on it. "He always 'ad that look in his eye when Mr Stern was about, especially at this time of the year. Go to the gallows he should!"

"They don't have gallows any more," pointed out Ethel.

"They should bring 'em back then!" Retorted Jenny.

Mrs Cummings tapped loudly on the table with her pen and brought the meeting to order.

"Ladies," she said, "this has been a most successful month I hope you agree. Elspeth Stebbings achieved an excellent turnout for her lecture on spineless gooseberries and Doctor Rotton was kind enough to give his time to talk about Villas of the Italian Lakes which was still a great success despite problems with the projector." She paused amid murmured agreement. Mrs Cummings continued: "now before we discuss the fete, we have one more event coming up: 'an evening with moths,' when we all gather round a bright light with the council moth expert and see what species appear. Of course refreshments in the form of a barbeque will be provided. Last year it was a great success.."

"More like an evening with mosquitoes," snorted Jenny Larcombe. "They all came up from the river. I got bitten to buggery; even got through me tights.."

"Remember poor old Mrs Baker," said Ethel, "she was bitten all over. People thought she got the pox."

Mrs Cumming ignored the laughter from the table. She looked at Jenny coldly.

"If we spray insecticide Mrs Larcombe, the moths wont come; we'll just have to cover up and there is such a thing as repellent. Personally I found the event to be very exciting."

Jenny fell quiet trying not to catch Ethel's eye. Mrs Cummings continued.

"Now then, the idea of combining our annual fete with the Beekeeper Show has met with approval from the organizing committee, so it is just a matter for us to plan the events. I'll do the herbal remedies booth again, it made sixty pounds last year."

"Can you see if you can make a remedy to stop people from complainin'," said Ethel. "They were even blaming me for the weather last year."

"I tell you I'm not doin' the White Elephant stall again that's for sure," Jenny was being assertive again. "It did my 'ead in last year tryin' to stop those kids from Ixdon from nickin' everythin'. Then them parents had the cheek to complain when I hit one of the little sods with a toast rack."

"I'll do the White Elephant," volunteered Mrs Price. "Anything's better than the wheel of fortune. Damn thing fell off twice last year. Rolled off down the field. People was accusing me of cheatin'!"

The debate was interrupted by a polite male cough from the direction of the hall door. The assembly turned.

"Father Simpson!" exclaimed Mrs Price, "excuse my language but it was very upsettin' to be called a cheat!"

"Don't worry Mrs Price," said the priest cheerfully, "It is quite understandable and to be honest, as long as the good Lord's name is not used in vain how can I object."

Mrs Price looked relieved.

"I am sorry to interrupt your meeting ladies but Mrs Cummings, I was hoping to have a word with you, at your convenience.?"

Mrs Cummings hesitated.

"Um oh of course Father, could we say after the meeting?"

"Go on!" Said Jenny, "we can have a tea break and come back in ten minutes." Jenny was more interested in the town gossip than planning the fete, in fact the only reason she joined the Women's Institute was to keep tabs on what was going on in Melbury. This morning she wanted to discourse on her theory that Melbury was somehow 'cursed'.

"Oh, very well," said Mrs Cummings. "We will meet back here at half past."

"Do you mind if we go outside," said Father Simpson. "It's such a splendid day again. It will only take a few minutes anyway."

Mrs Cummings led the way out of the hall. She was a little mystified as to why Father Simpson wanted to talk to her. She attended the Church of England services but more from a social standpoint than a religious one. She had little else to occupy her but the institute and it looked better if she was a churchgoer. She certainly had little to do with the catholic church.

Outside the hall Mrs Cummings walked onto the grass between the hall and the road and stopped beside the lichen covered brick perimeter wall, she turned to the young priest.

"What can I do for you father, is it something to do with the fete?"

Father Simpson got straight to the point:

"I'm sorry to interrupt your meeting Mrs Cummings but this is an important matter. As you probably know, Ronald Finch has been arrested for the murder of Albert Stern. I happen to believe that he is innocent and as Mrs Finch is one of my parishioners, I am trying to help. I was wondering, as you live almost opposite Mr Stern's house, if you had seen anything unusual the other night, the night that Mr Stern was killed?"

Mrs Cummings flushed slightly.

"I like to keep myself to myself father, I'm not like Jenny Larcombe, into everyone's business. I think people should keep their council."

"I understand Mrs Cummings," said Father Simpson diplomatically, "but this is very important, you may have seen something from your upstairs window perhaps?"

Mrs Cummings flushed again; she did not like to think that everyone knew about her preoccupation with looking out the window.

"Alright," she said finally with a hint of irritation, "I saw a few comings and goings, none of my business of course. I saw Bernie Small go to Stern's house; or rather stagger to Stern's house, he was obviously drunk. Debbie, from the Bell, she went to see him. Earlier on I saw a woman go to visit but I couldn't make out who: that's about it."

Mrs Cummings was clearly uncomfortable discussing what she had seen.

"You say you saw someone else visit, a woman, did you not recognise her?"

Mrs Cummings thought.

"She had her back to me, I think she had long dark hair. No, I didn't recognise her."

Father Simpson considered this new information, he knew about Debbie and Bernie Small but this woman visiting was news.

"I think that you should go to the police with this information, Mrs Cummings it could be useful to them."

Mrs Cummings shook her head emphatically.

"Nope. Mind my own business, that's me.. anyway father, If that is all I'd best get on with the meeting, sorry if I haven't been much help."

"Just one more thing if you don't mind Mrs Cummings," asked the priest, "was it usual for Mr Stern to have a lot of visitors in an evening?"

Mrs Cummings shrugged her shoulders.

"I wouldn't know father," she said, it was bad enough being considered nosy on one night, never mind every other night.

"You *have* helped Mrs Cummings," said Father Simpson warmly, "thank you for your time."

Mrs Cummings turned to walk back into the hall, then stopped.

"There was one other thing.." she said slowly, turning slightly.

"Yes?"

"There was a small grey car parked under the trees just up from Mr Stern's house, I noticed that because I had never seen it before."

Father Simpson was interested.

"You didn't see the make of the car I suppose Mrs Cummings?"

"No I'm afraid not, it was odd though, an odd place to park I mean, anyway excuse me Father I must get on with the meeting now."

Mrs Cummings walked back into the hall; Father Simpson looked after her and stood by the wall stroking his chin deep in thought.

Frank White drove through the country lanes picking a tortuous route back towards Melbury. For once he did not want to be recognised, difficult though it was in a bronze Bentley bearing the registration '2 FW'. Pavarotti lay dormant in the CD player and the euphoric mood of that morning had now turned to one of numb depression. Frank had checked Lenny for any incriminating paperwork and had wiped away his own fingerprints; not that it mattered he thought, because Lenny's death had been natural. 'Probably overdosed on chocolate,' fumed Frank. 'What a time to keel over; did Lenny really not kill Stern? Stern, that old bastard. Trust him to find out about my past. That club of Stern's in London had a lot to answer for. Bloody in cahoots with the rozzers the lot of them.'

Frank's thoughts were interrupted as his Bentley rode up onto a bank and through the Cow-parsley, which dominated the roadside at this time of year. Frank, cursing, struggled to control the car, eventually coming to a rest with a thump back on the road. He pulled over to the entrance of a field and switched off the engine. Frank's heart was beating fast, he took a deep breath and started to think: why did Lenny think that Jackie was having an affair? The man had only been in the area for a couple of days. It must be something to do with Lenny going to see Stern. Who could she be having an affair with, and who, if Lenny was telling the truth, killed Albert Stern?' Frank was baffled. What he did know, however, was that if the police found out about Stern blackmailing him, then *he* would become a suspect, and a pretty good one too bearing in mind his violent history.

Frank started the car and set off again for town. He had grasped the problem but the solution was eluding him. For the time being he would lie low.

Inspector Downs sat in his small office trying to come to terms with the developments.

He had, he thought, the murderer. The evidence was compelling: Finch sneaking through the woods to Albert Stern's house, a crazy story about pom pom dahlias. No, Finch did it all right, but what was all this other stuff: a drunken confession, someone breaking into the cottage and of course to top it all a suicide. What was that about documents..?

The inspector went to his office door and yelled down the corridor:

"Sergeant Price!"

"Yes sir?" The desk sergeant leaned over the desk to see the inspector.

"Send the forensic officers in to me immediately.. Oh and try to organize some coffee if you will.. and some sandwiches. I don't think I've had time to eat for about twelve hours."

Sergeant's Simpkins and Fred Brown dutifully appeared and sat in two chairs opposite the inspector. A woman from the canteen across the road followed them in with a tray of hot beef sandwiches, a coffee pot and some cups. Brown leaned forward and helped himself to one of the sandwiches. Downs scowled at him but had too many other matters on his mind to bother with a reprimand. He waited for the woman to pour three coffees, then, after thanking her and watching her leave, he addressed the two men, his hands held together, pressed against his lips.

"So you are both uniformed forensic officers, is that right?"

"Quite right sir," Simpkins agreed, "I am Detective Sergeant Bill Simpkins and this is Sergeant Fred Brown."

"Well first of all," said the inspector, reaching for the sugar bowl, "what are these 'interesting and relevant' documents that you claim to have discovered?"

"Ah!" Said Simpkins pulling some papers from a bag by his side. "These *are* interesting. In Albert Stern's bureau we found these records. Take a look inspector."

Simpkins pushed the papers across the inspectors desk.

Downs picked them up and perused the documents neatly detailing Frank White's criminal record, then he leaned back on his chair, stirring his coffee.

"Well," he said at last, "I must say these are a surprise! Frank White eh! A criminal record! Amazing! Still though, I can't see why Albert Stern should have had this information and I don't see what it has this to do with this case?"

Simpkins looked across at his colleague who was devouring another sandwich. He had heard about John Down's reputation. Simpkins picked up one of the documents.

"Look inspector," he said patiently, "what would happen to Frank White's local business if something like this," he waved the piece of paper, "became public knowledge in this part of Suffolk?"

Inspector Downs sipped his coffee and examined the document again:

'*1969 Seven years, Manslaughter of Derek Hatfield, Jamaica Club, Bethnal Green.*'

"I see," he said, "Yes, the locals would not be very impressed."

"Right," said Simpkins, now look at this:

Downs looked at what looked like a crumpled restaurant bill and read out loud.

"Cavalry Club Mayfair, very posh; six hundred and fifty pounds. Rather a big night I'd say."

Simpkins looking expectantly at the inspector; Downs returned his gaze, looking blankly at the forensic officers for a few moments.

Simpkins became exasperated. He pulled out more similar casino debits.

"Look at these inspector! Gambling debts! Stern had gambling debts! He needed money! I'll bet he either was, or was planning to, blackmail Frank White. By releasing this sort of information White's business around here could be ruined!"

Inspector Downs leaned back in his chair again to consider this.

"If that is true, then that means.."

Simpkins looked expectantly again. Downs grasped for inspiration, "er, that means.."

"Yes?" Said Simpkins encouragingly,

Downs examined the documents again, then looked at the two forensic officers.

"What does it mean?"

"That means," said Simpkins, "that Frank White must be a suspect in this murder."

Downs considered this; he looked at the sergeant thoughtfully, "what about this other fellow you have just brought in, what's the score there?"

Brown stopped eating for a moment and decided to have a say.

"His name is David Robinson, he happens to work for 'White's

Realty'. How is that for a nice coincidence? One of Frank White's employees breaks into Mr Stern's house apparently to steal evidence!"

Downs took a deep breath and placed his hands palm down on the desk.

"Look," he said, "I need to think about this. If I don't charge this fellow Finch soon I'm going to have to release him. I've got a drunk in custody who has confessed to the murder and I have to interview him otherwise Finch's solicitor will have me roasted in court. There is this chap Robinson who was obviously up to no good and last but not least, there is a suicide on the other side of town to be tidied up."

Simpkins looked at the inspector for a moment. He was beginning to feel a little sorry for Downs, although he was aware that Downs was not a great detective he did mean well and was certainly dedicated. Perhaps he could help.

"May I make a suggestion Inspector."

Downs looked up hopefully; any suggestion would be helpful right now.

"Go ahead."

"You *could* get help from Norwich, but I know that you don't want to do that because you want to run your own case."

Inspector Downs nodded, there was no point in denying what was probably common knowledge, Simpkins continued.

"A few years ago I joined this forensic training scheme because my wife was worried about me doing regular police work. Before that I saw a lot of action as a police sergeant working in East London. and at times it was quite hazardous. Anyway, the point is, I have a lot of police experience and I know the ropes believe me. In fact officially I am still a detective sergeant even though I am in forensic. If you like, Fred can finish the forensic investigation at the house and then go to the hospital to see the murder weapon and perhaps pick up the post-mortem report. I could then help you here, I've done plenty of interviews in the past, and with some fairly nasty characters too I can tell you. I reckon I can clear it with Norwich to stay here for a few days and help you out. To tell you the truth, I am becoming quite interested in the case."

Downs considered this. He would still be in charge of the enquiry, this fellow was clearly quite experienced and also, he had to admit, quite sharp. He couldn't manage with the motley team of well meaning idiots he had outside the door at any rate.

"Very well Sergeant Simpkins, I could use a hand I must admit, I will carry on with Mr Finch and you can talk to this chap Robinson, see what he was up to."

"I think that we should bring in Frank White at some stage as well," suggested Simpkins.

"I'll think about that, we have enough to occupy us right now," replied Downs.

"Also," added Simpkins, "you *can* keep Mr Finch in custody for thirty-six hours if you apply to the chief constable, or longer if you go a magistrate."

Downs considered this for a moment. Simpkins was right of course but he could just imagine the reaction he would get if he called Chief Superintendent Ross. The local magistrate was a different matter however: Ebenezer Wedgewood was old and really not very with it. He was sure that he could convince him to grant a custodial extension.

"He looked at the Simpkins for a moment.

"I appreciate your suggestions sergeant."

Then, as if concerned about a show of momentary weakness, he pulled himself upright from the desk.

"Right then!" Downs surveying the two men; "let's get to it!"

Nick and Amanda sat at a round oak table in the corner of the expansive wood clad hotel foyer. Fran Todd placed a white coffeepot in front of them and then two cups and saucers.

"I'll be back in a moment with milk and sugar," she said, looking benevolently at the young couple. Just like Larcum and me at that age, she thought.

Since the morning paper had been delivered, Nick had taken on celebrity status at the Bell. Instead of having to seek out people to interview, the townsfolk had been coming to him, some with genuine information and some to expound their theories on the murder. Jenny Larcombe had already given her version of the 'Melbury curse,' much to Amanda's amusement. Amanda was particularly happy today because Nick's editor had been impressed enough with his first report to allow Nick to stay in Melbury for a few days or until the story dried up. Amanda was enjoying the break and Nick, delighted to be getting front-page coverage, was assimilating facts on the story with even greater vigour and excitement.

Nick scribbled on a note pad in front of him whilst Amanda poured him some coffee.

"This is terrific," enthused Nick, "the town garage owner goes to the police station and confesses to the murder, then this chap Robinson gets arrested in Stern's cottage..brilliant stuff! I think I might free-lance some of my copy to the national papers!"

"Don't forget the doctors suicide," prompted Amanda.

"Oh yes, that too, and the 'cursed town' theory!"

Amanda laughed and shoved Nick's arm playfully.

"You can't possibly report that! You'll be a laughing stock!"

"Well, perhaps you are right," agreed Nick, "Still the tabloids love that sort of thing!"

Amanda adopted a forlorn expression and hooked her arm through Nick's.

"Ni-ick," Nick kept writing on the notepad.

"Hmm.. what?" He asked absently.

"Could we go on a picnic?" Amanda gave him her 'hard to say no to' look.

Nick turned to her in astonishment: "a Picnic! Are you mad, I'm here to report on a murder!" His astonished look turned to one of amusement as Amanda began to look disappointed.

"Tsk! A picnic!"

He went back to his notepad.

"Oh please Nick, it just looked so beautiful down by the river to-day!"

"I haven't got time to go on a picnic," explained Nick, "I told you, this is not a holiday, I'm here to work."

They sat silently, watching the early evening sky turn pink. In the near distance Melbury sat peacefully awaiting sunset. To the north, along the river, a row of pines, beautiful and still, leaned their sharp black heads against the pale sky. One or two determined stars glimmered in the approaching darkness.

Amanda breathed deeply, enjoying the sensuous scent of grass and warm clover that hung in the still air. The river lapped gently at the bank where they sat.

"This is heaven," sighed Amanda, leaning back against Nick, the remains of their picnic was strewn on the grass bank.

"Yes," Nick agreed. Somehow it did not seem right to break the silence.

"Do you believe in the stars?"Asked Amanda dreamily, looking up at the fading sky.

"What sort of stars?" asked Nick, only half interested.

"I mean birth signs," said Amanda, "I mean, for example, I was born in October and that makes me a Libra. Because of that I'm very easy going."

"Oh yes," teased Nick, "I'm sure that whirling pieces of granite, millions of miles away have a great effect on our lives."

Amanda jabbed Nick in the side to admonish him.

"Cynic!" She said.

"I was born in April," said Nick. "What does that make me?"

Amanda pulled Nick's hair, tilting his head toward her.

"It makes you a Bull," she purred.

It was still warm; a light wind blew up along the river and rustled the leaves in the willow tree beside them. Two mating dragonflies flitted past like pieces of blue thread caught in a turbulent breeze.

"Nick," Amanda wrapped both arms around his neck, he could feel her warm breath on his cheek.

"Yes?"

Amanda pulled Nick back with her onto the grass, she pressed her mouth firmly against his ear; her breath became hot and her voice urgent.

"Make love to me."

For a while the problems of Melbury were forgotten. A light mist grew over the river, and a translucent grey-golden moon appeared like a mirage, shimmering on the horizon. Another day came slowly to an end.

Chapter 8

Frank White was restless and agitated. He sat on his leather arm-chair jigging his knee and rapping his right hand against the back of his left. He looked at his wife opposite. She was equally agitated. She took a cigarette from a box and lit it.

"You don't normally smoke English cigarettes," observed Frank.

"I decided to change."

Jackie stood up and walked to the window.

"What are we going to do about David?" She asked coolly, her back to her husband.

"I dunno," replied Frank, "what was he doing breaking into Stern's house like that? I mean what was he playing at?"

Jackie thought for a moment. This business had gone too far. Frank was going to find out somehow.

"He was trying to protect me," She said quietly.

Frank stopped rapping his hands. He looked at Jackie suspiciously. "What?"

Jackie turned and faced her husband nervously.

"Albert Stern was trying to blackmail me. I went to see him the night he was murdered. Of course I had nothing to do with that, but I left some things there that could be traced back to me so David went to get them."

Frank looked incredulously at his wife.

"What! I'm sorry, I don't understand. I was the one being black-mailed. Stern was blackmailing me!"

It was Jackie's turn to look incredulous.

"Why was he blackmailing you?"

"Well!" Exclaimed Frank, with heavy sarcasm. "No! After you! By all means, though I think I know what's coming!" Frank clenched his fists, more with apprehension than aggression; he wasn't going to like this.

Jackie was beginning to feel a little frightened; Frank was clearly not going to be able to handle the truth. She started to think on her feet.

"Stern seemed to think that I was having an affair with David. I don't know how he got that impression, probably because he saw us going out to do surveys together, but you told me to take David with me, so it was nonsense of course. Anyway, I didn't want malicious rumours spreading about the town so I went to see what he was talking about."

Frank sprang angrily to his feet.

"You were having an affair! I had a man watching Stern's place.. he told me!"

Jackie was distraught; she lit another cigarette, her hands shaking. She decided to bluff it out.

"Don't be ridiculous! You know what I think of David Robinson, why would I have an affair with him when I have you!"

The logic of this statement appealed to Frank. His ego couldn't really conceive of Jackie preferring someone else to himself, certainly not Robinson and Lenny could easily be wrong of course, all that boxing; too many punches to the head. Besides he didn't want to believe that his wife was having an affair.

He sank back into the chair.

Jackie inhaled on her cigarette; the storm seemed to be over, she looked curiously at her husband.

"So why was Albert Stern blackmailing *you*?"

It was Frank's turn to be defensive. Jackie knew nothing of his past.

"I wasn't actually being blackmailed," Frank explained. "Stern was *trying* to blackmail me, it was to do with business. No big deal really, he was obviously not dealing from a full pack if he was trying to do us both. Must have been desperate I suppose, assumed that we were rich and tried it on."

Jackie was relieved that the pressure was off; she walked across to her husband and stroked his hair.

"Do you really think I would prefer someone else to you?" She said gently.

Jackie pressed home her advantage; she understood her husband and was even beginning to feel renewed affection for him in his temporary show of insecurity.

Frank reached up for her hand and held it tightly.

"No love," he said unhappily, "I don't. All I know is that all this," he gestured to the elegant surroundings, "would be nothing if I didn't have you."

Jackie felt genuinely moved. Frank had not spoken to her like this for a long time.

"That's alright then," she said quietly, "we just have to stick together."

Inspector Downs took his seat once again opposite Ronald Finch. Next-door David Robinson had refusing to discuss his actions without a solicitor present. The solicitor in question was in Norwich for the day and not due back until late, so Simpkins had cancelled proceedings until the morning. Downs surveyed the uncomfortable figure in front of him. At last, he thought, we might get somewhere with this infernal investigation. Downs looked hopefully at Ronald and pressed the start button on the tape-recorder.

"Present at this interview Mr Ronald Finch, Mr Rupert Crook his solicitor and.."

He was interrupted by a brief screech from the squawk box on the desk.

Downs groaned and lowered his head into his hands.

"Oh Gawd! What now?"

After a cursory tap on the door, the baldhead of the desk sergeant appeared again.

"Sorry sir, you aren't going to believe this!"

Downs wearily raised his head.

"No," he said, "I'm not. What is it sergeant?"

"Some kids have found a dead body, just out of town at a place called Boulmer Cottage. I've called for Doctor Rotton and there is a car outside waiting.."

Doctor Andrew Rotton had been looking forward to a quiet evening when his telephone rang. Taking on all of Doctor Vandersteen's patients had proved to be an administrative nightmare. Rotton had not been very well acquainted with Vandersteen. Indeed he had found Vandersteen to be what he could only describe as irascible and rude.

This contrasted uniquely with Doctor Rotton's own character, which was genial and benign. He had needed to be; throughout his life his surname had made him the butt of many jokes. As the school rugby captain his name frequently appeared on the team selection as:

'*A Rotton Captain.*'

Later at medical school he was always being introduced as: "Hello, I'm such-and-such, this fellow is Rotton." He even began doing it himself, especially with the opposite sex. It amused him to see the reaction as he extended his hand and with a smile said, "hello, you look lovely; I'm Rotton."

He grew a bit tired of it really, but even now he could not resist the occasional pun. The brass plate on his surgery door bore the engraving:

'*A Rotton. Doctor.*'

Doctor Rotton picked up the telephone, listened intently, and then, with a brief acknowledgement, he walked swiftly to his car.

The three men stood in the half-light looking solemnly at the large motionless figure lying on the gravel next to the small grey Volvo.

"Says here that his name is Leonard James, 42 Balham road, Hackney." Said Simpkins, examining Lenny's wallet in the orange glow of the police torch. He paused for a moment, looking quizzically at the name.

"That's funny. I'm sure that name rings a bell."

Inspector Downs ignored him and turned to Doctor Rotton.

"What do you think doctor?"

Doctor Rotton had made a brief inspection of the body.

"Well I can't be sure of course, especially in this light, but it looks like heart failure to me. There is no sign of violence, you can see where he has tried to loosen his clothing and he is very overweight. He's a prime candidate for it."

"What could he have been doing out here?" queried the inspector. "There are some very rum goings on around here I must say. What do you make of it sergeant?"

Simpkins put Lenny's wallet in a small plastic bag and contemplated the body.

"I really don't know. I'm inclined to agree with the good doctor. The best thing is to get a post-mortem underway, I'll get back to the

89

station and see if I can find anything out about him; relatives etceteras."

Inspector Downs suddenly felt very tired. He turned to Doctor Rotton.

"Could I ask you once again to do the honours doctor, I'll go back to the station with Simpkins."

"Writing death certificates is getting to be a bit of a habit in this town," observed Doctor Rotton ruefully, he looked at the police inspector for a moment.

"Inspector Downs, you are looking exhausted. I strongly suggest that you take some rest; you've been on the go for some time now. It's getting late anyway and you'll probably be more productive tomorrow."

"I must admit, I am a little tired," agreed Downs wearily, "I think I'll just go and finish off some bits and pieces and then get some sleep. I can't face trying to talk to Finch anymore today, that's for sure," he looked at the doctor. for support; "he's completely off his trolley you know."

Doctor Rotton did not know, but he shook his head in sympathy anyway.

"Good idea boss," rejoined Simpkins. "You go now and I'll tidy everything up at the station and make sure things are raring to go in the morning. I think that everyone has had quite enough to think about for one day."

The next morning Inspector Downs was up early. He had slept fitfully and the face looking back at him as he shaved looked no better than the haggard one that he had taken to bed the previous night.

He dressed, made himself a cup of strong coffee, then got in his car and set off towards the police station, pausing only to buy a doughnut from the baker shop just outside his flat. Down's devoured the doughnut as he drove thoughtfully to work, sprinkling a light layer of powdery icing sugar over his brown suit. As the inspector approached the road that led to Doctor Vandersteen's house, he slowed down, glanced at his watch and then turned left, stopping finally outside the smart beige house that had, until yesterday, been a busy doctor's surgery.

Parked in front of the house was the brown Mini that the inspector recognised as belonging to Madeleine Hart. He stepped up to the front door, dusted his suit, straightened his tie, wiped his hands on a pocket tissue and rang the doorbell.

Maddie answered the door, her troubled blue eyes suggested that she had slept no better than the inspector.

She seemed pleased to see him. "Inspector! Come in, I was just going through the patient's records, they are all getting transferred to Doctor Rotton's surgery for the time being. Father Simpson is here as well."

Inspector Downs walked into the reception room. Father Simpson was sitting casually dressed in slacks and an open neck check shirt; the inspector greeted him.

"Good morning father, you're looking very relaxed today. A dreadful business," he gestured generally to the surgery.

The priest stood to return the greeting.

"Good morning inspector, yes indeed, terrible! I've just come over to see if Miss Hart needed anything, it is always good to have company under such stressful circumstances."

Father Simpson looked sympathetically at Maddie who was grateful for the moral support.

"You are very kind father," she said demurely, then looking at both of them: "would you gentlemen like some coffee? It won't take a moment."

Father Simpson declined.

"Thank you Maddie, that's very kind but I must go." Turning to Inspector Downs, the priest continued:

"Inspector, I had another reason for popping in. Are you aware that Doctor Vandersteen visited Albert Stern sometime on the night that he was murdered?"

The inspector raised his eyebrows.

"No I didn't know that. Was Stern a patient?"

"That's just it inspector," replied the priest, "I assumed that he must be, but Miss Hart has done some checking for me. Albert Stern is not on the books here and is actually registered with Doctor Rotton not Doctor Vandersteen."

Maddie agreed.

"No, Mr Stern was never seen by Doctor Vandersteen, I would have known if he had been. Coffee for you inspector?"

Inspector Downs held up his hand.

"No thank you, I just have to ask a few procedural questions then I must go. How curious father, how did you discover that Doctor Vandersteen visited Stern?"

"Debbie, the new barmaid in the Bell told me, I suggest you chat to her at sometime. Also, You may be interested to know that Mrs Cummings, who lives across the road from Mr Stern, saw a woman with long dark hair visit Stern's house on the same night."

Inspector Downs eyebrows began to work overtime.

"Really father," he said, "how interesting. You have been busy. I must have a little chat with Mrs Cummings."

Then, as if to alleviate any possible doubts he added quickly: "Merely to eliminate other possibilities from my enquiry you understand."

Downs beamed smugly at his small audience.

"After this investigation there will be absolutely no question that I have arrested the right man!"

Downs was gratified by what he thought was an admiring look from Maddie.

"Inspector," Father Simpson, sounding uncharacteristically impatient, was clearly unimpressed. "Mrs Cummings also says she saw a grey Volvo parked rather suspiciously, just up the road from Stern's house."

Father Simpson was surprised at the effect this piece of information had on the inspector. Downs seemed thoroughly taken aback and reaching back, sank into one of the wooden chairs which were scattered around the waiting room.

"My God!" Downs saw Father Simpson scowl disapprovingly and looked suitably apologetic.

"Sorry father, but are you aware that we discovered the body of a man, lying next to a grey Volvo at Boulmer Cottage last night?"

It was Father Simpson's turn to look surprised. He stared for a moment at the inspector.

"Do you know who it is?"

Downs shook his head, "Simpkins is looking into that hopefully. We know that he is not from around here that's all."

"I don't know what is going on here inspector," said the priest with gravity, "but you *must* now be prepared to consider that Ronald

Finch may not have murdered Albert Stern."

Inspector Downs looked uncomfortably at the floor, saying nothing. Could his 'hunch', his 'gut feeling', be wrong? He considered the priest's words for a moment, then looking at his stretched out feet he made a pronouncement:

"Father, with respect, I have been trained in the work of criminal detection. Unlike you, I have had dealings with the criminal classes. I *understand* them. I appreciate what you are trying to do for Mrs Finch, but right now, Ronald Finch is our number one suspect."

Father Simpson was non-committal. He turned to Maddie.

"Please excuse me Maddie, I must go, I have my ministry to perform."

"Of course father," said Maddie warmly, "thank you so much for dropping in."

"My pleasure," replied the priest, then as she moved towards the waiting room door he put up his hand. "It's alright Maddie, I can find my way out." He walked towards the door, as he passed Inspector Downs he nodded to the policeman. "Inspector."

"Good-bye father," said Downs, happy that the priest was leaving, "I must be getting on myself shortly."

Father Simpson disappeared out of the waiting room door. Downs dearly wanted to stay. Maddie was looking refreshingly attractive in a floral dress, which did little to hide her voluptuous figure.

The inspector stood up and smoothed the creases in his brown trousers.

"Miss Hart," he began.

"Maddie, everyone calls me Maddie."

"Oh, er, Maddie."

He tried to sound professional; he was feeling self-conscious being alone with her like this.

"Ahem.. Maddie, did Doctor Vandersteen have any reason to visit Mr Stern, I mean were they friends or acquaintances?"

Downs once again tried to avoid a natural inclination to stare at Maddie's breasts.

"As far as I know they didn't even know each other," replied Maddie innocently.

"So you can't imagine why the doctor should have visited Mr Stern?"

Maddie pursed her lips; looking mystified she shook her head.
"No Inspector, I'm afraid that I really can't."

Downs nodded, then looked at his watch.

"I was going to ask a little more about Doctor Vandersteen but I'm afraid that I must get going as well." He looked at her hopefully, "perhaps we could talk about it when I have more time."

Maddie looked sympathetically at the policeman. He looked very worried.

"Of course Inspector, you have a lot on your plate." She looked apprehensively at the surgery door, "I will be fine here."

Downs got back in his car and drove on to the police station. Melbury was relatively quiet compared to the last couple of days. A light easterly wind from the direction of the small Ixdon brewery, five miles away, gave the town a pleasant pungent scent of boiled malt and hops. Once again there was not a cloud in the sky. Only the occasional passing lorry, brimming with sugar beet, marred the peaceful Suffolk morning.

Downs pulled up in his parking slot in front of the police station. Outside, on the main road, a large truck bristling with aerials was being unloaded of a cargo of thick black snake-like cables. The truck bore the inscription: 'BBC OUTSIDE BROADCAST.'

The inspector walked through the front door.

"What the dickens is going on outside Sergeant Price?"

The baldhead behind the desk jerked up in surprise, a copy of The Norwich Standard slid surreptitiously onto the floor.

"Good morning inspector," said the desk sergeant excitedly "It's BBC 'Look East'; they're here to report on the 'Beekeeper Show murder.' I've already seen that Jason Damagio, you know the presenter. He's much smaller.."

"Shut up sergeant and get rid of them," said Downs curtly. The desk sergeant looked abashed.

"See if someone can bring me a coffee. I'm going to make a quick call to Ebenezer Wedgewood, the magistrate, then I want Sergeant Simpkins to come and see me."

Price tried to look business-like.

"Yes sir! Sergeant Simpkins has been in for a while, he wanted to see you as soon as you came in."

Inspector Downs walked towards his office as the desk sergeant answered the telephone.

Sergeant Price recognized the deep London tones of Frank White. Frank asked to speak to David Robinson.

"Good morning Mr White, no I'm sorry but I can't let you speak to Mr Robinson just now."

At the other end of the line Frank was tense; he was used to getting his way.

"Right sergeant," said Frank lowering his voice an octave. "I want you to pass Mr Robinson a message."

"A message, yes I can do that Mr White go ahead." The sergeant, picking up a pen, a little intimidated by the authority in Frank's voice.

"Tell Mr Robinson not to worry and that I will sort him out, can you do that sergeant?"

"Yes sir Mr White: 'you will sort him out,' I'll pass the message on."

Simpkins had been busy. The previous night he had made several telephone calls to his old colleagues in east London and this morning he had been in early to prepare the sleepy rural police station for a full-scale murder investigation. Indeed the station did seem to have a buzz of excitement and anticipation since Simpkins had assumed the role of deputy to Inspector Downs. Simpkins appeared at the inspectors open door clutching a clipboard.

"Good morning sir."

Inspector Downs was sitting in his office writing on a pad of paper. He looked up.

"Morning Simpkins!" Downs gestured to the chair in front of his desk, "Take a seat, there are a few things I want to run by you."

"Ok sir, and when you have finished I have something for you. By the way did you have any luck with extending Ronald Finch's custody; he's been in over twenty-four hours now."

"I'm still working on it," said the inspector wearily. He couldn't be bothered to tell Simpkins that Ebenezer Wedgewood, the magistrate, had yet to answer his telephone. "Anyway," he said, "to address the task in hand: first of all Simpkins, to make this conviction stick, we have to eliminate all other possibilities from this enquiry. Don't you agree?"

Simpkins didn't see it quite that way: "Well sir I think we should keep an open.." Downs continued.

"To that end sergeant, to start with, I want you to interview this chap Robinson. I will deal with that awful Small fellow, if he's sober, and hopefully that will remove two red herrings from the pie."

Downs, unaware of his mixed metaphor, looked at Simpkins for approval before continuing.

"Well I.."

Downs held up his hand.

"In a moment Simpkins, hear me through: It has come to my attention that a woman with long dark hair visited Albert Stern on the night that he was murdered. Also that the man we found dead last night, Leonard James, parked his Volvo just up the road from Stern's house the same evening. To this effect we need to interview a woman called Mrs Cummings who lives opposite Stern."

Downs sat back to observe the reaction of this news on Simpkins.

"Additionally we should speak to the barmaid from the Bell again, she apparently believes that our deceased doctor also visited Mr Stern the day he was killed."

"Perhaps Stern was his patient," suggested Simpkins.

"No, he wasn't," said Downs, "I've discovered that Stern was actually doctor Rotton's patient." Downs could not actually bring himself to take the credit for these details but he hoped it had been implied.

Simpkins looked at the inspector with renewed respect.

"What you say sir, is very interesting, very interesting indeed. However, when you have heard what I have to say I think that you'll agree that there is definitely another angle to this case."

Downs waved his hand towards Simpkins to continue and leaned back in his chair.

"Go ahead sergeant."

"Last night I telephoned some old colleagues from Stepney, where I used to work. You remember I said that the name 'Leonard James' rang a bell?"

Downs nodded.

"Well I was right. He used to be a professional boxer in the east end and then got involved in collecting protection money for one of the gangs. He's got a long record of violence, strangely enough though he hasn't been up to much for years."

"Then he turns up in Melbury dead," interjected Downs.

"Quite," agreed Simpkins, "I asked the guys at Stepney about Frank White and I mentioned some of the stuff Albert Stern had in his bureau."

"And?"

"They are getting back to me this morning. In fact one of my old colleagues is contacting New Scotland Yard for the information."

"Excellent!" said Downs, "Well let me know what you find out. I must say it does seem very fishy. Meanwhile we have to interview Finch and get rid of Small."

Simpkins flicked over some sheets of paper on the clip file.

"Sir, before we do that could I just run through the state of play regarding the forensic evidence."

"Go ahead," replied Downs unenthusiastically. His idea of a solution to this case was a good old fashioned confession, extracted by his own skilful questioning technique and intellectual analysis of the facts. Still, he supposed, the forensic evidence could back it all up. It might even demonstrate what good intuition he had.

"Well," continued Simpkins, "first of all, the result of the post-mortem on Albert Stern should be ready by now, hopefully it will arrive shortly. That of Lenny James should be here this afternoon. Regarding the evidence from Albert Stern's house; Brown has discovered five or six set of prints, so, with your permission I will start fingerprinting all potential suspects.."

"Just a minute sergeant," Downs interrupted, he sprang forward from his reclined seating position and tapped his forefinger on the desk to emphasise his point.

"There is only one suspect in this case. I appreciate that there are some weird goings on in Melbury at the moment but do you seriously believe that the man we have in custody is not the killer? I mean, for a start, how many people do you know that run around the woods to someone's house wearing boot polish and a boiler suit late at night?"

Simpkins nodded.

"I admit that the evidence against Finch is compelling sir, however, to be thorough we must eliminate all other possibilities."

Downs knew it, had he not said so himself?

"Ok, go on, but don't lose sight of the facts."

"Well sir," Simpkins chose to ignore Down's condescending manner, "in support of your theory, pieces of blue overall, matching the one discovered in Finch's house, were found on Albert Stern's perimeter fence."

Inspector Downs gave a satisfied snort and leaned back in his chair again, adopting his former relaxed pose.

"We also have the lipstick stained Gauloise cigarette and glass that Robinson was trying to steal from Stern's house. It would seem likely, from what you say, that they are connected in some way to the dark haired woman seen by Mrs Cummings?"

Downs nodded thoughtfully. This was getting complicated. He was tempted to draft some more help from Norwich but if he did so the investigation could run out of control. What amounted to a relatively simple case could snowball, along with his own career. They would certainly have a more senior police officer in charge of the case if they knew that it was becoming this difficult. For the time being he would stick with it.

"I agree sergeant, there are lot of loose ends. For a start though, I would like you to talk to this fellow Small, then send him home. Make sure he's had a couple of coffees and an aspirin first or you'll get no sense from him. Then I want you to find out what Robinson was up to. I'll carry on with Finch and whoever finishes first can get statements from this Mrs Cummings and the barmaid from the Bell. She obviously did not tell us everything she saw the other night."

Simpkins stood up. "I'll get onto it, also, with your permission I'll draft in some secretaries to keep up with the paperwork; typing etceteras."

"Good idea sergeant," agreed Downs, by this time he was beginning to feel quite cheerful.

"Also I'll ask Sergeant Ellis to get someone to visit all the local tobacconists, see who regularly buys French cigarettes, it shouldn't be too difficult to find our mysterious lady visitor."

"Excellent!" Piped Downs.

Simpkins walked towards the door.

"Oh, Simpkins." Down added.

The sergeant turned, "Yes sir?"

"I won't let your efforts here go unnoticed."

Simpkins looked pleased. "Thank you sir." He walked back along the corridor smiling to himself, unlike Downs he was not concerned about promotion or career but the thought was there. Perhaps Inspector Downs wasn't such a bad fellow after all.

Ebenezer Wedgewood, the Melbury magistrate, was in a bad mood. He had sent his hearing aid to be repaired as a matter of urgency and for some reason it had still not been returned. He had a feeling it was something to do with this Beekeeper fiasco but anyway he felt totally frustrated. Ebenezer walked across the room and picked up the telephone, which, unknown to him, had been ringing for some time. Inspector Down's voice was at the other end.

"Hello Mr Wedgewood it's John Downs here."

The magistrates face frowned with concentration.

"Eh! You'll have to speak up, m' hearing aid's broken."

The inspector raised his voice.

"Downs, John Downs!"

Ebenezer looked alarmed.

"John's drowned! John who?"

Down's looked at the telephone in frustration.

"*Inspector Downs!*"

The magistrates look of alarm increased.

"The inspector's drowned! That's terrible! It's that river; people shouldn't be allowed to go in it! The inspector! Drowned you say! Listen, you've got the wrong man. This is the magistrate; you need the coroner. But anyway call me after ten; my clerk will be here then."

Ebenezer put down the telephone and walked across the room shaking his head. The inspector; drowned he thought, whatever next.

John Downs stared in disbelief at the telephone in his hand. Things simply weren't going his way. Even the simple things! He decided to have another chat with Ronald Finch.

Nick King was delighted. For the second day running The Norwich Standard was running his column on the front page. What pleased him even more was that two of the national papers had chosen to run his story, admittedly with slightly lower profile than The Standard. He hadn't had time to report details of the discovery of the body of Lenny James the previous night, but nevertheless the public imagination had been fired by the 'Beekeeper Show murder.' The third death in the town could only make the story bigger.

Dorothy Finch was distraught. Although the newspapers had been careful not to directly accuse Ronald, the implication was there for all to see. She dared not venture into town.

"What can I do father," she had cried unhappily. "Inspector Downs is determined to prove that Ronald did this awful murder."

Father Simpson was becoming increasingly concerned that a miscarriage of justice was about to occur. Inspector Downs was certainly looking for the conviction of Ronald, yet it was clear to the priest that something more sinister had occurred. Something to do with a fat man in a grey Volvo, a dark haired woman, young Robinson, perhaps even Bernie Small. Also there was the elusive connection with Doctor Vandersteen. Strange that Mrs Cummings hadn't mentioned the Doctor visiting. Perhaps she had not been looking at the time, or perhaps Doctor Vandersteen had gained entry to Stern's house discreetly; but if so why? Why would a country doctor want to behave in such a surreptitious way? Father Simpson was left pondering these matters as he prepared for the morning service. He needed to enlist some help, he would speak to Father O'Byrne in Norwich, he was always useful in a crisis; also he would talk to the young reporter from The Standard. Somehow he would get to the bottom of this.

Jason Damagio stood impatiently in front of the television camera as a young woman put the finishing touches to his make up. Sergeant Price had reluctantly sent the television crew away from the front of the Melbury Police Station, and the BBC truck was now cluttering up the street outside the Bell hotel. Damagio had been broadcasting for BBC Norwich for several years and was a famous face in the county. Dark haired and well past fifty, Damagio was popular with middle-aged ladies although his own tastes were for somewhat younger women, most of whom were not flattered by his frequent advances. Finally, apparently satisfied, the young make-up woman stood back and Jason, holding up a microphone, addressed the camera.

"This quiet Suffolk town has been shocked to the core by the recent murder of one of its elderly residents.." Damagio's voice tailed off as Deborah walked past the crew wearing tight jeans and an orange tank top. She glanced at Damagio and turned into the front door of the Bell.

"Here we go," the broadcast director was leaning nonchalantly against the truck holding a clipboard. "Close down the BBC, Jason's seen a woman."

"I'm sorry Andy," said Damagio feeling slightly embarrassed, "I was distracted."

"By a bare midriff and a pair of legs, I know," said the director; "try it again."

Damagio began again:

"Thus quiet Suffolk town.."

This time the slim figure of Jackie White stepped from her car across the road and walked into a newsagent. Damagio had been particularly impressed by an expanse of elegant calf as she climbed from the driver's seat.

"Oh for goodness sake!" The director tossed his clipboard onto a small collapsible chair.

"Can somebody give him some bromide or something, come on Jason, take your mind off women for two minutes and lets do this!"

"Yes! Yes..sorry Andy..ahem."

Damagio looked at the camera:

"This..."

Suddenly the broadcaster disappeared from view as the blue fumes of a passing sugar beet lorry enveloped him, Damagio emerged from the cloud of smoke coughing and gasping for air.

"That's it, I've had it!" exclaimed the exasperated director. "I've been buggered about all morning, then I try to get a sex maniac to string five words together, now we're being gassed with diesel fumes. Take a break everyone, come on Jason, I'll buy you a coffee in the hotel perhaps it will calm you down."

Inside the hotel a small crowd had been watching the antics being performed in the street through the bar window. As Jason and his director came in, the group politely returned to the oak table that they normally occupied at this time of day. Thanks to Constable Dobbs the Bell customers and therefore the whole of Melbury, were up to date on the progress of the police investigation.

"My sister in Ixdon tells me he was staying at the Red Lion," said Roy Barnes, watching Damagio sitting at a table across the bar, but actually referring to Lenny James.

"Wonder what he was doin' over at Boulmer Cottage?" Asked Ivan Hillsdon, "strange place to keel over and die."

"It's witchcraft!" Proclaimed Jenny Larcombe, "the town is cursed I tell you. Bernie Small's been and confessed to murder, young Robinson gettin' arrested. I'll bet they're under a spell or possessed or something. One of us'll be next." She looked apprehensively around the group for signs of demonic possession.

Roy Barnes laughed his woodbine laugh, "the only spirit possessing Bernie Small was from a bottle of Red Label, he was paralytic when he went to the police station. Didn't you see him in the corner of the bar!"

"Robinson was in that day as well," said Mrs Baker, "he was sittin' on his own, I noticed it 'cos he don't normally come in here; he's revolting."

Ivan looked perplexed. "What are you on about Mrs Baker?"

"I think she means he's a loner," Said Jenny, who, for once, was equally at a loss.

"That's right," agreed Mrs Baker, "He's a hippy!"

"How can he be a hippy?" Said Roy, "He's a property surveyor."

"I've got to go," said Ivan standing up, "I've lost the thread of this conversation anyway; see you at five o'clock for the next instalment."

Across the room Damagio was amusing himself by trying to flirt with Deborah who politely ignored him. As his director ordered coffee Amanda walked into the bar and sat at a table. She was wearing a short yellow summer frock and positively radiated youthful health. Damagio grabbed the director's arm.

"We've got to try to stay here a while," he hissed into the director's ear, "the women in this town are knockout, look over there!"

Andy glanced at Amanda, "must be the air," he said, "or the milk or something."

"Either way we've got to stay, tell them it's a great story and we need a stopover." Damagio let go of Andy's arm.

"I really don't think 'good looking women' is a very professional reason for spending a night in Melbury," said Andy slightly amused. There again he thought, the Bell looked most accommodating and the story did have some merit.

"I'll tell you what," he continued, "if you can take your mind off

the fair sex this afternoon long enough to do a   decent item for tonight's programme, I'll see if we can stay another night."

"You're on," said Damagio enthusiastically, "not only that, I'll buy
you a pint or two of Ixdon's finest beer."

"Over the road, outside the newsagent Jackie White was in her
car thoughtfully smoking a cigarette. So Frank had a man watching
Stern's house, then Stern had been murdered. I wonder. She thought.
She had to speak to David. She started the car and drove towards the
police station.

Chapter 9

To say that Bernie Small had a hangover when he woke up would be an understatement. Bernie was quite used to waking up with a hangover, but it was usually in his own bedroom or at least somewhere in his own house. There was something unfamiliar about the faded cream walls and the stark steel door, which loomed into focus as Bernie painfully opened his eyes. Bernie shook his head in order to refocus on the image that had appeared in his throbbing brain. He immediately regretted it, "yow," he muttered, as the same image reappeared. Then he remembered: he was a murderer! He was in prison!

"Yow!"

Trying to sit upright had caused his brain to rattle painfully in his skull. The cell door opened allowing bright sunlight to stream in from a window across the corridor. Bernie screwed up his eyes and looked at the large silhouetted figure of Sergeant Price holding a steaming mug of coffee.

"Morning Mr Small, how are we this fine morning! I thought you could probably use this."

Sergeant Price handed Bernie the coffee and then held out two white pills in the palm of his hand.

"Sergeant Simpkins says you should have these, then he wants to talk to you."

Small grunted and sat round-shouldered sipping the coffee.

"Your missus came in last night."

"Oh gawd!" said Bernie, "what did she say?"

"She said we could keep you here for as long as we liked for all she cared," said Sergeant Price cheerfully. "I don't think she was very pleased with you."

"Great," muttered Bernie.

"Anyway, finish your coffee and then I'll take you up to Simpkins."

Sergeant Price closed Bernie's door and opened the cell contain

104

ing David Robinson. David had not slept, partly due to Bernie's snoring but mainly due to his predicament. He had spent the night planning a story that would protect Jackie. It was implausible but it couldn't be proven wrong. He had assumed that Stern's house was to be sold by 'White's Realty' and he had gone to do an initial survey. Not having the keys at the time he had entered using the window. As a matter of habit he had naturally tidied up as he looked around hence the ashtray contents and the glass on his person when he had been apprehended. He was contemplating this far-fetched tale when Sergeant Price opened his cell door.

"Mr Robinson, just to let you know that Simpkins will see you as soon as your solicitor has arrived." David nodded nervously.

"Oh and Mr White telephoned and said he would 'sort you out,' whatever that means."

David felt a cold shiver run down his spine. 'Sort him out'! What did he mean! Jackie must have told Frank everything and now Frank was going to 'sort him out'! He clasped his forehead and rolled back on his mattress. This changed everything, now he would have to protect himself.

"Are you alright Mr Robinson?" Asked Sergeant Price concerned at David's reaction. "The colour's gone right out of you."

"Oh.. er yes I'm fine sergeant, I'll see whoever whenever."

Sergeant Price closed the cell door and walked back to his desk shaking his head. There were certainly some strange people about these days.

After finishing his coffee Bernie Small was led to Simpkins. He sat down opposite the policeman and looked unhappily around the room. His head still hurt. Simpkins doodled on a notepad in front of him.

"Mr Small, before we start taking formal evidence why don't you just tell me why you came in last night and what this is all about."

Bernie related his story, at first incoherently and then more eloquently as the gravity of his statement began to clear his head. He described the poker syndicate, explained the state of his garage business and how he had gone to Stern's house to collect his debt. His voice trembled a little as he described how he had grabbed Stern by the lapels and how the old man had slipped and hit his head on the chair.

"I didn't mean to do it honest," pleaded Bernie, "I was probably a bit rough but I didn't expect him to fall over and bash his swede!" He looked at Simpkins for understanding. The sergeant simply nodded impassively, he had been wondering about the bloodstain he had found on the chair. Bernie continued, "anyway then I just panicked and ran out of the house. I suppose I should have called a doctor," he added ruefully.

There was a pause as if Simpkins expected more.

"So that's it?" Asked Simpkins, somewhat surprised.

"That's it," agreed Small, wondering if he had missed something.

"You think you killed Stern by him falling and hitting his head?"

Bernie nodded unhappily.

"It was an accident honest!"

Simpkins shifted his position put the palm of his hands together and leaned across the desk looking Small directly in the eye.

"Mr Small," said Simpkins gravely, "would it surprise you to know that Albert Stern was murdered with a kitchen knife?"

Small sat back stunned. The door to the room opened and Sergeant Price appeared.

"A call for you from London Bill, you can take it next door."

Inspector Downs was making little or no progress with Ronald Finch. Finch was sticking to his story about the pom pom dahlia and whenever Downs tried some mild intimidation to force a confession Mr Crook 'objected.' Down's decided to formally charge Finch; he was clearly going to have problems keeping him in custody anyway. He was about to initiate the process when, after a cursory knock on the door, Simpkins appeared.

"I'm sorry to interrupt but something's come up I think you should know about. Could we go somewhere private."

Down's was grateful for the break and led Simpkins into his office. Simpkins got straight to the point.

"I've had a call from my colleagues in Stepney."

Downs adopted his customary position, slumped in his chair.

"Go on."

"Well" Simpkins continued, "the whole thing goes back a bit but apparently Frank White used to be involved with a bunch of thugs who took over a lot of the criminal activities of the Crays once Ronnie and

Reggie had been arrested. It was on a much smaller scale, but they basically operated a protection racket from Camden to Stepney. Albert Stern's information was right, White finally went down for seven years for the manslaughter of a small time crook called Derek Hatfield. White was in his mid twenties at the time, apparently he only did four years. Then when he came out he supposedly went straight. The police had their suspicions about him but they never got him for anything else."

"I see," said Inspector Downs rubbing his face, "then he came to Suffolk to set up a property business."

Simpkins flipped over his notes, "yes and with substantial starting capital it seems. Anyway this is the point: when Frank White was up to no good in the east end guess who his main henchmen was?"

Downs looked unblinking at Simpkins. He thought he knew what was coming. "Don't tell me," he said, "our man with the grey Volvo."

"That's it," continued Simpkins, "Lenny James was minder, debt collector and right hand man to Frank White. Then should appear on the scene here in Melbury when Frank has a little trouble? None other than Lenny James."

Downs grimaced. Lenny James was near the house when Stern was murdered; this was going to complicate matters.

Downs became the devils advocate. "We don't know for sure that Stern was blackmailing Frank White sergeant, we are only guessing."

"No sir but the circumstantial evidence is pretty strong. We should certainly interview White on the matter and perhaps search his premises."

Downs sat thinking for a moment.

"Sir," said Simpkins gravely, "I'm sorry to spoil your theory but it does look to me as if Lenny James is our killer and that Frank White employed him."

Downs rested his elbows on the desk and putting a hand on each temple and pressed so hard that his hands began to shake, he growled in frustration. This had all seemed so simple.

"Shall I bring Frank White in?" Asked Simpkins, looking rather concerned at the inspector's antics.

"I suppose we had better," replied Downs grudgingly. "But we are running out of manpower, we don't have the resources to interview all these suspects, search premises and run the police station."

"I think we can manage it sir," said Simpkins, Brown can take a break from typing up the forensic results, with you, him, Sergeant Ellis and a couple of the lads I thing we will have enough to apprehend Frank White. The rest we can work out later."

"We haven't even got cell space for all these people!" Protested Downs,

"That's all right sir, Small can go once I've got a proper statement from him. He didn't kill Stern but his evidence is important. That will release a cell."

Inspector Downs looked doubtful but after some thought he realized that there was little else he could do.

"Very well," he sighed, "lets get it organized; go and tell Sergeant Price to get the team you suggest together. We will just have to hope for the best. Perhaps when we have all the protagonists in this saga in the station we can get to the bottom of this case."

The party to arrest Frank White was gathered in the police station foyer chattering excitedly. Inspector Downs had his back to the reception desk and was discussing details with Sergeant Ellis. The desk sergeant spotted Simpkins walking up the corridor and leaned across to call to him.

"Ah Bill! I've found out that information you wanted. Didn't take long actually, young Dobbs went round all the tobacconists and news agents in town, only one stocks Gauloise cigarettes and that's Carvers opposite the Bell, apparently the only person in Melbury who buys them, apart from the occasional visitor, is Jackie White, Frank White's wife."

Inspector Downs froze in his conversation and turned slowly around.

"I don't suppose," he said, "that this Jackie White has long dark hair?"

"That's it," replied Price cheerfully, "good looking woman, long dark hair, in fact.."

He paused mid sentence and peered through the dusty window by the police station door.

"In fact, if I'm not mistaken that's her now, getting out of her car just outside the station.."

Father Simpson turned from the presbytery window and it's view of the town church and looked across at Nick King who was sitting on the sofa with Amanda. The priest had been telling the couple everything he knew about Albert Stern's murder.

"Phew," said Nick sweeping back his fair hair with his left hand, "so all these goings on in Melbury seem connected in some way, even perhaps doctor Vandersteen's suicide."

"That's what I believe," replied the priest. "I don't know what the link is but I am very concerned that Inspector Downs is determined to pin the crime on Ronald Finch. I was rather hoping that your paper could help prevent a miscarriage of justice."

Nick looked pensive. "It would be difficult to write opinion rather than fact."

Amanda joined in. "Oh come on Nick, all the serious papers campaign for one cause or another. It would add to the excitement for you to have an angle, besides, you heard Father Simpson, this case is not absolutely clear cut anyway."

Nick smiled at Amanda's enthusiasm. "I suppose it could be ok," he agreed and held up his hand to illustrate an imaginary headline: *"Beekeeper Show murder. Have they got the right man*, that sort of thing."

Father Simpson agreed. "In my opinion you would be doing this town and Ronald Finch a great favour if you were to suggest alternatives in your column," he said. "Not to mention Ronald's wife Dorothy. She is quite distressed with what you write."

"That does it," said Amanda finally. "Nick, one is supposed to be innocent until proven guilty, you are going to have to take a different tack."

Nick laughed and put his arm around Amanda hugging her playfully.

"Well then, that's it!" he said, "I suppose I don't have much choice! The Norwich Standard is going to become the New York Post, Watergate will be nothing after this!"

Jackie White walked into the police station and looked surprised at the gathering in the lobby, all of whom stared at her with what she thought were rather stupid expressions. She walked up to the desk and confronted Sergeant Price.

"I want to speak to Mr Robinson," she said with nervous authority, "I'm his boss."

Sergeant Price raised his eyes to Inspector Downs who had moved towards the desk.

"Mrs White," said Downs solemnly, "you can certainly see Mr Robinson, we would also like you to remain here to help us with our enquiries. To start with could you perhaps tell us exactly where your husband is right now?"

The arrest of Frank White went more smoothly than Inspector Downs could have hoped for. Being used to a certain amount of misfortune in his professional life, Downs was relieved to find Frank White opening his own front door. White looked taken aback by the impressive array of policemen on his doorstep.

"Mr White," began Downs, "I would like you to accompany me to the station. You need not say anything but anything you do say will be taken down and used as evidence against you."

Sergeant Ellis coughed politely.

"Er I think that's 'taken down and may be used against you' sir." Downs looked at Ellis disbelievingly.

"What?"

Ellis squirmed, "The caution sir, It's 'taken down and *may* be used against you'."

"What did I say?"

"You said.."

Frank White looked bemused.

"What the fuck are you nincompoops on about?" He boomed.

"Should I write that down sir?" asked young Constable Dobbs.

"You can't really," rejoined Sergeant Ellis, "he hasn't been properly cautioned yet."

Inspector Downs flushed red.

"*Alright! All right!* Mr Frank White, you need not say anything but anything you say will be taken down and may be used against you." He turned angrily to Sergeant Ellis, "happy now sergeant!" Ellis looked embarrassed. "The lawyer sir.."

"Oh yes," Downs mentally cursed himself. "You have the right to a lawyer and if you don't have one, a lawyer can be provided."

White glowered at the inspector.

"Of course I've got a lawyer, I'm a bloody property agent aren't I."

Simpkins turned to Dobbs.

"Recall the men from the back of the building constable." Sergeant Simpkins took an instant dislike to Frank White. He had met men of his like before and he knew how to deal with them.

Dobbs ran off around the house whilst Frank White was bustled to the waiting police car.

"What's this about?" Frank protested.

"We'll deal with all that when we get to the station; you can see your wife there as well," replied Downs. Simpkins shoved White unceremoniously into the car and climbed in beside him. White settled uncomfortably on the back seat, wedged between Ellis and Simpkins.

"My wife! What's she doing at the police station?"

"All will be revealed," demurred Inspector Downs, turning sideways from the front seat. "We have a lot to ask you and if I were you I would cooperate as much as possible."

White, seeing that protest was useless, sighed and slumped moodily in the rear seat. The police car sped along the hot Melbury streets towards the police station where a small crowd had gathered having heard that 'something' was going on. An excited murmur went through the assembly as they saw Frank White taken from the police car and led into the front door. By late afternoon most of Melbury knew that Frank White had been arrested.

After Nick and Amanda had left, Father Simpson finished his daily prayers and then took a long playing record from a small cupboard, carefully removed it from the sleeve and placed it on an old Garrard turntable, one of the few luxuries he allowed himself. Reclining back in his chair he closed his eyes and allowed his mind to relax to the gentle sound of Respeigh's 'Pines of Rome.' A ring on the doorbell startled him. Father Simpson went to the door to find Debbie standing, rather agitated, on his doorstep.

"Debbie! How good to see you," said Father Simpson warmly; "do come in."

Debbie was wearing the same jeans and tank top that had so distracted Jason Damagio earlier in the day. She stepped in the door and looked up at the priest with large unhappy eyes.

"I'm sorry to trouble you again father but I need some advice and you are the only person I could think of coming to."

"I'm delighted," said the priest, feeling guilty that he found Debbie's attire caused confusing feelings in him. He had taken vows of celibacy of course, but that did not change the fact that he was a man.

"Do come in." They walked into the lounge. The room was filled with the sound of the orchestral music.

Father Simpson lifted the tonearm on the Garrard and gestured Debbie to an armchair. She sat down and produced some papers from her shoulder bag.

"My father's solicitor came to see me this morning," began Debbie. "My father kept his will in the bank and the solicitor had instructions to retrieve it in the event of his death."

Father Simpson listened closely and nodded encouragingly; Debbie continued.

"He left me everything he owns, which is basically the house. He had no money in the bank just an overdraft, It's terrible, I didn't realize he was so hard up and there was I asking him for money."

"Well, you weren't to know Debbie," said Father Simpson, "don't feel bad about that."

"It's not *just* that I'm upset about. You see my father had large gambling debts and the solicitor says I will have to sell the house to pay off the people he owed money to."

Father Simpson considered this; his time in the monastery had not really prepared him for giving financial advice.

"Well," said the priest, at least you should have something left over when you sell the house. It wont be all that bad, that cottage will easily sell, just the garden alone will sell it."

Debbie rocked forward anxiously.

"That's the point! My father loved that house, look at the work he put into the garden; it must be almost an acre. I just feel that it shouldn't be sold. He wanted me to keep it, I mean it was his life."

"I see," said Father Simpson, "I can't immediately see a solution to your problem," he paused for a moment. "I'll tell you what, give me a list of those owed money, perhaps I can come up with an idea."

"I have it here," Debbie sifted through the documents in her hand and produced two sheets of paper, she handed them to the priest.

"Leave this with me, I might have a brain wave." Father Simpson smiled; Debbie looked relieved that she had unburdened herself. She reached out and squeezed his hand.

"You are very kind father."

"Call me William," replied the priest, "it sounds too formal for you to call me father. Apart from in church that is!"

"Alright William." Debbie studied the priest's even features; she couldn't quite work out his age, thirty something anyway. Debbie let go of the priest's hand and stood up. She looked at Father Simpson for a moment. He must have quite a lonely life really, saying mass and looking after his parish.

"Father, I'm sorry, I mean William, what are you doing tonight?"

"I'm not doing much," replied the priest. I'm going to visit Dorothy Finch and then I was going to have a quiet evening. I find I solve more problems relaxing listening to music than any other way. Why do you ask?"

"Well," said Debbie with a little mischief in her voice, "I know that you're a priest but I wondered if I could buy you dinner? There is a really nice pub on the way towards Ixdon that serves good food. It's the least I can do after all your help."

Father Simpson laughed aloud.

"Being a priest does not mean that I can't enjoy myself," he said. "I'm allowed to go out you know, even when it is with an attractive woman."

Debbie flushed, "There is only one thing," added Father Simpson, "perhaps we could go Dutch, I don't get much but I spend little and I know that you are hard up, you told me!"

Debbie laughed, "I don't know why but you seem to have a therapeutic affect on me," she said, "whenever I see you I feel, well, lighter somehow."

"I've told you, it is the holy spirit at work," said the priest, "you must come to my Pentecost vigil next year, then you will know what I mean. By the way wont you want to see your young man from Ixdon?"

Debbie turned down her mouth, "*him*," she said scornfully, "he wasn't interested in me. He was only after one thing and he got really aggressive when he didn't get it. I've given him his cards," she grinned at the priest, "he can go and sort out his testosterone problem somewhere else."

Father Simpson was rather taken aback at this frankness. Debbie looked at him and put her hand to her mouth.

"Oh, I'm sorry, I find it to easy too forget that you're a priest, you seem so, well so normal."

"I'm flattered," replied the priest amused, he really did enjoy Debbie's company although he was becoming concerned about the attraction he felt. He would just have to accept it he thought, after all, he couldn't avoid the company of attractive women just because of his vows.

Debbie turned to the door, "I'll pick you up at eight," she said waving her left hand gaily, "Larcum told me I could borrow his car one evening if I wanted to."

"I'll look forward to it," replied Father Simpson. He watched Debbie's slim figure walk back down the presbytery drive, then he walked back towards the kitchen; his mind went back to Ronald Finch, and the murder of Albert Stern. He must, he thought, make that call to Father O'Byrne..

Jackie White was feeling rather numb as she watched the police depart to arrest her husband. Had Frank been lying to her or was there some sort of genuine mistake? She stood in front of the desk dazed, having almost forgotten the reason for her visit to the police station. Sergeant Price walked around the desk and lightly touching her arm, spoke gently to her.

"This way Mrs White, you can sit in Inspector Downs office and I'll bring you a nice cup of tea."

Jackie suddenly recovered herself.

"No! I wish to see Mr Robinson, I will stay and answer questions but first I want to speak to my employee!"

Sergeant Price hesitated for a moment. "Well.. I don't know if you should see him under the circumstances."

"Look I'm not under arrest or anything. I could walk out the door now if I wanted to. I have every right to see my staff."

Sergeant Price relented and led Jackie to one of the cells at the end of the corridor.

"Another visitor for you Mr Robinson," he called through the small observation flap on the steel door.

"I'll leave the door open and get back to the desk, let me know when you've finished."

Then he peered into the other cell.

"You alright Mr Small, anything you need?"

"Yeah I wanna see Sergeant Simpkins!" Replied Small grumpily.

"He'll see you later, then I expect you can go. Get back to that lovely wife of yours."

"Gawd," muttered Small, relapsing back into silence. Sergeant Price glanced back then walked slowly back towards the front desk.

Jackie and David looked at each other uncertainly for a moment, then David Pulled Jackie to him and held her close. After the conversation with her husband, Jackie had been thinking of finishing the affair with David. It was just too risky. Now though, she felt the old feelings run through her like a light charge of electricity. Her lips found David's and they kissed passionately. Finally David released her.

"Jackie! I'm so happy to see you. I don't know what's been going on stuck in here."

Jackie regained her breath after the embrace.

"Who was your other visitor?"

"My solicitor," replied David, "I've been waiting all day to be interviewed, I don't know what's happening. First they are about to question me then they go and do something else. Then this morning the desk sergeant tells me that Frank is going to 'sort me out'. Have you told him about us? I mean I don't know whether to keep the facts quiet or tell the whole story!"

Jackie took a cigarette from her bag and lit it, blowing a thin column of blue smoke across the cell.

"I haven't told Frank anything; though I almost did I must admit. A lot has been going on. First of all Frank was being blackmailed by Albert Stern as well. He is suspicious that I am having an affair because he had a man watching Stern's house. Whoever it was must have seen us together as we drove to the cottage across the road."

Jackie inhaled on her cigarette again; David sat on the edge of his bunk absorbing this information. Jackie continued. "The problem is I am not sure that this doesn't all tie up."

David looked up, "what do you mean?"

"Well," said Jackie, "Frank has always been kind to me but he has something about him that I've never been able to get to the bottom of. He never talks about great chunks of his past and he has this vicious streak in him, with some folk anyway. Also he seems to know people who can come and do his bidding when required, at the drop of a hat sometimes."

"I'm still not with you," said David.

"I'm just not sure that Frank hasn't got a criminal connection, look at the way he frightened Arthur Well's into selling up. What I am saying is I have a feeling that Frank may be involved with Stern's murder."

David sprung to his feet. "But they have the culprit. This chap Ronald Finch running through the woods and getting into Stern's place, they've got it cut and dried!"

Jackie shrugged, "maybe, it's only a thought, I just happen to think that Frank is capable of it."

"Well if he was being blackmailed I suppose he had a motive," agreed David. "Are you going to tell the police?"

"I don't think I have to," said Jackie stubbing her cigarette out against the cell wall, "they have gone to arrest Frank now."

Along the corridor Bernie Small had become bored, the only interesting thing seemed to be the conversation in the cell further along. He couldn't hear it of course because of the thick walls, however he found that when he pressed his ear against the water pipe running through the back of the cell, the pipe acted as a microphone. He could hear every word. As Jackie finished her conversation with David Bernie stood up from the uncomfortable position of lying with his ear against the pipe. He had a curious grin on his face.

Chapter 10

At the police station Rupert Crook was waiting anxiously. When he spotted Inspector Downs and the contingent of excited policemen leading Frank White up the police station steps, Rupert walked alongside and tried to get the policeman's attention.

"Inspector Downs. I must talk with you!"

Downs ignored him and called to the desk sergeant.

"Sergeant Price, Mr White will be questioned in the interview room by Simpkins, I'll talk to Mrs White to my office."

Frank White scowled grimly at Downs; Rupert Crook became more persistent, grabbing Downs by the sleeve.

"I really must insist that I talk to you inspector!"

Downs shook Rupert's grip from his sleeve and stooping, pushed his face nose to nose with that of the solicitor.

"What do you want? I'm very busy, can't you see!"

Rupert Crook stepped back slightly alarmed.

"I..I must insist.." he began again.

"Oh shut up!" Shouted Downs, who was rather euphoric after the excitement of making the arrest. "Stop snivelling and get to the point!"

Mr Crook looked offended; he pulled himself to his full height, which was not actually very much.

"Either you charge my client, or you let him go." He said imperiously.

"Very well," replied Downs, "we'll charge him. Actually I've been trying to get round to it all day. Now get out of my way."

Mr Crook looked thwarted as the hectic procession made its way down the corridor.

Frank White sat down in the interview room. Simpkins closed the door behind him and walked, deliberately, to the chair behind the desk.

"Mr White," said Simpkins, "I presume that you will want a solicitor present for this interview?"

"Bloody right," Frank White said with feeling, "I want Mr Stone, the same fellow who's going to look after Mr Robinson. And I'll tell you what, you blokes had better have a bloody good reason for dragging me and my wife here or there will be a few careers in ruins."

Simpkins looked unperturbed, he had met characters like this all the time in east London. He leaned back nonchalantly in his chair.

"A reason?" Simpkins stroked his chin thoughtfully. "Well then, how about a dead hoodlum called Lenny James, blackmail and murder, Mr White."

Frank's reaction was just what Simpkins had wanted; he physically blanched.

"I didn't have nothing to do with murdering that old man if that's what you think!" insisted Frank White, with a little more humility this time.

"Well maybe you did! I reckon we've got you bang to rights Frank," said Simpkins casually. "We've got motive, we know about you hiring Lenny James and we know all about your past so why don't you just sing?"

Simpkins realized that he was pushing his luck but he also knew that it would be hard to prove that Stern had been blackmailing White. He might, however, be able to tempt White into admitting something. Frank was shaken; he looked at Simpkins with something verging on respect.

"I'm saying nothing until my solicitor arrives," said Frank quietly.

Simpkins grinned unkindly at his prey. He spoke again, a hard edge to his voice.

"I think you know where I'm coming from Mr White. We'll talk later.."

Simpkins opened the door and yelled down the corridor. "Sergeant Price send someone to keep Mr White company." He turned back to Frank, "I'm used to the likes of you White, Stepney wasn't it? I've got more dirt on you than you can shake a stick at, so you had better be straight with me."

A young policeman came to the door, accompanied by Sergeant Price. Price gave the policeman instructions and turned to Frank.

"Can I get you any refreshment whilst we await your solicitor Mr

White?"

Frank was still recovering from Simpkins verbal onslaught. He hadn't been spoken to like that since he left London. He looked blankly at the desk sergeant.

"Oh.. er yes, thanks, a cup of tea would be good."

Simpkins step was light as he walked back down the corridor; he had enjoyed his bit of play-acting. This was just like the old days, he thought.

Nick sat at the small table in the hotel room, the screen of his laptop glowed uninspiringly in front of him. Amanda lay on the bed, her right hand behind her head.

"I don't know," said Nick at last. "I can't imagine any connection between Doctor Vandersteen, Albert Stern and this chap Lenny James. I mean Stern wasn't a patient of Vandersteen's and Lenny James doesn't even live around here. I still can't help thinking it's just a coincidence and that maybe Ronald Finch did do it after all."

Amanda rolled over to look at Nick.

"One thing I do know Nick, is that investigative reporters don't solve things in their hotel rooms."

"Great!" Said Nick, "except all the people I want to talk to seem to be under arrest! PC Dobbs is keeping everyone informed more than The Standard. I don't know how he gets away with it; and now the BBC is here to steal my thunder."

Amanda rolled off the bed and stood behind Nick, massaging his shoulders.

"They won't steal your thunder if you get to the bottom of it. You will be the headline. Why don't you interview that Mrs Cummings? Debbie said that she might have seen something."

Nick reached over his shoulder and held Amanda's left hand; he turned to look at her.

"You're right. There is nothing to be learnt sitting here. Lets go and start asking some more questions."

Back at the Melbury Police Station, Inspector Downs had hastily convened a conference.
Sergeant Ellis and Bill Simpkins sat impassively as Downs explained the situation.

"Look," he said, glancing around the room. "I am on borrowed time. As soon as Chief Superintendent Ross gets the suspicion that this is not a straightforward domestic murder, he'll have a major incident squad down here and we won't get a look in. We have to get to the bottom of this enquiry and quickly. In fact if there is a big television report tonight, Ross could even send a team tomorrow."

Ellis and Simpkins considered this for a moment. Sergeant Ellis was an ambitious policeman, being involved in this enquiry was going to look good on his records, assuming it all went well of course. Bill Simpkins felt too involved now to let go, also he wanted to finish interrogating Frank White. His years in London had given him a hatred of these gangsters who always seemed to beat the rap. No one in the room wanted to lose the investigation to a bona fide murder squad. Simpkins thought for a moment.

"The trouble is," he said, "we can't interview Frank White until his solicitor gets here: Jack Stone or whatever his name is. It will probably end up as tomorrow morning by the time he gets briefed and so on. Also tomorrow we should have all the forensic and post mortem results. If we can stall Ross until tomorrow night I reckon we'll be home and dry."

Sergeant Ellis decided to have a say; he leaned forward almost apologetically.

"Sir, if you are going to charge Mr Finch with the murder you can tell Norwich that the case is effectively solved. We can say that Frank White and the others are just witnesses. It will give us twenty four hours and if we have sorted it all out by then no one will mind."

Inspector Downs nodded. "If we haven't sorted it out I'll be in deep shit," he said with feeling. "Mind you it's only the depth that has varied so far in my illustrious career so I don't suppose it matters." He looked morosely around the room. "I'll probably get sent to the Hebrides as traffic warden if I screw this up."

"We *will* sort it out," said Simpkins, surprised at Down's uncharacteristic display of self-doubt. "We have all the information we need; we just have to put it together so it makes sense. You wait, by tomorrow night we will have nailed the killer. Personally I'm pretty sure it'll prove to be Lenny James and that Frank White employed him."

Simpkins confidence in solving the case rubbed off on Downs, although he didn't agree with his conclusions.

"Very well," he said enthusiastically, "let's charge Finch now get it over with, then I'll call Chief Superintendent Ross and assure him that it's all in hand. It looks like we'll have to let Mrs White and young Robinson go home until tomorrow."

"What about Frank White?" Interjected Sergeant Ellis, "we don't want to let him go do we?"

"Leave him to me." Said Simpkins, "I think I can convince him that it is in his interest to stay in custody tonight.."

Downs looked blankly at Simpkins, then shrugged his shoulders.

"Ok, let's get on with it. Sergeant Ellis, bring Finch to the interview room to be charged and send Mrs White and Robinson away. Tell them we want them back here at ten o'clock sharp tomorrow morning."

"We still haven't chatted to Mrs Cummings," pointed out Simpkins, "also you mentioned that the barmaid from the Bell thought that Doctor Vandersteen visited Stern the night he was killed."

Downs squeezed his temples with his left thumb and forefinger.

"Gawd!"

"Don't worry inspector, these cases often get complicated before a simple solution appears. Perhaps Sergeant Ellis could take some evidence from Mrs Cummings at home tonight and I'll see Deborah, the barmaid, in the morning."

"No problem for me," said Ellis. He was flattered; normally Downs didn't trust him with anything important.

Downs agreed. He had enough today and his mind seemed awash with random disjointed facts. No wonder they usually put a full incident team on a job like this. He was trying to crack the case with a few urban policemen and a hastily recruited forensic officer.

After Simpkins and Ellis had left, Downs made the call to Norwich. Chief Superintendent Ross was relieved when the Inspector assured him that all was well. The aftermath of the football riot had left the Norwich cells full and had totally occupied all his manpower. Downs put down the telephone. After a moment he pulled out a telephone directory from his draw and flicked through it. Then he picked up the receiver and dialled another number. A woman's voice answered.

"Miss Hart? Hello it's Inspector John Downs here.. yes.. oh I'm fine; listen, I hope this isn't inappropriate, but I was wondering if you would like to have dinner with me tonight?"

Bernie Small stood on the steps of the police station and took a deep satisfied breath of the musty evening air. After signing the statement prepared by Bill Simpkins, Small was allowed to go. He walked down the steps and set off to the town centre humming cheerfully to himself. For the first time in weeks he felt happy. This morning he had been an almost bankrupt murderer; now he was free and if he wasn't mistaken, about to make some fast money. He might even, he thought, be able to deal with that young rat Weinstein and his unfair dismissal case.

The town centre was quiet. The shops were closed and the streets were deserted. It was not quite dusk but already small bats swooped over Bernie's head, skilfully feasting on the clouds of summer insects. Bernie strolled down the high street and stepped into the Bell Hotel. Instead of turning left as usual into the bar, he stood at the reception desk and confidently hit the small brass bell with the palm of his hand. The sound of the bell echoed down the passage towards the kitchen. Fran Todd appeared, wiping her hands on a towel. She looked surprised to see Small. His spell in the police station was old news in the hotel.

"Mr Small! I thought you were, well, you know.."

Small held up his hand impatiently.

I was, now I'm not. What room is that reporter bloke in, the one from The Standard?"

"He's in room five, is everything alright Mr Small.."

Fran was talking to an empty space as Bernie ran off up the stairs. As he walked down the corridor looking at the door numbers, Nick and Amanda appeared from their room. Nick was struggling to lock the door behind him.

"Ah just the man!" Boomed Bernie as he recognised Nick.

Nick looked up, surprised.

"Mr Small! I thought you were.."

"I was, now I'm not," interrupted Small. "But I happen have some information that you might consider; shall we say..valuable?"

"Well do come in," replied Nick enthusiastically, "I could certainly do with a bit of info."

They went back into the room and Small arranged himself on a cushioned chair in the corner. He grinned at Nick and then looked lasciviously at Amanda. Amanda uncomfortably shifted her gaze out of the window.

"Well what can we do for you Mr Small?" Asked Nick, irritated at Small's blatant ogling of his girlfriend.

Small returned his attention to Nick.

"How about," he said, "a tale of murder, blackmail and .." his mind struggled to find the right word, then he gave up. "Sex!"

Nick raised his eyebrows and glanced at Amanda, "well.. er.. yes, yes, excellent, go ahead."
He looked encouragingly at Small.

"Ah! There's the rub," said Bernie, emphasising the point by rubbing his palms together.

"This valuable information will cost.. shall we say..a grand."

Bernie sat back, waiting to observe the impact of this announcement.

Nick jumped up. "A thousand pounds, The Standard can't afford to pay that sort of money for a story! It's just a provincial newspaper!"

Small was unperturbed.

"That's ok, I'll see if that nice Mr Damagio from the Beeb is interested."

Small got up to leave.

"No wait!" Nick scratched his head anxiously; "you think you have something really hot?"
Small nodded confidently.

"Let me call my editor," said Nick, "then I'll get back to you. I've never been in this situation before, so I don't know what he'll say."

Small thought about this for a moment: "tell you what," he said, "I'll be in the bar: a large scotch on your tab would be ok I presume?"

"Yes..yes that's fine," agreed Nick, "I'll speak to you in a while when I've made a call."

Small got up to leave, as he approached the door he winked mischievously at Amanda. Amanda squirmed uncomfortably.

The door closed and Nick stood in silence for a moment. Then he looked across at his girlfriend.

"What do you think Amanda?"

"I think he's a dirty old man," she replied with feeling, "I feel like I need a shower after the way he looked at me."

"I'm talking about his story dozy."

"Don't call me that; anyway I think that you should hear what he has to say first, if it's that interesting perhaps Mr Bryant will pay."

"You might be right," agreed Nick, "if it's going to increase the circulation much he might consider it: I'll give him a ring."

Debbie arrived at the presbytery at seven o'clock. Father Simpson greeted her warmly; in the background his Garrard record deck sent the mellow sound of classical music echoing down the hallway.

"My you look radiant!" exclaimed Father Simpson, visibly impressed.

Debbie was certainly looking her best. In exchange for her usual jeans and casuals she had decided to dress up for the evening. In deference to Father Simpson she had attempted to keep her style unprovocative but the long yellow dress she had chosen seemed to provide a sense of concealed sensuality. She wore little make-up; just some eyeliner and lipstick but the effect on William Simpson was quite profound.

"Thank you," replied Debbie happily, she looked at the priest admiringly. He was dressed in casual slacks and a cream short-sleeved shirt.

"You don't look bad yourself! What wonderful music, what is it?"

"Vivaldi; 'Concerto for viola d'amore' to be precise." Father Simpson smiled.

"That sounds romantic," Debbie stepped into the hallway.

"That was Vivaldi's intention I think." Father Simpson couldn't help smiling again. He showed Debbie to the lounge where the music was emanating from a small pair of second hand Spendor loudspeakers.

Debbie stood by the fireplace. "I didn't know priest's were allowed to be romantic."

Father Simpson's smile broadened, he was enjoying himself.

"Then it will probably surprise you to know that Vivaldi was also a priest!"

Debbie felt young and silly now.

"Oh. I didn't know that of course, and yet he still wrote such beautiful romantic music."

"Absolutely," Father Simpson agreed, "apparently it was not uncommon for Antonio Vivaldi to leave the alter in the middle of mass complaining of chest pains, just to scribble down a few bars of music that had sprung into his head."

It was Debbie's turn to smile.

"No! You are teasing me now."

"Really! It's true, but then I do have the unfair advantage of having been taught ecclesiastical music at the Ospedale della pieta, the very place where Vivaldi himself taught music. I'll tell you more about him over dinner if you like, he was quite an interesting character."

"I'd like that." Replied Debbie. She meant it. In fact, she thought, this charming young priest could talk about what he liked over dinner, she really didn't mind.

"Would you like an aperitif?" asked Father Simpson, "unfortunately I can only offer you Benedictine or a rather ordinary white wine."

"I'd better not if I'm driving," said Debbie, "I'm taking you to an out of the way pub near Ixdon. It's called The Trowel. I thought you might feel uncomfortable if you knew everyone and we were together."

"That's very thoughtful Debbie, but it isn't a problem. Can we just wait for a few minutes though? I'm expecting a call from Father O'Byrne in Norwich. He's a very smart man; I've been talking to him about your father's death. He came down this afternoon as a matter of fact; he seemed very interested, especially as your father came from his area some years ago."

"Can he help?" Asked Debbie doubtfully

"He seemed to think that he could. Apparently he knows a bit about your father when he used to live in the parish..excuse me there's the telephone. That's probably him now, come and sit in the lounge, I won't be a moment."

Father Simpson was longer than a moment and Debbie amused herself by looking around the room. She could hear the subdued and indistinct conversation in the hallway. The record on the Garrard came to an end and the stylus clicked monotonously on the lead out groove. Debbie leaned forward and tentatively lifted the delicate tonearm.

Father Simpson was deep in thought as he came back into the room. Debbie smiled.

"I turned off you record, it had finished."

Father Simpson looked worried.

"Oh.. no that's fine.. thank you."

Debbie picked up on the priest's mood.

"Was the 'phone call helpful? It sounded important."

"I'm not sure," replied the priest, brightening up as he looked again at Debbie in her smart yellow dress. "I'll tell you some of it over dinner. Father O' Byrne is doing some checking up for me, it is probably irrelevant."

Father Simpson switched off the turntable and carefully returned the record to its sleeve. He looked really quite handsome and 'unpriest like,' thought Debbie. It struck her as unusual to see a clergyman so casually dressed.

"Do they mind you dressing so normally?" She asked tactlessly. "Oh, I'm sorry, I mean do they.. "

Father Simpson laughed, "If you mean am I allowed to dress like my parishioners occasionally, then yes." Answered the priest happily, "however, I think that there might be some rumblings from the bishop if I were to celebrate mass dressed in denims and a tee-shirt!"

"Well anyway, you look very nice," said Debbie. Suddenly she felt young and awkward. Usually, with men, she felt so confident and 'in control.' "Anyway," she added briskly, "if you are ready, we'll go. It takes a little while to get to The Trowel. You can tell me about your telephone call from Norwich on the way."

Nick and Amanda walked into the bar where Bernie Small, on his third scotch, was enjoying the attention of the Bell regulars. "Yes," Bernie was saying, waving his whiskey glass wildly, "of course the police were only doing their job, but I think I've pointed them in the right direction." He spotted Nick coming through the door. "Ah Nick m'boy! 'Scuse me everyone," he looked at the assembled audience and assumed a posture of exaggerated self importance, "I've got to talk to Mr King here."

Nick manoeuvred Bernie into the corner of the bar where there were a few vacant seats, they all sat down and Nick, glancing around, began in a confidential tone.

"My editor has authorised me to negotiate a five hundred pound fee, *if* your story is good enough. He's left me to decide that. What do you think?"

Bernie thought it was fine. Five hundred pounds right now looked a lot better than the few years for manslaughter that he was contemplating that morning. He recounted to Nick the conversation between Jackie and David that he had overheard in the police cell earlier that day, embellishing the story here and there when he thought it appropriate. Nick, busily taking notes, was impressed. He sat back in his chair and swept a hand through his hair.

"Phew!" He said at last, "This is hot stuff! I don't know if we can print details of the affair between Jackie White and David Robinson, but blackmail certainly provides a possible motive for White to murder Finch. You think that Stern was blackmailing Mrs White as well?"

"Yup," said Bernie looking wistfully into his by now empty glass. "She said 'as well', that Frank White was being blackmailed by Albert Stern 'as well.'"

Amanda joined in. "And the dead man up at Boulmer Cottage: *he* was driving the grey Volvo that Mrs Cummings told Father Simpson was parked near Albert Stern's cottage the night he was murdered. So *he* must be the man that Jackie said was working for her husband watching Stern's house."

"It certainly ties up," agreed Nick.

"Great!" Said Bernie who was more interested in solving his financial problems than a crime. "So when do I get paid?"

Nick laughed, "Well I guess it's a good enough scoop. Pity we don't know why White was being blackmailed, but if his wife says he was, I guess he was! I'll get the money sent from Norwich."

Bernie gave an embarrassed cough.

"Would there be a possibility of a small advance? I mean it's not easy for me to get to a bank tonight. I've had a very stressful day you know."

It was Nick's turn to look embarrassed.

"I've got about twenty pounds, that's all."

Bernie mentally converted twenty pounds to eight whiskeys and one of Fran Todd's meat pies.

"That'll do my son!" He stood up and winked at Amanda again. "That'll keep the wolf from the door, for a night at least!"

Small took the money and retreated back to the bar. Amanda turned to Nick.

"The police should know this," she whispered urgently.

"They probably do know it by now," replied Nick. "Look, lets go over to Mrs Cummings, then I'll type up some copy for the next edition."

"Do we ever get to eat?" Asked Amanda petulantly. She was on holiday after all. "I want to go for a proper meal somewhere. Somewhere outside Melbury for a change."

Nick looked unsympathetic. "No chance, too much work to do. Come on we're off to see old snoopy."

Inspector Downs was late arriving at Madeleine Hart's home. Charging Ronald Finch had proved to be hard work with Mr Crook continuously interrupting. Eventually an unhappy Mr Finch was taken back to his cell and Downs, feeling exhausted, left the hastily commandeered secretaries to type up the days work. He was still sure that the events surrounding Frank White were coincidence and that Finch was the killer, despite what Simpkins thought. Perhaps the forensic evidence tomorrow would shed some more light on the case.

Madeleine opened her front door and Downs caught his breath. She had dressed for an evening out, but it wasn't so much what she was wearing but how she was wearing it that caught his attention. Madeleine, in all innocence, was incapable of disguising her sexuality. Somehow she personified the term. She didn't know it of course. In fact she was quite critical of herself: she thought her hair was never right and she really *was* a bit overweight. She had decided this latter point because the magazines she read always had pictures of emaciated girls who, to Madeleine's eyes, were beautiful. Tonight she wore a long black skirt, fashionably split to the thigh and a white cotton blouse through which Downs could see 'something lacy'. She also wore more make-up than usual. Perhaps she had been a bit too heavy on the lipstick, but her lips were very full and it would appear that way. Anyway Madeleine's lack of guile prevented her from seeming "tarty'. Madeleine was also very slightly myopic which gave her eyes a vulnerable "searching" appearance. In fact she was just trying to focus. At work she sometimes wore glasses but she hated them and found contact lenses irritated her eyes making them stream. The inspector looked at her and struggled to find something to say. Eventually he found his tongue.

"You look.. well.. you look wonderful!"

Madeleine flushed. She couldn't really say the same of Inspector

Downs. He had worked late and his only gesture to the evening out was a shave which he had indulged in at the police station, using one of the cheap razors normally reserved for overnight 'detainees.' Nevertheless she found him rather endearing in his crumpled brown trousers and tired jacket.

"Thank you," she said. "Are you sure you can face an evening out? You must be very tired with everything you have on your plate right now."

Madeleine looked genuinely concerned. The inspector assumed a burdened expression.

"Oh well, no, I'm fine." Then he added modestly, "murder investigations are always a bit stressful." He didn't mention that this was his first murder investigation, or that he was only allowed to do it because Norwich was doing it's best to have a civil war and his chief thought the small problem in Melbury was a simple domestic case. Cut and dried.

"Where shall we go?" asked Madeleine happily.

"Somewhere quiet," replied Downs. "Somewhere I can forget about all this for a few hours." He gestured, without looking, towards a large hawthorn bush behind him. Maddie peered at the bush, puzzled for a moment. The inspector continued. "I would like us to have a splendid evening and, maybe tomorrow, I can approach this case with a fresh mind."

"I think I know just the place," said Maddie. "Come on, I'll take you there."

Sergeant Ellis knocked on Edith Cummings door a little after seven thirty. After some while the door opened and Mrs Cummings peered suspiciously at the policeman.

"Mrs Cummings?"

"Yes."

"I'm sorry to bother you this late Mrs Cummings but I wonder if you could answer a few questions about a car parked near here on the night that Mr Stern was killed."

Mrs Cummings reluctantly showed Sergeant Ellis to the living room. A sweet cloying smell pervaded the house.

"I'm making some herbal beverages for the show," she explained, "they are very popular; cure all sorts of ailments."

Sergeant Ellis was interested; he sat, uninvited, on the cream and red floral sofa.

"Really? Do you have anything for rheumatism? My poor wife suffers terribly. Mind you it's not quite so bad at this time of year."

Mrs Cummings seemed to brighten up.

"Boil the bark of a willow tree in a pot and then get her to drink the liquid when it's cooled down a bit."

Ellis raised his eyebrows and made some notes on his pad.

"Make sure you get the bark from a tree in a nice damp spot by the river mind," added Mrs Cummings. "It will have more resistance."

Sergeant Ellis seemed impressed.

"I don't suppose there's anything for hay fever is there? It makes my life a misery at this time of year."

Mrs Cummings was enjoying the sergeant's attention and forgot her normal reticence. She clasped her hands together.

"Oh yes. Put some borage, hyssop and.." she unclasped her hands and clenched her fists as if racking her brain for the information. "Yes fennel or sage leaves, that's it, put them in a bowl, pour on hot water and inhale the steam under a towel."

Ellis scribbled frantically,

"Marvellous!" He exclaimed, "I'll get the missus to try all these, how did you learn all this sort of thing Mrs Cummings?"

Barbara sat down in a matching chair next to Sergeant Ellis.

"Herbal remedies are wonderfully natural you know sergeant, I have always had an interest since I was a child in Norfolk. When my daughter was young.." she tailed off and began to look very sad. Then looking up she continued. "Anyway it's just a hobby. What was it you wanted to see me about?"

Sergeant Ellis returned to the subject of the grey car that Edith had mentioned to Father Simpson. Mrs Cummings described the car she had seen under the chestnut trees, no she hadn't seen it before and she couldn't identify the make, she didn't know much about cars she explained.

Sergeant Ellis dutifully noted all this down. Then sat thinking for a moment, his pencil at the ready on his notepad.

"Was there anything else that you saw that evening that could help our investigation," he asked.

Mrs Cummings reluctantly repeated the story she had given the priest. She really did not want the reputation of a busybody. Ellis was surprised when Mrs Cumming's mentioned that Debbie had visited Albert Stern the night he was killed.

"That's curious," mused the sergeant, "what was a barmaid doing visiting an old man at that time of night?"

Mrs Cummings eyes narrowed.

"It doesn't surprise me," she said with feeling. "That man was always up to something woman-wise.."

She caught Sergeant Ellis looking at her strangely.

"I'm sorry," she added quickly, smoothing her skirt, embarrassed. "This is a small town; people notice things."

Sergeant Ellis nodded; indeed, people 'noticing things' was often the greatest asset a police force had. He pursued the topic.

"Was there a woman involved with him now do you know?"

Mrs Cummings looked more embarrassed.

"I wouldn't know that sergeant, I doubt it, he was seventy something you know..mind you," she added knowingly, "I wouldn't put it past him.."

Sergeant Ellis got the distinct impression that Albert Stern did not conform to her view of how a seventy-year-old should behave, she was obviously an old fashioned sort, he thought. He looked at his watch.

"Well, I must be going, thank you for all your help Mrs Cummings."

Sergeant Ellis stood up.

"Before you go let me get you some of my elderflower and yarrow elixir, it sold very well last year at the show. People keep telling me it worked wonders in the winter, for fever and colds, it might do something for your hay fever."

Sergeant Ellis thanked her profusely and stepped back out onto the street. Across the road Albert Stern's house looked dark and ominous in the low light of the grey hazy moon. The chestnut trees rustled in a light gust of wind. Ellis shivered and walked quickly back towards the town centre. He thought about Albert Stern and Debbie. Why had Debbie visited Stern? Was it possible that this young woman was responsible for the old man's violent death?

Chapter 11

The Trowel public house was one of the few thatched pubs left in Suffolk. The art of thatching was a dying trade and higher insurance costs tended to make landlords replace old thatch with tiles. The Trowel, whilst off the beaten track, was popular with connoisseurs of 'real beer'. Indeed The Campaign For Real Ale, CAMRA, somtimes organized a bus trip to visit and sample The Trowel's offerings. Also the pub's food, under the auspices of a new Italian chef, was beginning to get a good name in the area.

Jason Damagio and his director sat near the Trowel's Inglenook fireplace. Jason looked moodily around the almost empty bar.

"What did you bring me out here for Andy, there's bugger all here."

Andy puffed happily on a small cigar. "I presume," he said loftily, that by 'bugger all here,' you mean there are no women."

Damagio looked miserably around the bar again.

"Well if twee horse brasses and bits of old farm tool hanging on the wall are your scene, I suppose it's perfect. Just because three of the best looking females I've ever seen in my life happen to be over in Melbury, why not go to some remote pub for the evening I say."

Andy smiled.

"This pub," he said patiently, "happens to sell some of the finest beer in the known universe. In fact CAMRA come here on specific visits just to try it."

The Trowel landlord, a stooped elderly man with untidy grey hair was collecting glasses on the adjacent table.

"Isn't that right landlord," called Andy, "The Trowel is very popular with CAMRA."

The Landlord turned, beer glasses in hand and scowled.

"Don't you talk to me about bloody CAMRA." He shook the glasses menacingly at Andy. "Said they were coming here last week to try me mild, I got it just right, perfect in fact, took me all week. Know what they did? Turned up in a big bloody bus, drank about ten pints

132

of 'Ixdon Peculiar' each and got back on their bloody bus pissed out of their wits." He shook the beer glasses again "I'll give you bloody CAMRA."

He turned back to the bar muttering.

Jason rocked back in his chair chuckling.

"So much for your so called ale experts! Come on let's go somewhere with a bit of action."

Jason and Andy had sent a dramatic piece of broadcasting to Norwich for transmission that evening. As a result, they had managed to get yet another day in the area to gather more information and send another item on 'The Beekeeper Show Murder.' Like Nick King they did not have to go far to put another item together: the town was full of people ready to expound theories and motives as to the crime. With little left to do for the evening Jason and Andy had left their crew in Melbury to visit The Trowel Public House.

"Lets just have one more pint of Ixdon," Andy protested, " then we can head back. The night is still young."

Jason was about to insist that they leave, when he noticed Debbie walk through the entrance, closely followed by Father Simpson. In contrast to the drab decor of the pub, Debbie looked positively radiant in her yellow dress. She approached the bar, held Damagio's eyes for a split second, then turned to the landlord.

"You have a table booked under the name of Deborah Smith I believe?"

Jason looked at Andy's empty glass.

"It's my round I think."

He swept up both glasses and made for the bar. Andy spotted Debbie and chuckled to himself, *"and a small cigar please Jason!"* He called.

Jason approached the bar and stood next to Debbie, waiting his turn to be served. He half turned towards her.

"Hello Miss.. er Smith we met in the Bell in Melbury I believe?"

Debbie could hardly forget Jason's clumsy attempt at flirtation earlier that day. She fixed him again with her large brown eyes.

"Yes Mr Damagio, I remember you. This is Father William Simpson, a friend of mine."

Jason had difficulty dragging his eyes away from Debbie's. He looked at Father Simpson, the slim figure in the cream open neck shirt looked anything but a priest.

Jason extended a hand. "Jason Damagio, pleased to meet you, er, father."

"Call me William," replied Father Simpson. "An interesting broadcast you made tonight Mr Damagio."

Jason looked pleased; he smiled at Debbie.

"You enjoyed it?"

"Well," Father Simpson chose his words carefully; "If I were you I would be careful assuming that Ronald Finch is Albert Stern's murderer. All this 'Beekeeper Show Murder' stuff is very good sensational news but you might begin to look foolish if Mr Finch proves to be innocent."

"Of course he did it." Jason tried unsuccessfully to hold Debbie's gaze again. "We've got the whole story, anyway he was officially charged with the murder tonight, didn't you know?"

Father Simpson did not know. He looked troubled.

"Table two madam," said the stooped landlord. Debbie glared at Damagio and pointed Father Simpson towards a pine table in the corner of the room.

Damagio returned to his place by the fireplace and slopped a dimpled glass in front of his colleague.

"She's crazy about me," he said breathlessly taking his seat.

"She looked at you as if she couldn't stand you," suggested Andy.

"Ah, that's just women for you.. 'spare me your indifference' as they say."

He adjusted his seat so as to see Debbie.

Debbie squeezed Father Simpson's hand and leaned forward looking worried.

"I'm so sorry," she said, "I thought that this place would be quiet."

Father Simpson squeezed her hand back.

"Don't worry," he said, "right now I'm more concerned about Ronald Finch, it will be interesting to see if Father O'Byrne comes up with anything else.."

Inspector Downs sat uncomfortably in Madeleine's car. It wasn't that the car was uncomfortable, but Maddie's black skirt had ridden well up her leg provocatively exposing a stocking top, suspender and as much female thigh as the inspector had ever seen, never mind sat next to. He shifted his position to try to avoid looking, as Maddie leaned forward peering myopically down the dark Suffolk lanes.

"Ah, I think it's left here."

She threw the steering wheel to the left causing the inspector to slump against her; he put out his hand to straighten himself only to find it straying onto her exposed thigh.

"*Oh!* Oh sorry!" He exclaimed, withdrawing his hand and slumping against her again.

Maddie turned and smiled at him.

"LOOK OUT!" Yelled Down's as a sharp right hand bend appeared. Maddie spun the wheel hard right and the inspector slumped gratefully the other way.

"Are we nearly there?" Asked Downs, praying that his ordeal would be soon over.

Maddie accelerated unnecessarily down an extremely narrow section of lane, finally negotiating an almost impossibly tight right turn into a small stone courtyard.

"Yes," replied Maddie, hitting the brakes and sending the inspector on a close examination of the windscreen.

"In fact, I think this is it here."

Down's looked up. In front of them was a thatched building with a sign, swinging in the breeze, depicting what looked to him like a mediaeval instrument of torture. The sign proudly declared the premises as 'The Trowel Inn: Purveyor of fine food and ales'.

David lay on his back, gazing at the sloping ceiling. Jackie lifted herself up on one elbow and gently caressed David's cheek with the back of her right hand. She looked worried.

"The police will want some answers tomorrow David, what are you going to tell them?"

Jackie and David had taken advantage of Frank White's detention to return to the cottage next door to Mrs Cummings. As soon as they entered the cottage they embraced passionately and succumbed to frantic lovemaking on the hallway floor.

"Well!" Jackie said as they recovered. "What brought that on?"

"Must be the tension." David was feeling rather foolish with his trousers around his ankles.

Jackie looked at him and laughed.

"Lucky the postman didn't come!"

David feigned a rueful expression.

"He's about the only one who didn't."

They both began to laugh uncontrollably and staggered together up the stairs, the laughter echoing around the sparsely furnished cottage.

Now they lay on the bed in the main bedroom; it was familiar territory to them.

"*David!*"

David seemed to snap back to the present.

"Wha' oh yes, the police. I've just been thinking. I'm going to tell them the truth."

"Great!" Said Jackie, sitting up now. "That will drop us all in it nicely."

David eased himself up and sat, hunched, on the side of the bed, his shoulders tense. He turned to look at Jackie.

"Look, there has been a murder, your husband may well be involved, you said so yourself. There is no point in fabricating a story just to keep our little secret. Before you know where you are we will be suspects, we might even be now."

"So you are going to tell them that you broke into Albert Stern's house to steal evidence implicating me with Stern," snorted Jackie. "Brilliant! Don't forget to mention that I was being blackmailed. That way you can give them enough circumstantial evidence to charge me straight off."

David was beginning to feel annoyed with Jackie's heavy sarcasm. He stood up and walked across to the window.

"OK smart ass, *you* come up with a plausible explanation for me being in Jasmine Cottage nicking evidence."

He lifted the curtain and looked absently out of the window. He could see Albert Stern's house, sombre and dark. The light from Mrs Cummings cottage illuminated the road. He was just thinking how much darker it was tonight than last time they were here, when he suddenly remembered something.

"My God!" David dropped the curtain and turned his back to the window.

Jackie looked concerned.

"What's the matter David? You've gone quite pale."

David looked intensely at Jackie.

"I've just remembered: the other night, when you went to the bathroom, I lifted the curtain to look out of the window."

Jackie was puzzled.

"So?"

David became agitated.

"I saw someone running across Stern's lawn."

Jackie thought about the significance of this; then the penny dropped.

"David!"

"Quite! It was quite late and whoever it was did look quite furtive. I'll bet anything that whoever I saw was Albert Stern's killer."

Jackie looked alarmed. "Did you recognize them, I mean was it Mr Finch?"

David thought about this.

"I don't know.. it could have been. Whoever it was seemed quite small, but they were running sort of hunched so it may have just looked that way."

"You'll have to tell the police!" Jackie rolled off the bed and walked around to the window. She looked across at Albert Stern's house. To Jackie the light from Mrs Cummings window cast an eerie shadow over the lawn. Despite the balmy night Jackie shuddered. She turned and folded her arms around David's neck and glanced apprehensively out of the window again.

"I don't like it here, lets go somewhere cheerful, perhaps some clever solution will appear and we can get out of this mess."

David agreed and having secured the cottage they made their way around to the barn and to David's car. David started the engine. "Where to?" He asked.

"Somewhere out of the way," said Jackie.

"I know just the place!" David crunched the Vauxhall's gear stick into first and put his foot down. The rear wheels spun on the gravel and the car lurched forward and towards the yard entrance, kicking up a cloud of dust as it accelerated towards the main road. "Had lunch there a few weeks ago when I was showing a client a place outside Ixdon. It's called The Shovel or something like that, it should be nice and quiet."

A little after nine p.m. Bill Simpkins walked unannounced into the cell in which Frank White was trying to make himself comfortable. Frank was not entirely unfamiliar with overnight detention in police cells, although after his newfound comfortable life in Suffolk, he had not expected to encounter the experience again. Accompanying Simpkins was a tall middle-aged man with a large curved nose and thinning grey hair. The nose supported heavy black-rimmed glasses. The tall man, seeing White, grinned and held out a large hand. His husky voice hinted of a southeast accent.

"'Ullo Frank, long time no see! What 'ave you been up to then?"

Frank White rose wearily to his feet, glanced apprehensively at Simpkins and shook Jack Stone's hand unenthusiastically.

"Ullo Jack, there's been a mix up that's all." He turned to Simpkins, "sergeant do you think you could leave Mr Stone and me for a while?"

Simpkins agreed but with a caveat: "of course Mr White, however I would like to make it clear that although you are quite entitled to return home tonight, I would prefer it if you stayed here."

Jack Stone looked sharply at Simpkins.

"If my client is entitled to return home, then return home he shall!" He said sternly.

"That's fine, but presently people round here know nothing of Mr White's colourful background. I have no reason to brief the press, and I shall have even less reason if Mr White is co-operative. As it happens I would prefer it if he stayed as we feel he may be able to assist in our investigation into a very serious crime."

Jack Stone looked at Simpkins in well-practised indignation.

"You can't threaten my client! This is outrageous.."

Frank held up his hand impassively.

"Jack..Jack, relax, I'll stay if it makes them happy." He looked around the sparse yellow walled cell. "I've spent the night in worse places. The main thing is that we clear this mess up."

Stone shrugged his angular shoulders and dragged a wooden chair from the other side of the cell. Simpkins looked satisfied.

"Right then, I'll leave you to it. We haven't got a lot of staff on tonight so when you've finished just wander back to the desk. The door won't be locked. Then I would like to question Mr White about the circumstances surrounding the murder of Albert Stern."

Simpkins left closing the cell door behind him. Jack Stone looked for a second at the austere door then stood up and looked around the cell distastefully.

"Seems like a right bastard," he said, tilting his head towards the door.

"He's certainly giving me a hard time." Agreed Frank. "Unfortunately though he does have some ammunition. Let's go through it and get you in the picture. I'm relying on you getting me out of this."

Jack Stone grinned and slapped White on the back.

"Always have Frank. Always have.."

Jason Damagio practically dropped his beer as Madeleine Hart walked into The Trowel, accompanied by Inspector Downs. Maddie peered into the dark bar and Downs steered her to a table not far from Jason.

Damagio grabbed his director's sleeve. "My God!" He hissed, "have you seen that?"

Andy had to admit that the woman in the black skirt and white blouse was something.

"She's gorgeous!" Continued Damagio, still clutching Andy's sleeve; "look at those.."

"Alright!" said Andy, exasperated. "She is lovely, but just calm down will you. Just behave yourself for a change and admire from afar."

It was too late. Jason had already left his seat and was in the process of introducing himself to Inspector Downs and Madeleine Hart.

Across the room Debbie covered her forehead with her hand.

"Oh no!" She whispered, "it's Inspector Downs. So much for a quiet place!"

"Interesting." Observed Father Simpson. "Our inspector has obviously taken a shine to Miss Hart; Doctor Vandersteen's receptionist."

Debbie looked up. "You mean the poor man who committed suicide? How awful. The poor girl! She found him didn't she?"

Inspector Downs noticed Father Simpson. He was finding Damagio rather tiresome so excusing himself he made his way across to the priest's table.

"Good evening father, what a surprise to see you here. Difficult times for Melbury don't you think?"

"I certainly do." said Father Simpson cordially. "Inspector Downs this is Miss Deborah Smith, a friend of mine."

Downs nodded at Debbie.

"Indeed Miss Smith, it is fortunate to meet you. Sergeant Simpkins would like to have a few words with you tomorrow morning at the station if it is not inconvenient."

Debbie looked flustered, "I've already told the police what I saw in the woods."

Inspector Downs looked at her unsympathetically.

"I think this has more to do with your late night visit to Mr Stern the night he was murdered. Do you think that you could come along at say, nine o clock?"

Debbie looked uncomfortable. "Of course inspector," she demurred.

"Thank you Miss Smith." He nodded to the priest. "Enjoy your meal father."

Downs returned to his seat to find it occupied by Jason Damagio. Damagio was leaning over Maddie to her obvious discomfort. Downs stood behind Jason and coughed. Damagio turned.

"Ah my good inspector, I was just telling Miss Hart here what a fine job you are doing on the 'Beekeeper murder' case."

"Why don't you piss off." Downs said with feeling. Damagio looked shocked.

"I beg your pardon?"

"I said.." At that moment Nick and Amanda appeared through the entrance and approached the bar. Damagio scuttled back to join his colleague and Downs sat back in his chair to the admiring gaze of Maddie.

Jason leaned across to Andy. "This is amazing. One minute we're about to leave, next thing every good-looking bird for miles comes in! Look, that's the barmaid I was chatting to. You know, from the Bell. Looks a bit classy tonight."

"Must have heard you were here Jason.. look here comes another of your fancies."

Andy gestured to the bar. Jackie White and David were looking for somewhere to sit and Jackie was becoming more and more concerned as she saw first Father Simpson and then Inspector Downs.

She grasped David's hand urgently and spoke quietly between clenched teeth.

"Lets get the hell out of here!"

David looked surprised. "What's the matter?"

"Only that everyone from the press to the police are in this place: look!"

David glanced casually around. "Oh.. I see what you mean."

Jackie turned her back to the room and curved in her shoulders, as if it might make her less conspicuous.

"What are we going to do?" She whispered sideways.

"Well, we're here now so we'll just draw attention to ourselves if we rush out. Let's just sit over there out the way."

David ordered the drinks and manoeuvred himself and Jackie self-consciously across the room.

Damagio, impervious to his curt dismissal by Downs, was in his element.

"That's the one with the legs that got out of the car across the road!" He exclaimed. "I tell you there is definitely something in the air round here producing all these good looking women."

Andy grabbed the beer mugs and stood up.

"I notice that none of them are taking any notice of Jason Damagio, the famous broadcaster, wit and raconteur." He observed wryly. "Same again?"

Jason looked hurt. "Give me a chance! I've only just arrived in town. You probably have to live here ten years before anyone takes any notice of you."

"You've probably got about two days."

Andy left for the bar. At their table Father Simpson and Debbie had ordered the 'Linguine al forno,' as recommended by the waitress who also happened to be the chef's girlfriend and the landlord's daughter. The waitress nonchalantly handed the priest the wine list.

"Dad says the wine is on the house what with you being a priest." Father Simpson looked taken aback.

"That's very generous of your father," he said warmly. The waitress looked unmoved. "Well he drinks enough of it 'imself so he might as well give it away. He always says that if the good Lord thought enough of wine to turn water into it, it must be alright."

The priest laughed. "Quite right! The wedding of Cana! Approval

141

indeed! In that case," he looked inquisitively at Debbie. "Do you have any preferences?"

Debbie shrugged. "You have seen how unsophisticated I am already! You choose, I really don't mind."

Father Simpson glanced briefly at the card in his hand.

"The Bardelino then," he said decisively, "and please say thank you to your father." He smiled at the waitress, "I approve of his motives for wine appreciation."

The girl shrugged took the card and casually wandered back towards the bar.

Father Simpson turned back to Debbie.

"I went to Bardelino when I first became a priest, an Italian Benedictine monk that I knew invited me. It's a lovely town by Lago di Garda, a huge lake in the north. They were having a wine festival at the time. The town was going mad, with baskets of grapes and vats of the New Year's wine everywhere, so we had to try it." He winced at the thought. "It was only about a month old. I hope this one's better."

Debbie laughed. "There doesn't seem to be much that you don't know about."

Father Simpson frowned.

"I'm afraid I don't know who killed your father."

They both fell silent for a moment. The priest rested his palms on the table and looked seriously at Debbie.

"You will have to tell the inspector about your situation you know Debbie, I mean I really respect you for confiding in me but.." Debbie reached across and squeezed his hand again.

"It's alright William, I'll tell them about Mr Stern being my dad. They had to find out sometime. Don't worry." She felt a little self-conscious calling the priest by his Christian name.

Father Simpson instinctively squeezed Debbie's hand back. "Actually," he said, "It isn't you that I'm worried about." Debbie looked slightly abashed. The priest realized his lack of tact. "Oh! No I didn't mean it like that, it's just that I'm sure that you will be ok. I'm really worried about Mr Finch and Dorothy and justice of course. There is something very odd about all the circumstances surrounding your father's murder. I mean are they linked or is it just coincidence? For example why did Doctor Vandersteen visit someone with whom he had no apparent connection, work or otherwise and then, on the same night, kill himself?"

Debbie considered this for a moment.

"Yes, it is odd, especially for him to visit so late at night."

A voice from behind them interrupted their conversation.

"It's all very bizarre isn't it father, I agree!"

Father Simpson and Debbie looked up to see Nick King standing by their table; Amanda hovered discreetly behind Nick's right shoulder.

Father Simpson greeted Nick cheerfully; he was genuinely pleased to see him.

"Nick! And Amanda! Do join us for a moment; you might shed some light on the problem. I believe you've both already met Debbie."

Nick nodded to Debbie and pulled a chair across for Amanda.

"Of course; the lady in the woods." He sat down on a stool by the table.

"I'm sorry to interrupt but I couldn't help hearing what you said. I must say I'm as mystified as you, but actually I've just had some rather illuminating information from Mr Small."

"Perhaps we could compare notes," said Father Simpson, "between us there might be some sense to be made of all this!"

Nick agreed and proceeded to recount the result of Bernie Small eavesdropping in the police cells. As he came to the possible affair between Mrs White and her assistant, Debbie looked across at the couple in question, sitting in the corner. Jackie and David were deep in conversation.

"They don't seem to be very concerned about people knowing," she observed, a note of disgust in her voice.

"Well they do work together," said Nick, looking across the room. "Besides, I'm sure they didn't expect this place to be so full of people from Melbury tonight."

"Quite the contrary," agreed Amanda, looking pointedly at Nick. "Some people probably come here for a quiet evening for two."

Nick looked rather helplessly at Amanda. "Yes, well." Then he turned to the priest. "Anyway, the suggestion is that Albert Stern was blackmailing Jackie White *and* her husband. Jackie because of her affair with David Robinson and Frank White for some other reason."

They sat in silence for a moment. Debbie bit her bottom lip and began to sob. Father Simpson put a comforting arm around her. Nick and Amanda looked surprised at Debbie's unexpected display of emotion.

"What's the matter Debbie?" Asked Amanda anxiously.

"I think you had better tell them why you are upset Debbie." Said the priest.

Debbie looked, red eyed, at Nick and Amanda.

"Albert Stern was my father," she explained. Nick sat up in surprise. Amanda gave Nick an 'I knew there was something,' look.

Debbie briefly outlined the circumstances that brought her to Melbury. Nick listened intently. He made a mental note to get to the telephone and amend his evening's report to The Standard before it went to the printers. This was something that Jason Damagio and the BBC would not have discovered. *Murdered man had secret daughter!* Nick visualised the headline.

"I'm sorry," he said, as she finished. He was genuinely moved. "I must have seemed very tactless."

"You weren't to know," conceded Debbie wiping her eye with a tissue.

"Look," said Father Simpson, "I would like to talk more and we don't have much time, Ronald Finch has already been charged with murder. Why don't you join us?"

Amanda scowled at Nick.

"Good idea!" Said Nick, deliberately ignoring her unsubtle attempt to influence him. "We can discuss the crime over dinner."

The conversation paused for a moment as the waitress appeared with two large plates of steaming pasta.

"Chef's choice?" She asked rather disinterestedly.

"Yes please!" Chorused Debbie and Father Simpson.

The waitress presented them with their meals.

"Pepper?" She asked brandishing a huge wooden mill at the priest.

"Er no, thank you."

"Just a little for me please," said Debbie politely.

Nick turned to the waitress. "Could you bring the order from table six to this table please?"

The chef's girlfriend looked perturbed, but reappeared shortly with two more steaming plates. Once again she waved the pepper mill, a little more threateningly this time.

"Pepper?"

Nick declined.

"Yes please." Said Amanda, managing a smile. After all she might as well make the best of the evening.

As the waitress left Amanda leaned forward and lowered her voice to confidential tones.

"They always give the impression that pepper is some rare commodity in Italian restaurants, it always tickles me."

Debbie laughed; pleased to be able to break the tension.

Across the room Jason was beginning to get a little drunk and was conducting a belligerent conversation with his director about the influence of freemasons in the BBC.

"I tell you it's riddled with the buggers, *riddled!*" He thumped down his beer glass to emphasise the point. The bar fell quiet and Andy looked around sheepishly.

Inspector Downs looked scornfully across at Damagio, then glanced up as Jackie White and David Robinson began to make their exit. He wondered for a moment what the two might be scheming. It would be a full day tomorrow, but *he* would get to the bottom of it. Madeleine Hart looked beautiful sitting opposite him. He couldn't help his thoughts going back to the police station; he was equivocal about leaving Simpkins and Ellis on their own with so much at stake. Still he thought, looking across the table at Maddie, policemen had to have a break sometime.

Chapter 12

As Inspector Downs enjoyed his meal in The Trowel, Bill Simpkins, under the experienced eye of Jack Stone, was just starting his interview with Frank White. Frank and Jack sat on slatted wooden chairs, whilst Bill Simpkins remained standing, walking to and fro a little as he developed his theme. Sergeant Ellis sat attentively by the door.

"I want you to appreciate just what a serious situation you are in Frank."

"Mr White," corrected Jack Stone. "My client is a wealthy local businessman and should be spoken to with respect."

Simpkins fixed Mr Stone with a withering look.

"Your client is an ex-con. I know exactly what he is and I am also getting a pretty good feeling about you as well Mr Stone. You are here to advise your client on points of law, not to teach me etiquette, ok?"

Jack Stone looked sulkily at Simpkins, the solicitors tall figure seemed out of place, sagging uncomfortably on the small chair. Simpkins turned his attention back to Frank White.

"As I was saying, although for his own reasons Inspector Downs has charged Ronald Finch with the murder of Albert Stern, I still consider the case very much open, and you," Simpkins stopped pacing for a moment and fixed Frank White with an unwavering gaze. "You are a prime candidate for suspicion."

White squirmed and glanced hopefully at his lawyer. Jack Stone looked impassively at the faded yellow wall in front of him.

"Perhaps to begin with Frank." Simpkins continued, "You could explain the presence in Melbury of your old 'fixer' Lenny James? What was he hired to do?"

Jack Stone's languid body came to life, his tone was reproachful.

"Now then Sergeant Simpkins, you have no direct link between these two men. For all we know Mr James may, like many other folk, have been here to admire the countryside and to get away from the smoke and grime of the city." Stone sat back casually, as if he had effectively dismissed Simpkin's argument.

Simpkins held up his hand impatiently.

"Wait wait! Are we going to waste our time here tonight?"

He looked incredulously from Frank to Jack Stone.

"What have we got.."

He began counting off the items on his right hand using the index finger of his left.

"We've got witnesses to say that on the night of the murder a car similar to Lenny James Volvo was seen under the trees next to Mr Stern's house. We have proof that Albert Stern had gambling debts, we find detailed accounts of your criminal background in Stern's bureau. We have a strong suspicion that your wife went to see Stern the same night he was killed and if that's not enough we catch your employee David Robinson apparently removing evidence from Mr Stern's cottage!"

Simpkins looked around the room satisfied.

"It all adds up to one thing to me!"

Jack Stone looked unimpressed. He had extricated clients from worse predicaments than this.

"You may think it adds up to what you like sergeant," he said, twisting to find a comfortable position on his chair. "The fact is, that a gentleman found camouflaged and breaking into Mr Stern's property on the night he was killed, sits in a cell down the corridor. This gentleman has been officially charged with Albert Stern's murder. Now either you release *him* and charge Mr White here, or you drop the whole matter and cease this ridiculous circumstantial line of questioning."

Simpkins looked curiously at the lawyer. Stone gazed back defiantly.

"There is nothing to prevent two men being charged with murder Mr Stone. Perhaps we would be making more progress if Mr White here explained these 'ridiculous circumstantial' events."

The detective put both hands, palm down, on the table. He leaned forward, looking Jack Stone straight in the eye; his tone became slightly menacing. "Let's put it like this. We have some important forensic evidence coming tomorrow. If I have to charge Mr White with murder to keep him here overnight, I will. Is that clear?"

Frank blanched; the prospect of the community finding that he had been charged with murder did not appeal. As it was he was going to have a damage limitation exercise to preserve his business reputation. Frank sighed.

"Alright," he said with a tired air of resignation, "I'll try and make as much sense of it as I can."

Back at The Trowel the strong local beer was continuing to have an effect on Jason Damagio, much to his director's embarrassment. He was now venting his view of the competence of the 'national' BBC current affairs presenters. Having been 'passed over' for such positions himself it was a particularly sore subject. He leaned forward talking very loudly.

"D'yer know why I wasn't chosen for prime time news. Eh? D'yer know?"

Andy, by this time had long lost interest and was looking across at Madeleine Hart, perhaps it was the beer but she looked even more beautiful now than when she had made her impressive entrance. Damagio became annoyed at the lack of attention. He tugged on Andy's sleeve and raised his voice again.

"Oi! Red nose! I said D'you know why.."

Andy looked at Jason with a long-suffering expression. "Alright! I can hear you. No I don't know why you weren't chosen for prime time news, enlighten me."

Jason's voice was still conspicuously loud.

"It's because I'm not a bloody nig-nog that's why...!"

Andy winced and looked around the room in horror. Most of the customers had become silent and looked distastefully at Damagio. Andy reprimanded his colleague who was now trying, without much success, to direct his half full beer glass towards his mouth.

"Shhh! Keep your voice down will you; this is embarrassing! You can't make racist comments like that in public!"

Inspector Downs glared across the room.

"If he doesn't keep quiet I'll arrest him for causing a disturbance. I fully intended for you and I to have a peaceful evening."

Maddie put down her fork for a moment. "It's alright, it was my idea to come here anyway. Besides," she smiled disarmingly, "I'm having a lovely time."

Inspector Downs flushed with pleasure.

"Well that's the main thing. It's helping to clear my mind as well. If I solve this case I think there may be a career move in it for me."

Madeleine looked disappointed; her full lips turned down for a moment.

"Does that mean you might have to leave Melbury?"

Inspector Downs hesitated.

"Well possibly. One things for sure, if, by this time tomorrow night it isn't sown up, I'll be sent a long way from here, some remote out-post I expect. Falklands or something."

The inspector looked morosely at the table as he contemplated this. Maddie looked positively alarmed now. She reached out and lightly touched the policeman's forearm.

"Oh," she said, "I hope that doesn't happen."

Behind them there was a commotion of scraping chairs and loud voices as Jason Damagio and his director made to leave. Jason lurched up to Down's table and stood unsteadily in front of Madeleine.

"Mish Hart," he began, "I would like to say," he tottered slightly sideways, "I would like to say that you are the most.."

Andy grabbed Damagio by the shoulders and pulled him away.

"He would like to say that the Ixdon beer is very strong," he said nodding politely at the couple. Andy shoved Jason towards the front door.

"Come on old boy, time for bye byes.."

The door crashed open and Jason was propelled outside.

The stooped Trowel landlord came across to the inspectors table. He began wiping it with a damp cloth.

"Bloomin' people," he said, glancing at the now closed door. "Come in here and can't take the Suffolk beer. Just as well they left," he shook his fist with bravery that was no longer required, "I was gonna chuck 'em out if they hadn't."

"Very good," approved Downs, "do you think we could have the bill now please landlord?"

The stooped figure disappeared toward the bar muttering.

Across the room the waitress was clearing the table in front of Father Simpson's party. On the advice of the house they all ordered the 'Tiramisu' desert. Nick returned to the subject.

"I must say," he said. "There appear to be a number of people who could quite possibly be suspected of the murder. I mean if not for motive, then for the fact that they saw or rather visited Mr Stern the evening he was killed."

"Even me," added Debbie sadly, "I saw him that evening."

Nick looked surprised.

"You did?" He corrected himself. "Oh well I wouldn't include you in my list of course."

"Why not," Debbie continued, "he had ignored my existence all my life, and I stood to gain any inheritance as his next of kin."

Nick looked uncomfortable. There was an embarrassed silence around the table; there was after all some truth in what Debbie had said. Amanda broke the spell. She put her hand on Debbie's lap.

"Alright Debbie you can be a suspect as long as you don't mind joining the queue behind rest of the inhabitants of Melbury."

Debbie smiled. Father Simpson was pensive. "You know I had heard a very unsubstantiated rumour that something was happening between Mrs White and David Robinson. I get a lot of gossip as part of my offices, but I ignore most of it."

The waitress arrived with four generous portions of desert, precariously balancing on a tray. Amanda seemed the only one interested in eating and she eagerly tucked in.

"Mmm," she enthused; unaware that she had coated her top lip with the creamy pudding. "Delicious!"

Nick looked indifferently at his plate.

"Father, time is getting short, as you've already pointed out. If I'm going to write a convincing article to suggest that the police are wrong we need some pointer as to whom the real killer is. Do we have *any idea?*"

"I wish I did Nick. As you say there are a lot of possibilities. I am sure however that it is not Ronald Finch." He paused for a moment, absently rolling his napkin. "I would like to know a bit more about the poor fellow they found dead at Boulmer Cottage though."

Amanda grunted through a mouthful of Tiramisou.

"Ah, the infamous grey Volvo!" Agreed Nick, "we tried to speak to Mrs Cummings about that tonight."

Amanda swallowed quickly and found her voice.

"She was so rude, said she has spoken to the authorities and didn't want to talk to nosy newspapers! Nosy! I mean she can talk!"

Amanda became aware of the large figure of John Downs approaching their table. She fell quiet, intimidated by the policeman's presence.

"Don't let me stop you," said Inspector Downs cheerfully. "Miss Hart and I were just about to say goodnight. I'm afraid I have a bit too much on my mind to really relax tonight."

"I was just talking about Mrs Cummings," said Amanda coyly. "She was being rather difficult when we tried to ask her about the grey Volvo."

"Don't be too hard on her," advised Father Simpson. "She has had rather an unhappy time of it. Her husband died last year."

Amanda looked embarrassed. She put her hand to her mouth. "Oh!"

"Yes. It is very sad. Apparently he had a car crash some years ago. He had been in a wheelchair and poorly for some time. My colleague Father O'Byrne from Norwich told me. Actually he didn't even know she had moved here, obviously she wanted to get away from it; as a matter of fact he and I were talking about it on the telephone earlier. She was getting medical help for depression when she lived in Norwich. He was rather concerned that she was being looked after down here."

"You appear to know a lot about problems in your flock father," said Inspector Downs. "I wish I had access to such a mine of local information. No one seems to confide in the police."

"She *was* getting medical help here."

Everyone turned to look at Madeleine Hart.

"Mrs Cummings," explained Maddie. "She was seeing Doctor Vandersteen. She used to see him about once a week. In fact she was the only patient he would see whenever she wanted to. I was always cancelling appointments to fit her in."

"I had heard that doctor Vandersteen was very good at counselling," said Father Simpson. "Father O'Byrne will be pleased when I tell him."

"Pity he couldn't counsel himself," observed Inspector Downs wryly.

"I don't know why he used to go to such trouble for Mrs Cummings," continued Maddie. "She used to make him herbal remedies for his migraine, perhaps it was because of that."

The table fell quiet.

"By the way Nick." Father Simpson broke the silence. "Do you think you should tell Inspector Downs about the information that Bernie Small gave you."

"Sold me," corrected Nick.

"Quite," acknowledged the priest. "Anyway it is clearly important with the blackmail implications. Better that he knows now than reads about it tomorrow."

Nick felt irritated to be put on the spot. It went against his journalistic sense of propriety to pass information from a source. Nevertheless he clearly had little choice, so he took the inspector to one side to outline the conversation Bernie Small had overheard in the police cells. Maddie Hart remained hovering by the table.

"Please join us Madeleine," Father Simpson gestured to Nick's empty chair. "Have you met Amanda and Debbie?"

Maddie smiled and shook their hands.

"Pleased to meet you."

"We still have a little wine left over," said Father Simpson lifting the bottle of Bardelino and squinting through it. "May we offer you some?"

"Thank you, that's very kind," demurred Maddie, gracefully settling into the chair. He turned over an unused glass and poured Maddie the remains of the Bardelino.

"Madeleine.." The priest seemed hesitant, his right hand fiddled nervously with a wine cork.

"This is going to seem like an unusual request." He dropped the cork. It rolled across the table onto the floor.

"I wouldn't ask if it wasn't important, but would it be ok to glance briefly through some of Doctor Vandersteen's medical files? It will be entirely in confidence of course. I can assure you of that."

Maddie hesitated.

"Actually I'm just in the process of sending the files to Doctor Rotton."

She looked doubtful, her dark eyebrows furrowed.

"It doesn't seem right really." Maddie looked at the priest's anxious expression.

"Still I suppose in view of the strange goings on around here it would be ok. You are a priest after all! How can it help you?"

"I'm not entirely sure," replied the priest. "It's really just to clear something up."

He bent down to pick up the cork. Debbie looked quizzically at Father Simpson, before she could say anything Nick and Inspector Downs had made their way back to the table. Downs looked thoughtful. He caught a look in Father Simpson's eye.

"Curiouser and curiouser eh father!"

"Indeed Inspector," agreed the priest. "Certainly curious enough to open one's mind."

Father Simpson was too gentle a person to be unkind but Ronald Finch's liberty was at stake. It was time for broad hints. Downs was not slow to miss the innuendo.

"I am always open to ideas or suggestions," he said defensively.

"That's very wise inspector," agreed Father Simpson.

"Anyway," said Downs feeling somehow that he had lost face. "We must be on our way. I have a feeling that tomorrow will be somewhat taxing."

Madeleine stood up.

"Thank you for the wine father."

"You are very welcome Maddie." The priest stood politely. "I'll pop around to the surgery tomorrow morning if that's alright."

The inspector and Madeleine bade everyone goodnight. Maddie linked her arm through the inspector's and the couple made their way around the maze of tables to the exit.

"Well!" Said Father Simpson looking at the bar door. "The inspector's armour is cracking! There's hope for us all!"

"And perhaps salvation for Ronald Finch!" added Nick. "I wouldn't go that far," said Amanda, "I don't think the inspector likes to change his mind."

Everyone was becoming uncomfortable in the interview room at the police station. Sergeant Ellis squirmed on his chair by the door and began to amuse himself by counting how many times Jack Stone changed position in a minute. He was rather enjoying the proceedings to start with, but he had heard Frank White's version of events several times now and despite Simpkins sceptical cross examination, Frank could not be swayed from his story: yes, he had seen Lenny James, Lenny had visited for old times sake and was only in the area for some healthy country air. Furthermore, he insisted, despite the circumstantial evidence, that Albert Stern was certainly not blackmailing him.

Sergeant Ellis was dying for a cup of tea but dare not mention it and Jack Stone was convinced that a disc had finally popped at the bottom of his back, so excruciating was it for him to sit on that little chair.

Stone uncrossed his legs and twisting around threw his right arm over the back of the chair. 'Seven' thought Ellis. Stone had kept fairly quiet after Simpkins earlier onslaught, but he could take no more.

"Really sergeant, we have been over and over this. Clearly my client has nothing to answer for. Furthermore we are all very tired and uncomfortable."

To emphasise the point he reversed his position.

'Eight.'

Simpkins finally sat down himself and considered the situation. He had to bear in mind that they only really had one day left before an incident squad was certain to be sent from Norwich. Finally, he made a decision.

"Very well." He surveyed his weary audience and looked at his watch. "We can stop the questioning tonight but I would still like Mr White to remain overnight pending forensic evidence. He may wish to return home but then I might be inclined to press charges in order to keep him here."

Simpkins was bluffing of course. Jack Stone could smell a rat. He levered himself out of the chair. He would have sprung to his feet in earlier days but three hours in that chair had put paid to any possibility of that.

"This is preposterous! What about Mr Finch? You've already charged him! This is quite without precedent. You are a bunch of amateurs! You aren't even a murder squad! Just a hotchpotch of village bobbies! I will sue every.."

Frank White became alarmed. He knew he was on fragile ground and did not want to alienate Simpkins too much. He joined the others standing up.

"Hold on! Hold on!" He said irritated. "Lets not get carried away, it's already very late and I've agreed to stay anyway. Let's just stay calm about it."

Sergeant Ellis was relieved; he too was on his feet.

"How about a nice cuppa?" He said brightly.

"An excellent idea Sergeant." Jack Stone flashed a wicked smile at Simpkins. "At least someone in this police station has a career ahead of them."

Inspector Downs journey home was no less exciting than the earlier adventure. A slight mist had descended over the narrow lanes and Madeleine adopted her customary driving position, hunched over the steering wheel peering into the night. A couple of glasses of wine had given her new valour and she obviously felt it best to deal with the fact that she could hardly see, by negotiating the journey as quickly as possible. Downs was once again thrown from one side of the car to the other. When his face found itself pressed against Madeleine's right breast she simply turned and smiled benignly at him. Unfortunately the distraction was enough to cause the car to depart from the road into a sugar beet field.

Maddie accelerated and swung the wheel violently. The car skidded its way back towards the road across the field. It bounced across a ditch and landed back on the lane with an unceremonious thump. Inspector Downs, who had investigated most of the car interior already, struck his right cheek on the doorpost, or rather on a 'bunny' shaped scent dispenser, hanging on the doorpost.

"Oww!"

Maddie stopped the car on the road and switched off the engine.

"Are you alright?" She asked turning on the interior light. She leaned across Inspector Downs, looking anxiously at a bruise appearing under his eye.

Downs touched the bruise tentatively.

"I'm fine. Really, It's just a bump."

"Oh dear," said Maddie unhappily. "I'm terribly sorry, I don't know where the road went."

"That's all right, carry on, just drive a bit more slowly that's all."

"I'll look at that bruise when we get back."

"It's alright."

Madeleine started the car and drove sedately, until at last the glow of Melbury and then the town itself came into view. Downs gave a sigh of relief, vowing inwardly never to let Miss Hart drive him again.

Maddie eventually pulled up outside her cottage.

"Come in," she said, peering anxiously at the bruise and squeezing the inspectors hand. "I'll make some coffee and administer some serious first aid."

Father Simpson and Debbie had a less eventful journey back from the Trowel. "Alright," said Debbie, as she turned out of the car park and onto the main road, "I can't stand the suspense. Why do you want to look at Doctor Vandersteen's medical files?"

Father Simpson smiled.

"Actually, I don't want to see Doctor Vandersteen's medical files."

"But you said.."

"I just want to look at *one* medical file."

Father Simpson turned slightly to look at Debbie's profile; she glanced at him, frowning with annoyance.

"Well why?"

The priest leaned back in his seat again.

"I was going to talk to you about it over dinner, but to be honest, it is such a vague line of enquiry that I'll see what Father O'Byrne and myself can discover before I say much. Also, I suppose I shouldn't discuss personal information gained through the job."

Debbie was dissatisfied.

"What has a Norwich priest got to do with it?"

"Ah," replied Father Simpson, in a mock Irish accent. "You don't need the internet as a priest. The web of information in the church reaches far and wide!"

Debbie sat in silence for a while, feeling slightly snubbed. She drove past the church and pulled up outside the presbytery.

"Yes I will come in for a night-cap," She said curtly, not waiting for an invitation. "But if you are going to be mysterious and patronising all night I won't stick around!"

Father Simpson laughed as Debbie petulantly stepped from the car.

"Really!" He said, "I didn't mean to be like that; come in. I'll try and make amends. Please don't take offence."

The priest smiled disarmingly. He really was most unpriest-like, thought Debbie again. He was certainly difficult to stay annoyed with for long.

"Alright," agreed Debbie, "You can entertain me with some of your music."

"And some Benedictine!" Added Father Simpson.

"I'd rather have a glass of wine."

"Before the wine jugs are made of our clay?" The priest added.

"I beg your pardon?"

"Omar Kayam." William Simpson was grinning happily. "Most of his poetry seemed to involve wine: rise up my love and solve our problems with your beauty, let us drink wine together, before the wine jugs are made of our clay."

Debbie shook her head and crossed the threshold of the house.

'*Most* unpriest-like,' she thought.

David Robinson and Jackie White made their way back to the cottage. As David parked the car in the barn Frank called Jackie on her mobile. He explained that he was remaining at the police station overnight to 'clear up a few problems. 'No he didn't want her to visit him. She had enough to sort out the next day.' Jackie switched off the mobile and sat with her own thoughts for a moment.

"Frank's in big trouble you know, he's always been so confident. He sounds really worried."

They walked slowly to the back door, their feet crunching noisily on the gravel.

"Do you really think he would have killed that old man?" Asked David, struggling to unlock the door in the dark. "It seems rather extreme."

"The police think he was involved," replied Jackie, stepping into the hall. "And they also think that we are."

David wrapped his arms around Jackie from behind and nuzzled his face into her hair.

"Ah," he whispered confidentially, "but we have our story now and however weak it is, they can't disprove it."

Jackie smiled and she squirmed as David kissed her neck and tried to pull her to the floor.

"Not here," she said, resisting. "Upstairs."

"Correlli, Mozart or Haydn?"

Father Simpson stood by a shelf thoughtfully studying some record sleeves. Debbie, in a much happier mood, was sitting on the sofa sipping a glass of white wine.

"Oh you chose. You're the expert."

"Haydn it is then. Now then," Father Simpson browsed the record collection for a moment. "Do we play the unlucky but beautiful cello concerto or the unlucky but equally beautiful trumpet concerto?"

Debbie laughed. "You make it so difficult! I've a feeling I'm going to regret asking this but why unlucky?"

"Well," said the priest picking up the two records. "Haydn never actually heard either of them; for different reasons mind. The cello concerto wasn't played until two centuries after he wrote it. The original concerto manuscript was eventually discovered in a museum in Prague in the nineteen-sixties."

"You mean he lost it! How could he lose his own music?"

Father Simpson smiled. "Oh, he didn't lose it, it just wasn't published and therefore never played."

"And the trumpet?" Debbie was amused, she rolled onto her front on the sofa, clutching her wine glass in both hands and swinging her legs up behind her.

"Ah the trumpet!" William Simpson held up his forefinger in mock importance.

"The trumpet, unfortunately, hadn't been invented when Haydn wrote his trumpet concerto."

"No!" Debbie was Laughing again. "You are teasing me again, you're very cruel!"

"Really," said the priest. "He wrote the concerto for a Viennese court trumpeter who convinced him that the instrument he was building could play all the scales. Haydn dropped everything, wrote the concerto and then found that the instrument this chap finally made couldn't play it."

Debbie sat back. "He must have been cheezed off!"

"History doesn't record his reaction, but it wasn't until after Haydn died that a trumpet was finally built that could play the piece, which, incidentally, is one of his finest."

Debbie was suitably impressed. "Well," she said, "I lie here in uncultured amazement. The trumpet concerto it is then, and my wine glass is getting empty." She was feeling rather heady.

Father Simpson picked up the bottle of blanc de blanc.

"You had a few drinks earlier." he said, concerned. "Are you ok driving?"

Debbie's eyes twinkled mischievously and she stretched out alluringly on the cushions.

"Who said anything about driving," she said, languidly holding out her glass.

Inspector Downs sat in Madeleine Hart's neat lounge sipping a cup of tea. He looked around the room, marvelling at the way women managed to be so tidy. There wasn't a speck of dust or cobweb in sight. Unlike his own flat, which was in a permanent state of bedlam.

Maddie appeared at the door with a bowl and some cotton wool. She sat down next to the inspector and looked closely at his right cheek. The bruise was just below his eye on the bone and it was turning a colourful shade of purple.

"Oh dear! That is nasty."

Maddie dipped the cotton wool in the bowl and gently dabbed the wound. Maddie was no nurse and she had misread the antiseptic bottle with the result that the solution was ten times stronger than it should have been. As she applied the cotton wool Downs jerked backwards throwing the hot tea over his lap.

"Yow!" He yelled, leaping up.

"Whoa!" He yelled again, as the hot tea seeped through his trousers.

"What are you trying to do, kill me?"

Downs hopped around the room, much to Maddie's dismay. Finally the scolding tea became too much for him and without thinking the inspector quickly undid his belt and pulled his trousers to his knees.

As the pain subsided Downs began to appreciate his predicament, standing in the middle of the room with his trousers around his ankles. He hopped self-consciously to the side of the room and flopped into an armchair.

"Are you alright?" Asked Maddie anxiously.

"Oh no, I like having boiling tea down my trousers," replied the inspector miserably.

"Almost as good as having acid put on a bump on my face." He touched the bruise tentatively.

"I'm terribly sorry," said Maddie, holding her hand to her chin. "I must have made the antiseptic too strong. Did it sting?"

The inspector was inconsolable.

"No, I normally jump about throwing hot tea over myself."

It had not been a terribly good night. Apart from his current plight, the news that there was even more evidence to incriminate Frank White did not please him. Of course he wanted the right man, but it had all seemed so tidy to start with. He had a suspicion that tomorrow it was all going to go horribly wrong.

"Let me have those trousers," said Maddie, standing up. "I'll soak them and they will be dry by the morning. You can't possibly go home like that."

She looked at the inspector's hairy knees and began to think how ridiculous he looked. Despite herself she started to giggle. Downs looked at her and tried to assume a dignified expression. Maddie found this just too much and tears of laughter ran down her cheeks.

"I'm sorry," she dabbed her eyes with a handkerchief. "Its just," she looked at him again and began to roar, eventually having to sit down. She dabbed her eyes again.

"Oh, I am sorry, it's just that I don't often get a police inspector sitting in my lounge with a black eye and no trousers!"

She started rocking with mirth again, and Downs, who could now see the funny side, began to find her laughter infectious.

"I suppose it is quite funny," he chuckled. Eventually, to Madeleine's relief, they were both laughing heartily, the inspector making the occasional "ouch!" as he was reminded of his tender cheek.

"Well," said Maddie, finally standing again. "I must say, you certainly know how to entertain a lady inspector!"

"John," replied Downs. "You should call me John."

"Very well," said Maddie efficiently, "but now I'll do your trousers and you can stay in the spare room." She looked at him sideways, smiling. "I'm sure that you are a gentleman."

Father Simpson was having trouble steering Debbie to his own spare room in the presbytery. She had insisted on hearing the 'cello concerto' as well as finishing the wine and she was now wrapping her arms around the priest's neck as he tried to gently guide her up the stairs.

"I wanna stay with you," said Debbie, stumbling on the stairs.

"You are staying with me," replied Father Simpson, "you are staying in the spare room."

"I don't mean the spare room," objected Debbie, hanging limply in the priest's arms. "I wanna stay in your room!"

At the threshold of the bedroom Debbie turned and tightened her grip around the priest's shoulders. Father Simpson could feel her smooth cool arms against his neck.

"Whoa! Steady!"

Debbie rubbed her face against William Simpson's neck; he caught the musky scent of her perfume. Her voice, husky, whispered in his ear.

"Come on William, come and hold me for a while, I need a cuddle."

Father Simpson disentangled himself. He was finding Debbie very hard to resist. He could feel her lithe body pushing against him under the yellow dress.

"No, No, please, this is very hard for me Debbie. Now you've had a bit too much wine, you'll regret it in the morning. Just have a good night's sleep and you'll feel fine. Don't forget you've got to see the police tomorrow."

Debbie walked into the room, spinning with her hands held above her head.

"I want to hear about Haydn," she said swinging her figure provocatively and looking the priest seductively in the eye. "I want a bedtime story."

Father Simpson laughed. "I'm glad that you like my composer stories," he said. "I'll tell you some more when you are a little more with it!"

Debbie fell forward against the priest again, she held him for a moment. Her voice became sad.

"I like you William," she said against his shoulder. She sounded resentful, pouting. "I like *you* very much, but you're a priest and I can't have you."

"I like you too Debbie."

Father Simpson extricated himself again and held her at arms length. "I like you very much."

He dropped his arms. "look, I cannot allow myself to feel like this, don't make it harder for me please."

He smiled kindly at her.

"Don't look so sad." He went to the door and looked back, "I'll see you in the morning; I make great real coffee. One of the few vices that I allow myself." He hesitated, she had not moved.

"Are you alright?"

Debbie sighed and looked around the room for the first time.

"I'll be fine," she said. She put a hand on his shirt and looked deeply into the priest's eyes.

"I'll see you in the morning." She hesitated for a moment. "Why is religion so obsessed?"

Father Simpson looked perplexed. "Obsessed with what?"

Debbie pouted slightly; disappointment clouded her blue eyes.

"Obsessed with pleasure. Not all pleasure is a vice you know, not even coffee.. you guys should loosen up!"

Father Simpson smiled. "You might have a point." He stepped forward and holding Debbie by the arms he kissed her gently on the forehead. "Now go to sleep and I'll see you tomorrow." He left closing the door to her room gently. Debbie touched her forehead where the priest had kissed her and smiling to herself slipped out of her dress and crawled under the cool sheets of the small single bed.

Chapter 13

The next Morning Father Simpson was up early. He had drifted in and out of sleep and had finally woken with a start. All the events of the previous day had rearranged themselves in his mind into an obscure 'Dali-like' dream sequence. He had finally woken up as Debbie, clutching a bloodstained dagger, stood naked over the mutilated body of Albert Stern. He lay in bed for a while, grateful that reality was different to the bizarre realism of his dream. Eventually he climbed out of bed and padded quietly to the bathroom looking apprehensively at the closed spare bedroom door as he passed. The dream had troubled him. He washed, dressed and walked down the creaky presbytery stairs. The Norwich Standard lay on the doormat: 'BEE-KEEPER SHOW MURDER. MYSTERY DEEPENS,' shouted the dramatic headline from the front page. Father Simpson picked up the journal and read through Nick King's article. He was satisfied to see that Nick had put a different slant on the enquiry, suggesting that Ronald Finch was not the only person in Melbury with a motive for the murder. The priest was mildly amused at a subparagraph: *Wealthy Businessman held for questioning. Could blackmail be the motive?* He was less amused by Nick's reference to Debbie: *Daughter grieves.* He must have been quick to get that in, thought the priest. Sixty miles away Chief Superintendent Ross was also unamused. He read Nick's article in his office at the Norwich Constabulary. In fact his level of amusement was at a lifetime low after the football riots. The way he felt, he may never be amused again. He reached for the telephone.

Inspector Downs drove to work pondering the problems of the day ahead. He hadn't slept well, partly due to the murder enquiry but mainly because he was all too aware that Madeleine Hart was in the room next door. She had unselfconsciously changed into a pink nightdress and popped in to his room to make sure that he was all right.

He had been, up to that point, but the image of Maddie in her night-dress had kept him awake for hours. He had never before shown much interest in the opposite sex, but now he was smitten. As if he didn't have enough on his mind. Still he thought, at least his trousers had been pressed for the first time in days.

Downs parked outside the police station, glanced at his watch and leapt out of the car. He noticed that a small crowd had already gathered outside the station, including the BBC Look East outside broadcast contingent.

"I thought I'd told Price to get rid of them," Down's muttered under his breath. As he walked towards the crowd a camera turned on him and Jason Damagio stepped forward thrusting a microphone in the inspector's face.

"Inspector Downs, Jason Damagio, BBC. I wonder if I could ask you a few questions about the Beekeeper Show killing."

Downs stopped impatiently and glared at Damagio. Jason squirmed uncomfortably. A little make-up had failed to disguise Damagio's red-eyed hangover.

"You're lucky I didn't arrest you for disturbing the peace last night you dunderhead," stormed Downs. "Never mind answering your stupid questions."

The inspector turned up his nose at the uncomfortable reporter.

"And you smell like a brewery. Now come on, out of my way, I've got work to do."

Jason glanced uncertainly at his director as the inspector brushed past him.

"I think we'll cut that bit out Andy, what do you think.. I mean the bit about me smelling like a brewery.."

Downs was greeted at the front desk by Sergeant Price.

"Good morning inspector," boomed Price cheerfully. "Chief Superintendent Ross has been calling. He sounds a bit upset."

"Gawd, that's all I need." Muttered the inspector.

Price peered at the purple bruise on the inspector's face. "Are you alright sir that looks like a nasty bump?"

"Never mind that. Get the chief inspector on the line and tell Simpkins and Sergeant Ellis to come and see me in ten minutes." He turned away and remembered his conversation with Nick King. "Oh yes, I want that fellow Small back here; he knows something.."

Downs headed for his Office, tentatively rubbing the purple swelling on his cheek. This phone call, he thought, was going to be very difficult.

The smell of freshly percolated coffee greeted Debbie as she came sheepishly down the stairs of the Presbytery. She walked into the kitchen with a hand to her forehead. Father Simpson met her with his usual warm smile and held up the coffee pot.

"Good morning, do you take sugar?"

Debbie thought about her seductive overtures the night before. It was quite out of character. What had come over her?

"Sugar?"

Father Simpson brought her back to earth.

"Oh, er, yes, one please. L-look William, about last night.."

"You were quite right, I've been thinking." Said the priest, stirring Debbie's coffee and handing her the steaming mug.

Debbie looked puzzled; she took the mug and looked at William Simpson expectantly.

"We guys need to loosen up," he reminded her.

Debbie laughed nervously. "Oh, I didn't mean.."

"No you were right, sometimes it needs to be said. Religion should not trade on guilt. As you pointed out, not all pleasure is a vice."

The priest caught her looking at him and turned to pick up his own mug.. that feeling again..

"Manners are more important than morals," murmured Debbie mischievously. She sipped her coffee.

"I beg your pardon?"

"Oscar Wilde. He said that in a civilised society, manners were more important than morals."

Father Simpson leaned his back against the kitchen counter.

"Ah, dear Oscar, another convert."

"Really," said Debbie. "You surprise me, I thought Wilde was most anti-establishment."

"Baptised in Rome just before his death." The priest adopted an air of mock superiority and gazed at the wall. "Most intellectual agnostics become catholic eventually you know."

Debbie laughed. "You continue to outdo me, you will convert me at this rate. That is if I don't corrupt you first. You know what they say, when there's trouble there's always a woman behind it somewhere."

Father Simpson laughed. "You are no trouble Debbie, indeed I find your company most stimulating. As for you corrupting me, well, perhaps as you say, I'll convert you first. Meanwhile we have a problem to solve: who killed poor Albert Stern."

Sergeant Ellis knocked politely on Inspector Down's door.

"Come!" shouted Downs. Ellis and Simpkins entered the office as Downs was finishing another trying telephone conversation with Chief Superintendent Ross. Downs gestured them both to the chairs in front of his desk and continued with the call.

"No sir, as I said it's not turning to worms. I have several people in custody but it's all to the same end. I'm quite sure that we can resolve it quickly."

He rolled his eyes at his colleagues in front of him.

"Yes sir, I know that Frank White is a very important man but he is helping us voluntarily."

Ellis and Simpkins could hear the raised voice at the other end of the line from across the desk.

"Yes sir, Mr White is in one of the cells; one of the better one's." He added quickly, "merely as a.."

Downs held the receiver away from his ear for a moment as Ross berated him. "No sir, an incident squad is not nec.." He winced as Ross hit new decibel levels.

"Very well, yes sir. We will expect them tomorrow. Yes..yes.. goodbye sir."

The inspector put down the receiver and sighed. He looked, resigned, at the two policemen in front of him.

"That's it. Chief Superintendent Ross is assembling a full murder squad. They will be here tomorrow. I've been told to just keep things from boiling over, whatever that means."

He slumped back unhappily in his chair.

"This time tomorrow my 'career' will be just that: downhill and out of control."

"That gives us twenty four hours." Sergeant Simpkins, ignoring the pun, sounded upbeat. "We could have it in the bag by then. I mean we've got a mine of information. The forensic and post mortem report will be here shortly. All we need is a bit of analysis and we've got our man."

Downs brightened up and sat upright.

"You're right, let's be positive. The forensic evidence should prove Finch murdered Stern, though I have to admit there are some curious goings on around here." He looked pensively at his audience. "For a start apparently our man Bernie Small overheard a conversation between Jackie White and Robinson in the cells. Not only are Mrs White and Robinson having an affair but also Albert Stern was blackmailing both Mrs White and Frank White. Mrs White and Robinson because of their relationship and Frank White possibly because of his past; as you suspected."

Sergeant Simpkins nodded. "That ties in neatly with the paperwork we found in Stern's house. It also gives White a motive for killing Stern; presumably through his henchman Lenny James."

"Possibly," agreed Downs, "although according to this conversation, White was suspicious of his wife and had a man, James no doubt, watching her. He hadn't necessarily hired him to kill anyone."

"That could explain Lenny's presence near Stern's house Wednesday night," agreed Simpkins. "We know from the Gauloise cigarette ends that Jackie White probably visited Stern, no doubt to discuss his blackmailing her.." He paused thoughtfully for a moment. "Or perhaps to kill him."

The room fell silent. Suddenly Jackie White had appeared as another likely candidate for the murder. She had a classic motive *and* she had probably been at the crime scene sometime that Wednesday night.

"It also explains the trouble taken by Robinson to collect the evidence left by Mrs White," added Simpkins. "The cigarette ends and the lipstick stained glass. I guarantee that the lipstick brand is the one used by Mrs White."

Downs squeezed his face with his left hand, and yelped with pain as he suddenly remembered his bruise. Ellis looked at the purple bump curiously.

"Gawd!" said Downs. "We can't charge three people with the same crime. Frank White's solicitor will have a heyday."

"I have something of interest as well." Sergeant Ellis felt it was time for him to contribute. He was enjoying being involved with such an important investigation.

"Go on," Downs looked at Ellis unenthusiastically. The 'Bunny scent dispenser' imprint was beginning to throb. He touched his cheek gently.

"Well, continued Ellis. "You know that I went to see Mrs Cummings last night, because she had seen the grey Volvo and so forth. Anyway, she was a bit reticent but she did tell me that she saw the barmaid from the Bell visit Mr Stern the night he was killed."

Downs muttered frustrated expletives under his breath.

"I want some solutions not more suspects." He stormed. "Is there anyone in Melbury who didn't go to Mr Stern's on Wednesday night?" He warmed to his theme. "Why don't we just arrest the whole town. Save a bit of time. That would really impress the incident squad.. Melbury empty.. 'Sorry, we don't have the killer but we've arrested everyone just to be sure.' In fact why stop at Melbury. I expect half of Ixdon went to visit him as well.. I can see the papers: *Murder enquiry: population arrested.*"

Sergeant Simpkins tried to stop the flow of sarcasm. "With respect sir, we have little time and Constable Ellis has provided possibly important infor.."

His point was drowned by the howl of the squawk box on the inspector's desk.

"That clodhopper!" Downs flew to the door and yelled down the corridor. "What do you want Price!"

Sergeant Price peered over his desk at the inspector. "Oh, sorry Inspector. I keep forgetting about that box. Mr Brown is here with the post-mortem reports; he's got Dr Rotton with him."

"That man is a mine of information."

Father Simpson had just spent fifteen minutes on the telephone to Father O'Byrne.

Debbie had finished her coffee and was helpfully washing the cups and generally tidying the sparse presbytery kitchen.

"What does a Norwich priest know that is so important?" She asked, drying her hands on a kitchen towel, which, inappropriately, bore a festive Christmas design.

"Well for a start he knows about you and your mother." Replied the priest.

"Impossible!" Debbie held the hand towel up and looked at it quizzically. "My mother and I are anglicans, and not very good one's at that."

Father Simpson shrugged. "So what? Jesus was a Jew. So was Saint Paul. We are not so parochial in the church you know."

"But Saint Paul became a Christian," laughed Debbie incredulously. "Even I know about the road to Damascus!"

"There were no Christians in 40AD." replied the priest. "Saint Paul lived and died a Jew. He just happened to be a Jew who proclaimed Jesus Christ the resurrected Lord. He effectively started Christianity, but he himself was not, technically, a Christian."

Debbie laughed again. "You always win! It's too early for me to have a theological discussion."

"I apologise," agreed the priest, smiling. "It's not very sporting of me as I have a slight advantage."

He looked at his watch. "Look, I've got a few enquiries to make. Will you excuse me if I dash off."

"Can't I come?" protested Debbie.

Father Simpson shook his head. "No, I am hoping to look at some medical files at Doctor Vandersteen's surgery. It is a rather delicate matter, so I had better go alone."

The priest thought for a moment, then he held Debbie's arms and looked seriously into her eyes.

"Debbie, don't think me insensitive but by visiting your father the night that he was murdered you may be a feature in the investigation. You must go to the police station and tell them about your relationship with your father and that you saw him on Wednesday night." Debbie nodded sadly. "I know," she said quietly, she looked apprehensive. "I don't think Inspector Downs will be very surprised though, after the article in the Norwich Standard. I'm amazed! That Nick King only found out about me being Albert's daughter last night."

"He must have telephoned it through," said Father Simpson. "They don't print until late these days in case of some exciting breaking news."

"Fame at last!" Exclaimed Debbie. "Andy Warhol was right, this is my ten minutes of fame! Debbie Smith! Breaking News!"

Father Simpson smiled. "You'll go then," he urged.

Debbie looked sideways at the priest. He looked rather tired. Vulnerable somehow.

"On one condition." She said mischievously.

The priest looked curiously at Debbie, naivety causing him to miss the temptation in her eyes.

"Go on."

Debbie stroked Father Simpson's arm and smiled innocently. "You must come to dinner with me again, I want to find out more about William Simpson the man, not the priest."

The priest laughed loudly. This woman certainly amused him.

"Very well." He agreed, "but you might be disappointed. The man and the priest are probably the same thing."

"I'll decide that," demurred Debbie. "We shall see, anyway. I'll pop back to my room at the Bell, change and then make an appearance at the police station. According to the Standard I must be one of the few people in Melbury not there anyway. I'll speak to you later." Debbie pulled Father Simpson by his sleeve kissed him on the cheek. Before he could reply she hastened to the hallway and out of the front door. The priest went to the door and, slightly bemused, watched her walk briskly towards the town centre. Before she reached the end of the road she turned, waved cheerfully, then disappeared from sight.

After Debbie had gone Father Simpson spent another fifteen minutes on the telephone talking to Father O'Byrne. Then deep in thought he walked to Doctor Vandersteen's surgery, arriving a little after 9.30am. He glanced curiously at Maddie's car as he opened the surgery gate. The little brown Minnie was wearing the effects of its adventure the previous night. Foliage from the hedgerow was caught up in the wheels and bumpers and the sides of the car were streaked with earth. Maddie had arrived at the surgery early and had been busy sorting out the medical files for transfer to Doctor Rotton's practice. It made her feel uncomfortable to be in the building alone. She still had horrific visions of David Vandersteen, lying grotesquely on his bloodstained bed. It made her shudder to think of it. She was quite relieved, then, when the doorbell rang.

"Hello father." Maddie greeted the priest warmly as she opened the door. She looked bashfully at her car. "I went into a field by accident last night. These roads are so poorly lit."

"No one was hurt I hope?" asked the priest, concerned.

Maddie thought about the inspector hopping about her lounge with his bruised cheek and his trousers around his ankles.

"Nothing serious." She smiled. "Inspector Down's bruised his head."

Uncharitably the priest couldn't help thinking that a blow to the head might do the inspector some good.

"Come in," said Maddie ushering Father Simpson into the reception room. Despite the circumstances she still managed to look fresh and composed in her floral summer dress. "I'm glad you've come. It's horrible here on my own."

The priest sympathised. "You should have someone to help you." He walked in and surveyed the piles of beige files. "Can't Doctor Rotton's receptionist give you a hand."

"I asked her," replied Maddie, "but she's snowed under with all the extra patients they have now that Doctor Vandersteen's gone." She looked sadly around the surgery. "Poor Doctor Vandersteen, I had no idea he was so depressed."

"Don't blame yourself Maddie, depression is a strange thing. Some people can tolerate it for so long and then, at a low moment, they can do something unexpected. You weren't to know."

He thought for a moment that perhaps, if anyone, he should have known about the doctor's state of mind.

"Maddie, are the files still in alphabetical order. I know it is improper, but I would like to look at a couple. It might help clarify a few things."

Maddie looked puzzled. "I've been trying to work it out, I always kept everything very orderly but some of the files seem to be missing, a few under 'B' and some of the 'C's."

Father Simpson stroked his chin. "Interesting..very interesting.. and a pity, that was just where I wanted to look."

They stood in silence for a moment.

"I'll make some tea," said Maddie, perhaps I can think where they went.

She disappeared into the kitchen whilst Father Simpson sat on a surgery chair; chin in hand, looking thoughtfully at the piles of folders.

Maddie returned shortly carrying a tray laden with two steaming mugs and a sugar bowl.

"I've just had a thought," she said handing one of the mugs to the priest. He politely refused the proffered sugar.

"Is it recent medical information you are looking for?"

"It could be. Thank you." He cupped the mug in his hands. "Why?" Maddie sat down next to him.

"Well, Doctor Vandersteen was a bit old fashioned, but he has just bought a computer and was learning how to use it. He was planning to put patient's details on it. It could be he's already started. I know he used to spend a lot of time sitting at it. It made him quite bad tempered actually."

Father Simpson looked interested.

"Where is this computer?"

"In the corner of his surgery next door, come, I'll show you.."

Chapter 14

Sergeant Simpkins ushered Brown and Doctor Rotton into Inspector Down's office. They all stood around the inspector's desk as Fred Brown spread an array of photographs and documents over the top. "Good afternoon everybody," began Fred. "I have the bare bones of the forensic and post-mortem reports here. I have brought Doctor Rotton with me because he has been talking to the pathologist and can hopefully shed light on some of the more technical aspects." Andrew Rotton grimaced modestly.

"If I could go over the forensic area first." Continued Brown. "I have to say the boys have worked very long hours on all this, as has Mr Haddon, the pathologist." He picked up a clipboard with several sheets of typed paper attached. "The finger prints inside the house belong to.." He peered at his notes: The victim, Mr Small, and two unknown females. One of whom had her prints on the glass." He looked up at his audience. "Outside, Ronald Finch's prints were all over the window sill of the house and the door of Mr Stern's greenhouse but nowhere else."

Inspector Downs muttered unhappily at this news.

"There were no fingerprints on the murder weapon, which was a Sheffield steel carving knife, corresponding to the one missing from the set in Mr Stern's kitchen.. also," Fred Brown turned over to a new sheet of foolscap paper. "As I think we already know, pieces of overall, matching the boiler suit belonging to Mr Finch, were found, caught on the fence surrounding Mr Stern's property."
Downs gave a contented grunt.

"Finally," said Brown, "though I will bring out another piece of forensic evidence in a moment, the lipstick on the glass in Mr Stern's is a proprietary brand known as L'oreal."

"Very nice too!" Said Downs dismissively. "What about the post-mortem results?"

"Some of the post mortem reports are a bit complicated," explained Fred. "So in view of the limited time," he glanced at Downs, "Doctor Rotton here will come in now and hopefully explain them."

There was an air of tension and excitement in the room; Downs prayed that at last something conclusive would be revealed.

"First of all," continued Brown. "The straightforward bits."

He produced a bright flash photograph of a large figure, lying prone on a shingle path.

"Lenny James," he announced theatrically, "died of a massive heart attack."

"Myocardial infarction," added Doctor Rotton. "The report says that his arteries and heart were in terrible condition. Lucky to have lasted this long."

"Unfortunately," said Sergeant Simpkins, "that doesn't explain why he was at Boulmer Cottage."

"I can help there as well." Fred Brown shuffled through the paperwork. "I hadn't intended to mix the forensic evidence with the post-mortem reports but..ah here it is.." He produced another photograph, this time of what appeared to be an area of the same shingle. "These tyre tracks were found next to the grey Volvo. We looked at them after you left inspector. They have been analysed as coming from a recent model of a Bentley Mulsane."

"Frank White!" Exclaimed the inspector excitedly.

"It would be easy to prove whether or not the tracks are from his car." Simpkins frowned at the photograph. "Hardly goes along with Lenny James popping in to see his old boss whilst getting a little country air does it? Meeting outside a deserted cottage in the middle of nowhere."

"Go on anyway," Downs encouraged Brown. "This is getting interesting."

Brown next produced a gruesome photograph of Albert Stern lying in a pool of blood.

"Cause of death: knife wound." He pointed his index finger at the figure in the picture. "The knife entered above the fifth intercostal rib space, piercing the heart."

"Surprise surprise." Said Downs laconically.

Brown ignored the inspector. "The knife, as I have said, matched the set in the victims kitchen and was the one missing from the set. It

174

is conclusively one of Mr Stern's own knives. Once again there were no fingerprints on the handle or blade. Additionally," continued Brown, "Stern had a severe head wound to the right temple. Sufficient it is suggested, to render him unconscious for some time. He had a little internal haemorrhaging, but this was not the cause of death. The head wound happened before he was killed."

"That would tie in with Bernie Small's description of Stern falling and hitting his head on the chair," said Simpkins. Downs studied the photograph.

"Does that mean that he was murdered whilst he was unconscious?"

"It's possible," agreed Brown, "but it doesn't explain why he was found in the hallway."

The assembly contemplated this for a moment.

"This is the interesting one." Said Fred picking up a photograph of another grotesque figure, this time lying prone on a bed.

"Doctor Vandersteen died.. Brown paused dramatically, looking around at his colleagues. "Due to a fatal administration of a poisonous drug, which although difficult to identify, is, in all probability one with the generic name 'Paclitaxel'."

There was a pregnant silence for a moment.

"Poison!" exclaimed Inspector Downs. "Poison! But he slashed his wrists! Surely he died through loss of blood?"

Brown picked up the post-mortem notes. "Apparently not." He peered at the small print. "Although the effect was dramatic, Vandersteen actually lost very little blood from his severed arteries. In fact the report suggests that the lack of bleeding indicates that his heart must have stopped within a minute or two of his wrists being cut. The blood simply stopped flowing."

Inspector Downs looked at Brown and Doctor Rotton blankly.

"How extraordinary! I suppose that a doctor *would* know how to poison himself." He thought for a moment. "But why slash his wrists as well? Very odd. What is this 'Paclitaxel' anyway?"

"That is most perplexing," said Doctor Rotton. "The pathologist considered that there were signs on Vandersteen's body which indicated the misuse of a cytotoxic drug. There are apparently not many things that produce some of the visible symptoms Mr Haddon could identify on Vandersteen's corpse. For example Doctor Vandersteen had a purple rash on his chest and a very swollen and inflamed face, throat and mouth. Indeed his final demise was assisted by what is known as 'angioedema', that is blocking of the upper airways. I say assisted because the pathologist suggests that Doctor Vandersteen had underlying cardiovascular disease and that, he also suffered a heart attack. "

The assembled policemen listened intently. Rotton continued.

"In view of the unusual symptoms on the corpse, Mr Haddon came to the conclusion that poisoning was likely, so he screened initially for cytotoxic drugs. To cut a long story short, an assay for Paclitaxel came up positive and he has put the cause of death down as 'a severe hypersensitive reaction to an overdose of Paclitaxel'."

Inspector Downs paused for a moment to consider Andrew Rotton's presentation. Then he summed up the reaction of the room.

"Doctor Rotton," said Down's patiently. "Assuming that what the pathologist has concluded is correct. Could you please, in layman's English, tell me what we are to draw from it? I mean why this poison etc?"

Andrew Rotton produced a thick medical volume and turning to a flagged page he addressed the room again. "Paclitaxel is a prescription only drug for treating some forms of cancer. It has saved many lives, however in large doses, like many drugs, it is very toxic. It is, of course, only administered by specialists. Indeed normally intravenously. You certainly wouldn't want to swallow the stuff as Doctor Vandersteen appears to have done. It is, in my opinion, most unlikely that a doctor would have some of this particular drug around his surgery. Also any doctor could find a hundred easier ways to kill himself. Even if he insisted on taking poison there are better ways: for example it would be simple to obtain a fast acting medicinal poison. There are plenty of dangerous drugs available." His audience looked blankly at him. "What I mean is: Paclitaxel would not spring to mind as a means of self-administered poison." Doctor Rotton leaned forward, his forefinger on the side of the desk. "There is something else though.."

Inspector Downs sighed. He didn't think he wanted to hear 'something else.' It was bound to complicate everything.

Doctor Rotton pushed the medical book to one side of the crowded desk and picking up the photograph of the stricken Doctor

Vandersteen, he waved it at his audience. He spoke slowly and emphatically.

"If Vandersteen died from a reaction to the poison, he would have lost consciousness quite some time before his death. Indeed he would in all probability been in a sort of coma for at least half an hour before his heart eventually stopped."

Downs, who felt that he was being rather inactive in the proceedings, agreed.

"Of course!" The inspector beamed confidently around the room. "Makes sense. Poor chap probably didn't feel a thing. Bit unnecessary cutting his wrists really.. anyway.."

"With respect inspector, you've missed the point." Doctor Rotton continued patiently: "Doctor Vandersteen must have been unconscious when his wrists were cut. It has been shown that he lost relatively little blood because his heart actually stopped very soon after the wound was inflicted. He must at that point, have been unconscious. It is inconceivable that he was compus mentus just before the poison killed him."

"Good Lord!" Inspector Downs exclamation reflected the mood of astonishment in the whole room. "You mean that someone else cut Doctor Vandersteen's wrists."

Doctor Rotton nodded patiently. "That is my conclusion and the one implied by the pathologist."

"So.." Downs pronounced the word slowly as he thought out-loud. "He either had an assistant in his suicide..or."

"Or he was murdered." Sergeant Simpkins ominously completed the sentence.

"Inspector Downs considered this inevitable conclusion for a moment.

"Why would anyone want to murder a country doctor?"

"I have no idea," said Simpkins. "But the facts are there."

Downs stroked his chin thoughtfully; then he turned to Ellis.

"Constable Ellis. Take Doctor Rotton over to Doctor Vandersteen's place and see if there is any of this.. Tax.. what's it called?"

"Paclitaxel." Interjected Doctor Rotton helpfully.

"Yes, Quite, go and see if there is any of this drug lying around." Downs gestured vaguely with his hand.

"Also," added Simpkins, "get Sergeant Price to check with all the local hospitals and dispensaries. See if Doctor Vandersteen has asked for this Paclitaxel stuff recently."

"You don't mind going do you doctor?" asked Inspector Downs.

"Not at all." Doctor Rotton looked at the pages of his book. "I'll give some thought as to why a practising country doctor should take, or be administered, 'Paclitaxel' of all things." He shook his head in bemusement, then he and Constable Ellis left the room, Doctor Rotton still muttering and shaking his head.

"What do you make of that?" Asked Downs, gesturing with his head towards the door through which the doctor had just left. "I suppose he's right but it doesn't help much does it?"

"I thought you'd like that little lot inspector." Said Fred Brown grinning.

"I don't like it!" Downs was irritated. "I want some answers not more blasted mysteries. The whole damn thing is mysterious enough." He started to pace up and down behind his desk, stopping to contemplate the curious crowd that he could see through the office window.

"If Doctor Rotton is right, we have to consider it likely that this stuff was administered to Vandersteen by a third party."

Simpkins agreed. "We have to keep an open mind, but it seems virtually proven to me. The death may even be connected to Albert Stern's murder. Don't forget, we still haven't explained why Doctor Vandersteen visited Albert Stern on Wednesday night. Stern wasn't one of his patients.. indeed as far as I can gather they didn't even know each other."

"Maybe *Vandersteen* murdered Stern and then committed suicide." Added Fred Brown helpfully.

Downs scowled at Brown and was about to say something scathing when, with his customary knock, the desk sergeant made another bald appearance around the door.

"Some visitors for you," he said cheerfully. "Mrs White and Mr Robinson. Also Jason Damagio is requesting an interview, oh and ITN have arrived outside as well."

Father Simpson clicked with the mouse and watched intently as the screen of Doctor Vandersteen's computer changed in front of him. Maddie peered myopically over his shoulder.

"It all looks very complicated," she observed, looking at an array of icons on the screen.

Uncharacteristically, Father Simpson ignored her. He moved the mouse deftly, clicking occasionally to look into the various files.

"We had a computer in the monastery," he said, as the various documents were called up. "It was almost as big a mess as this one.. Ah.. that might be interesting."

He looked into a word document called 'Pat Confid' paging down slowly. Finally he stopped and digested Doctor Vandersteen's text.

"What have you found?" Asked Maddie. From the side the writing on the screen was unclear to her. Father Simpson leaned back in the chair, gazing, dismayed, at the display.

"Oh my prophetic soul!" He gasped. He studied the screen for another moment.

"Could it be?" He exclaimed to no one in particular.

Maddie was alarmed. "What's wrong father, you've gone quite pale!"

The priest shook his head.

"Father!"

He looked at Maddie absently. Then he noticed her frightened expression.

"Oh! I'm sorry, yes.. Look Maddie, this is important. Did anyone arrange to see Doctor Vandersteen on Wednesday night? Any of his friends or patients perhaps?"

Maddie thought for a moment.

"Well, no.. I was never here late of course but as far as I know he didn't see anyone. Why?"

Father Simpson stood up, pushing the stool back.

"I think I may have found Mr Stern's killer. It doesn't all make sense yet but.. look."

He reached out and held Maddie's wrists urgently. "I want you to do something for me Maddie. Please call Doctor Rotton and ask him to meet me at St Peter's Church in about half an hour. Tell him it's urgent. I've got something important to do meantime."

Without asking he picked up the telephone on the desk and dialled a number. There was no answer. Father Simpson looked harassed. He reached for his car keys.

"I must go now Maddie," he said, "I'll explain it all later."

Chapter 15

Inspector Downs decided to interview Mrs White and David Robinson himself. He walked to the front desk and invited the nervous couple to follow him. He also took the opportunity to glance menacingly at Damagio, who hovered optimistically at the entrance.

Down's turned into his office and gestured Jackie and David to the chairs opposite his desk. He then sat down himself, rubbing his hands together in a business like manner. Constable Dobbs followed the group into the room and stood quietly by the door his hands held behind his back. Since his solitary stint at Albert Stern's cottage, Dobbs considered no job too onerous. Robinson looked apprehensively at Downs as the inspector struggled to start his tape-recorder. Finally it whirred noisily into life and Down's looked up, surveying the pair sceptically.

"I think you two owe us an explanation." Said Downs, narrowing his eyes and pressed his fingertips together. Jackie and David looked at each other. Jackie reached in her handbag and took out a packet of cigarettes. She had decided to be the spokesperson.

"Inspector."

Downs held up his hand. "Before you continue, I must tell you, we do not allow smoking in the building."

Jackie angrily dropped her cigarettes back in the bag. She dearly wanted to say: "are you going to charge me with smoking? Reflecting ruefully that as she was wearing underwear she couldn't totally mimic Sharon Stone. She took a deep breath.

"Look inspector," she explained, "I know this all seems strange but basically Mr Stern originally bought his cottage through 'Wells Properties.' Naturally as 'White's Realty' took over from Wells some years ago we anticipated that we would become sole agents for the sale now that Mr Stern was deceased. Normally in these sorts of cases properties are required to be sold quickly, what with people wanting their inheritance and all that. Anyway, A cottage like Mr Stern's is in demand around here, so, to get ahead of the game I asked Mr Robinson to do a peremptory survey."

"Unfortunately," added David, "the keys I had didn't fit but as I walked around the building I found an open window. Rather than run around looking for the keys I entered the house through that. The rest you know." David sat back; his expression suggesting that the problem was solved and no more need be said.

Down's stroked his moustache with his left hand and looked distastefully at David. He leaned forward across the desk; fixing David with what he hoped was a menacing look.

"The day after Albert Stern was murdered you decided to do an unsolicited survey on his property! Do you think that I'm stupid!"

David looked uncertainly at Jackie. Downs, worried perhaps that they might take the question too literally, gave an embarrassed cough, leaned back in his seat and continued.

"Mrs White," he asked. "May I see your lipstick?"

Constable Dobbs suppressed a snigger in the corner. Inspector Downs glowered at him, and turning back to Jackie rephrased the question.

"Mrs White what brand of lipstick do you use?"

Jackie knew what was coming.

"Lóreal," she replied, resigned.

Downs looked triumphantly at his notes. "And I believe, despite the brand that you just produced," he nodded towards her bag, "that you have a penchant for French cigarettes also?"

Jackie wanted a cigarette now. "Go on." She looked worried.

Downs pushed his chair back. He had difficulty sitting still at the best of times, now that he was closing for the kill he was quite animated.

"Time is short, and you are both lying!" He said tersely, fidgeting in his seat again. "You had better tell the truth and quickly. Presently we know that Albert Stern was blackmailing you because of your affair. We also know that you, Mrs White, visited Stern on the night that he was murdered." Downs turned to David. "The reason for your presence in the cottage the next day is open to very suspicious interpretation; especially as you were stealing evidence pointing to the presence of Mrs White in the cottage the previous night. In short you are both in it up to your necks, so if you want to avoid a fairly convincing murder rap, you'd better start telling the truth!"

Inspector Downs emphasised the last point by bringing his fist down firmly on the table. Constable Dobbs, less than vigilant in the corner, jumped at the noise; then composed himself, hoping no one had noticed.

Jackie and David looked stunned. There was a brief silence. Jackie looked at the inspector with new respect. He knew it all, she thought. Jackie glanced at David. "It's no use David; we will have to explain." She turned to Downs again.

"Please inspector," she had lost her earlier arrogance. "We had nothing to do with the murder, I swear it. I'll tell you everything, but could Frank be spared all the details. It would break his heart to find out about David and I."

"I'll promise nothing," said Downs. "You are not in a position to negotiate." He saw a look of anguish cross Jackie's face. "However, I am not an unreasonable man, so if what you say makes sense I'll see what I can do. My concern, I must emphasise, is with the truth. A man has been murdered and quite frankly," he regarded Jackie sternly, "your domestic situation ranks a poor second."

Nick King flung the newspaper on the floor in disgust. Throwing back the duvet he stepped out onto the well-worn hotel room carpet.

"I don't believe it! I just don't believe it!"

Amanda had been curled snugly against Nick in the small bed, she looked up, somewhat irritated.

"What's wrong?" Amanda rubbed her neck, which had suffered somewhat from Nick's hasty exit from the bed.

"They haven't printed half of it" He gestured towards the newspaper in frustration. We pay Bernie Small five hundred pounds and they leave half of what he said out! My report has been completely changed. I mean they only allude to blackmail and they haven't even mentioned Mrs White and David Robinson having an affair. I mean it's not bad but my original report was dynamite!"

Amanda propped herself up on her elbow. "Perhaps Mr Bryant was worried about possible libel action. After all, we only have the word of one rather unsavoury man for all those facts."

Nick glanced at Amanda disparagingly.

"You were there," he reasoned, "Small was genuine enough. He didn't make it all up."

Nick walked to the window and rested his hands on the sill, indifferently surveying the peaceful street outside the hotel.

"I don't know," he sounded exasperated. "This whole 'Beekeeper Murder' thing is getting me down."

Amanda looked uneasily at Nick. This was unlike his normal up-beat mood. She stepped out of bed herself and padding across to the window rested a comforting hand on his shoulder.

"Look," she shook Nick's shoulder gently. "You should be really pleased with yourself right now! You're editor is delighted with your work. You're getting front page coverage on The Standard and coverage with two national newspapers." She peered round to catch his eye. "Plus," she added, "you've got the best girlfriend in the world. So what have you got to worry about?"

Nick smiled at her and rested his hand on hers. "Oh I don't know. I just feel as if I'm missing something. I mean, we have all these snippets, little bits of a jigsaw: Ronald Finch, apparently caught nearly red handed. Lenny James, dead outside Boulmer Cottage. Bernie Small's information.."

"Debbie, don't forget Debbie." Added Amanda, helpfully.

"Yes, Debbie. Who is apparently Stern's daughter," agreed Nick. "All these facts and people." He gestured out of the window in frustration. "I mean, I'm supposed to be an investigative journalist! I should be able to figure it out. I just think that I've been offered an opportunity here and I'm not taking advantage of it." He turned to look at Debbie earnestly. "I would also, surprisingly enough, like to see justice done. Just think how good it would be if I could expose the killer. He's there somewhere, amongst all this.." he gestured again, at a loss for the word. "This rubbish."

Nick seemed inconsolable.

"Why don't we just sit down and think it through." Said Amanda helpfully. "Instead of rushing around town, let's just talk through the facts to see if we can come up with something."

Nick walked back across the hotel room and flopped onto a Victorian button-back armchair in the corner. The chair creaked dangerously.

"Alright," he agreed, running his hand through his hair in frustration. "Let's have a bit of lateral thinking. Lets start with poor old

Ronald Finch. We know that he was at Albert Stern's house on Wednesday night and that he, apparently, hated Stern because of losing to him at the Beekeeper Show every year. Who's next?"

Jason Damagio was becoming agitated. Apart from his hangover and his apparent rejection by the women of Melbury, he was frustrated because he could not gain access to any newsworthy information. There was an atmosphere in the police station that suggested something important was about to happen, but Damagio could glean nothing.

"Look," he pleaded with the desk sergeant, "at least tell me why Frank White is in custody."

"Sorry sir," Sergeant Price was feeling rather important, "it's all 'inter alia' at the moment. I'm not permitted to say anything." Neither Sergeant Price himself, nor Damagio, had the faintest idea what he was talking about. Indeed, Sergeant Price didn't know 'what was going on' anyway, but he wasn't going to let Damagio know that.

"Sergeant," Damagio continued, "must I remind you that this is a democracy, not a police state. As a journalist I am entitled to be kept informed. You must.."

Much to his consternation, Jason was suddenly brusquely pushed to one side. Father Simpson, unusually agitated, appeared at the desk.

"Excuse me," said Father Simpson. "I need to speak to Inspector Downs urgently!"

"Sorry father, the inspector is conducting an important interview. I can't disturb him." Price wasn't going to risk Downs wrath with another interruption.

William Simpson was exasperated. "Well how long is he going to be?"

Price adopted a patient, long suffering expression. "I don't know sir. If you'd care to take a seat?"

Father Simpson looked around. "Did Miss Deborah Smith come in this morning?"

Sergeant Price looked at the book in front of him and shook his head. "No, the only people who have checked in today are Mrs White and Mr Robinson."

The priest looked flustered. "Never mind. Look, tell the inspector that I have some very important news, some information for him. I'll

184

be back in half an hour. Alright?" Price nodded, slightly bemused.

"What is it?" Asked Damagio. "Can I help?" He was talking to an empty space as Father Simpson rushed off down the road. Price shook his head again. Even the clergy are in too much of a rush these days..

"I told you we wouldn't find any of the stuff in a GP's practice." Said Doctor Rotton. He and Constable Ellis had scoured Doctor Vandersteen's surgery, looking in every cabinet and drawer for any sign of Paclitaxel. Doctor Rotton had supplied Ellis with every branded name for the drug and between them they had turned the house upside down looking.

Maddie looked on with consternation as she saw the mess that was being made. She had been rather shocked at Father Simpson's reaction to whatever he had seen on the computer earlier and felt it her duty to make Doctor Rotton go to see the priest.

"Doctor Rotton." She positioned herself in front of the GP to emphasise her point. "Father Simpson seemed quite adamant that it was important you meet him." She paused. "He actually said in half an hour, which was some.." She looked at the surgery clock. "Some half an hour ago. I really think you should go." Doctor Rotton looked at Maddie. She seemed flushed and adamant.

"Well, you are very persistent young lady, but there is very important work to be done. I am sure that Father Simpson has an important reason for seeing me but.."

"You go ahead Doctor." Interrupted Constable Ellis, who didn't see any need for a doctor to be involved in anything other than an advisory capacity. This was police work after all and that was the end of it. "We have proved that there was no Paclitaxel here so I can report back and you can follow on later."

Doctor Rotton considered this: perhaps a break would give him time to figure out what had happened. It was very odd, very rum indeed in fact.

"Very well," he agreed at last. "You take the car, I'll walk back to the station shortly. I might get some inspiration from the fresh air."

"I'll call Father Simpson and tell him you're coming," said Maddie, happily.

Chapter 16

Rupert Crook was another Melbury resident who was becoming agitated. Back in the offices of Crook and Tritton he had been avidly reading up any criminal law that he felt pertinent to his role as lawyer to Ronald Finch. Ronald was still insisting upon his innocence to anyone who would care to listen. As it was, this proved only to be his wife and Mr Crook, as the rest of Melbury Police Station were otherwise engaged dealing with the ever increasing number of detainees and complications that the murder case was throwing up. Mr Crook initially thought the idea of representing Ronald a nuisance that interfered with the serious business of making money. This to him meant conveyancing or divorce. Gradually though, he was being seized by the excitement of a real case. It reminded him of the reason he went into law all those years ago. He had, in his youth, held high-minded ideals about seeing justice prevail. He soon discovered, however, that most work undertaken by country solicitors such as him, involved not so much the pursuit of justice but the pursuit of paperwork and minutiae trivia. It wasn't so much that he became disillusioned but he looked at the lawyers in provincial business and decided that a fine house and a smart car might just compensate him for the lack of excitement that he had expected from the profession. With this in mind he approached George Tritton, a colleague from law school, with the idea of setting up a legal practice.

Over twenty years or so Crook and Tritton had become very successful. They occupied a listed building on Dean Street, the most expensive and prestigious road in town. The premises boasted an imposing Georgian façade and a pilloried entrance. Inside the walls of the corridors and offices were adorned with oil paintings and watercolours of local scenery. Some of these paintings were commissioned but the majority were Victorian antiques, purchased at auction. Most clients, admiring the art in the waiting room, failed to consider that previous client fees had paid for the ostentation. Instead they assumed that the prosperous interior meant that Crook and Tritton, meant business.

Rupert Crook paced his office. The high media profile that the so-called 'Beekeeper Show Murder' had become, was worrying him. His reputation was now at stake as indeed was that of 'Crook and Tritton.' If he could get Ronald Finch freed, the publicity could produce a lot of lucrative business. He had got off to a poor start on the TV interview the previous day with Jason Damagio. Ronald Finch had forbidden Mr Crook from telling the public that his purpose in visiting Albert Stern's greenhouse late at night was in order to inspect Stern's horticultural prospects for the Beekeeper Show. The humiliation for Ronald would be too much to bear. Instead, when pressed as to why his client was dressed in overalls and covered in boot polish on Wednesday night, Mr Crook was reduced to filibustering and muttering that his client would undoubtedly be proven innocent in a court of law. Crook, to whom reputation purely meant business, couldn't understand Ronald's reasoning. He had already explained that the facts would all have to come out in court anyway, but Ronald had insisted and so that was that.

Bernie Small looked admiringly at a watercolour on Mr Crook's office wall. The scene depicted an inlet on the coast with small sailing boats stranded on a sandy beach.

"You've got some nice pictures here Mr Crook I must say; Rockland Dyke isn't it?" He asked, nodding at the painting. "Used to go there for picnic's. When the old nagger an' I was getting on that is," he added with a wink.

Rupert Crook looked at Bernie distastefully, a look Bernie was actually quite used to.

"Leslie Moor," said Crook loftily. "From Norwich. We have several of his watercolours actually. Anyway." He stopped pacing and sat down on the oak swivel chair behind his desk. "Judging by your telephone call you did not come here to discuss art. You said you have some useful information for me."

"For a fee," said Bernie, "I can give you some information that could assist your client." Bernie scanned the walls again. "Probably wouldn't do you any harm either."

Rupert ignored Bernie's last comment, whilst mentally acknowledging that this drunken garage owner was acute, regardless of his reputation.

"If the information is that vital why don't you inform the police?" He asked.

"Police didn't ask," said Small laconically. "Besides they don't have deep pockets."

Crook wasn't slow getting the message. "Just how deep do you mean Mr Small?"

Small shoved his hands in his pockets as if gauging just how deep pockets should be.

"A grand!" He announced. Actually he was going to ask for five hundred like the Norwich Standard had offered but Mr Crook's surroundings worked against him.

"Preposterous!" Said Rupert; "I won't even get that from my client I don't suppose. Tell me what you know anyway. Obviously I can't use it unless you agree to appear in court. I might add that it is quite disgraceful selling information pertaining to a murder, not to say illegal." He gave Small another look of aversion. "Though no doubt if pressed you'll say you know nothing.."

Bernie was beginning to feel angry. What did this ponce know about being on the brink of a precipice, with your business going to the dogs being surrounded by debtors and scoundrels.

"If you can make money from people's misfortune Mr Crook, why shouldn't I? Besides," he allowed himself a smile, "regarding my fee, judging by your television performance this morning you could do with some help. Your reputation could be on the line."

Crook winced at the thought of his interview with Damagio.

"I'll tell you what," said Bernie, smiling magnanimously. "I'm going to be sued for unfair dismissal by a chap called Weinstein, one of my mechanics. If you represent me for nothing I'll call it five hundred."

Rupert Crook looked unimpressed but he needed all the help he could get. With all this publicity, getting Ronald Finch released could lead to some quite lucrative work. He sat down at his desk and surveyed the unsavoury figure in front of him.

"Ok Mr Small, tell me what you know, we'll go from there.."

Doctor Andrew Rotton was deep in thought as he walked across the town. For the first time in weeks there was a haze of cloud on the eastern horizon and a faint land breeze drifted across the flat countryside towards the coast. Doctor Rotton turned up the slight rise towards St Theresa's church. He wondered why a catholic priest should want to see him so urgently. The Presbytery, a modest and for Melbury, relatively modern house, was just past the church on the left. Doctor Rotton glanced at the brick church as he walked past. The unkempt branches of the churchyard yew rustled in the light breeze. At the same time something stirred at the back of the doctor's mind. A subliminal thought that he could not yet grasp. It troubled him.

Father Simpson was already on the step of the Presbytery waiting to greet his guest. He shook the doctor's hand warmly and ushered him into the lounge where once again the Garrard turntable was playing.

"Thank you for coming doctor." Doctor Rotton sat down, he looked at the Spendor loudspeakers. "What wonderful music. Though I must confess I don't recognise it."

"Berlioz." Father Simpson lifted the tonearm of the deck and silence permeated the room. "L'Enfance du Christ." He explained. "Music is one of my passions. It also helps me think through a problem."

Doctor Rotton relaxed into the chair and adopted the benign manner that put his patients at ease. "And what 'problem' can I help you with today father?"

William Simpson smiled ruefully. "Am I so transparent doctor?" He sat down in the chair opposite.

"Well," Doctor Rotton folded his hands over his fairly ample stomach. "What with one thing and another in Melbury at the moment, I doubt that you have invited me for a social chat, delightful though I'm sure that would be."

Father Simpson admired the doctor's intuition. "You are quite right doctor. I do have a problem; or rather a question." He looked worried, as if hesitating to say what was on his mind. "It's about your colleague Doctor Vandersteen." The priest hesitated again. "Look, I'll get to the point; is it possible that Doctor Vandersteen's death was not suicide?"

Doctor Rotton sat up and looked at Father Simpson in astonishment.

"How extraordinary! Earlier today I was explaining the post-mortem results to Inspector Downs. It seems very possible that the doctor did not commit suicide. It appears that the cause of death was not through loss of blood, although clearly Doctor Vandersteen's wrists had been cut. The pathologist has concluded that somehow or other, the good doctor took, or was administered, a large quantity of a drug called Paclitaxel. Normally of course, under supervision and with routine premedication it is harmless, but like many drugs, when taken in excess it is very toxic."

Father Simpson raised his eyebrows in surprise. "That does seem strange when combined with doctor Vandersteen's cut wrists, but it doesn't rule out suicide surely, indeed perhaps it makes it more likely; I mean how many laymen know of this drug. I for one have never heard of it."

"Ah!" Said Doctor Rotton, wagging his finger zealously, "there is more. You see the reason we know Vandersteen died from the effects of the poison is that, although dramatic in appearance, he did not lose enough blood to cause death. In fact his heart must have stopped within a few minutes of having his wrists slashed."

Father Simpson looked puzzled.

"Otherwise the room would have been awash with blood," explained Rotton patiently. "But this is the crux." He narrowed his eyes and spoke slowly to emphasise the point. "If the drug overdose killed Doctor Vandersteen within minutes of his wrists being cut, it is inconceivable that he was conscious *when* his wrists were cut. The toxic effects would have rendered him comatose for some time prior to his death."

"So someone else cut his wrists," added Father Simpson.

"And possibly even administered the drug overdose." Agreed Doctor Rotton.

"So are we saying this was murder?" The priest seemed excited and alarmed at the same time. Andrew Rotton looked impassive.

"Technically yes. There is no evidence of the drug in the surgery, and someone clearly cut the doctor's veins with a surgical sharp."

Father Simpson picked up the caveat. "What do you mean 'technically?'"

"Well," continued the doctor. "There appears to be no sign of forced entry to the surgery *and* this is a *very* unusual drug to use as a poison. *Very* unusual." Doctor Rotton seemed lost in thought for a moment. "Absurd in fact! Anyway," he returned to the present. "The substance is probably only known to someone in the medical profession. So my conclusion is that although technically murder, a third party actually assisted the doctor in taking his own life."

Father Simpson considered this for a moment.

"By the way," Doctor Rotton added. "What made you ask the question in the first place?"

William Simpson stood up and walked pensively over to the fireplace.

"You may have heard that I do not believe that Ronald Finch killed Albert Stern." Doctor Rotton nodded. "Anyway some facts have come to my attention which suggest a possible alternative suspect and which would also include the murder of Doctor Vandersteen, bizarre though that may seem. I cannot say much more yet, firstly because your theory suggests otherwise and also because much of what I have found out is confidential information."

"You mean something from the confessional?"

"Not quite." The priest smiled. "It's just my source is a fellow priest in Norwich. It would be wrong for me to go into detail when I could be quite wrong."

Doctor Rotton seemed offended; he sat forward again in his chair.

"But father. I'm a practising Doctor," he protested. "Confidentiality is my business. Surely you can trust me. Besides we could work together on this." The doctor warmed to his theme. "We both have a similar vocation in life. You deal with spiritual welfare, I with physical well being. Our combined understanding of the human condition could provide some answers to this problem."

Father Simpson considered this for a moment. Time was of essence, he thought. Perhaps he could do with some help.

"Very well," agreed the priest. "I'll tell you what I know. Quite frankly this post-mortem report has thrown me somewhat. Perhaps we could start with you telling me more about this Paclitaxel, I mean what exactly is it?"

Nick King and Amanda were still sifting through the mountain of information relating to the 'Beekeeper Show Murder.' They were sitting cross-legged on the hotel room carpet. Amanda was wearing a rather drab courtesy dressing gown that she had found behind the bathroom door. Nick had donned a pair of red shorts that Amanda bought him earlier in the summer. The shorts looked incongruous in the Elizabethan room. Nick's fair hair flopped untidily over his forehead as he scribbled notes on a pad and sheets of the pad were spread neatly on the floor in front of him. He leant back and swept the offending locks of hair back with his left hand.

"So! We've written the name of each possible suspect with all the known facts associated with that person .." Nick looked at the sheets of paper. "What conclusions can we draw?"

Amanda peered at the morning's work.

"We've made a lot of notes about Frank White." She said helpfully.

Nick picked up one of the sheets and perused it.

"He does fit the bill rather well," he agreed. "He certainly had motive."

"And he's nasty," added Amanda with feeling. "In fact apart from one person he is the only one I think capable of killing someone."

Nick looked surprised. "Who else then? The rest are much of a muchness if you ask me. I think Frank White stands out as the man most likely."

"That's because the killer was a woman," said Amanda succinctly.

Nick looked blankly at his girlfriend. "Go on."

"The killing suggests hatred and anger," continued Amanda. "The accepted story is that one of Mr Stern's own kitchen knives was used in the murder. If that is true it means that whoever killed Mr Stern did not plan it. Otherwise surely they would have taken a weapon with them. I think that whoever murdered Mr Stern, did so on the spur of the moment."

Nick considered Amanda's point.

"Hm, what you say has some merit, but why does it suggest a woman?"

Amanda pursued her logic. "Let's assume that I am right and that the killing was unpremeditated and impulsive. What weapon is a man likely to use, bearing in mind that his victim is old?"

Nick tried to picture the scene.

"Anything I suppose," he said vaguely. " A knife? Whatever is at hand I guess."

"Think about it Nick," said Amanda exasperated. "A man could use his strength. The victim was over seventy. A man would be more likely to pick up a blunt object like a poker or bottle or something, I mean he could even have strangled him. A knife needs more thought. Whoever did this took the trouble to go to the kitchen, find a knife and then return to the lounge. I just don't see a man doing that. No, this murder suggests hatred. A woman's hatred..and there is something else."

"What?" Nick was intrigued.

Amanda sat up on her knees. "This might sound daft but I remember reading about women killers in a magazine. You know: what provoked the gentle sex to murder etc."

"Well?"

Amanda warmed to her theme and began to speak breathlessly. "Well the article was written by a criminal psychologist. He found that almost all murders by women were family orientated. You know, wife kills violent husband etc." Nick tried to interject but Amanda continued. "He also wrote specifically about murder weapons used by women. Do you know the knife is actually quite common, primarily because these were normally crimes of passion. Unpremeditated."

"That is interesting," said Nick, go on.

"The next part is more interesting." Amanda pressed her palms together excitedly. "There is apparently a difference between the way that a man kills with a knife and a the way that a woman does. The article suggested that in almost all knife murders by men, there are multiple stab wounds. Must be some primitive thing takes over; anyway, invariably a woman only uses the knife once. Perhaps she finds it too much or something, whatever, women do not have the frenzied attack that is the hallmark of a man. They just stab once and that's it. That is just how Albert Stern was killed. One knife wound."

Amanda stood up and held out a clenched fist, mimicking clutching a dagger. "I can picture it now," she said dramatically. "Our killer is filled with hatred, she gets the knife, she talks to Stern, threatens him. Finally she breaks and *whoom*." She thrust her mock dagger forward dramatically. "She stabs him."

Nick flinched back and looked at Amanda. This girl never ceased to amaze him.

"Very Macbeth!" He observed. He struck a theatrical pose. "Is this a dagger I see before me."

"Stop it," protested Amanda. "You are always teasing me. I'm serious."

Nick leaned across and kissed Amanda on the cheek. "I know and you have a good point. I never considered it but the kitchen knife does suggest unpremeditated murder; perhaps a crime of passion. But who would be passionate about an old man?"

"His daughter," stated Amanda succinctly.

Nick looked blankly at his girlfriend.

"You mean Debbie?"

"You heard her story," Amanda explained. "Her mother was dumped by her father, then more than twenty years later she tracks her father down to Melbury. Albert Stern made no effort to get to know or even find his daughter until she appeared in this town. Mrs Cummings has told us that Debbie visited her father the night he was killed and finally who do you think will inherit Mr Stern's estate. I mean that cottage is quite valuable."

Nick thought about Amanda's logic.

"Do you know," he said excitedly, "I think you could be right! Debbie came to live here just to get to know her father. Perhaps she grew to hate him."

"I think she hated him a little before she came to Melbury," said Amanda. "Also Mrs Cummings seeing Debbie visit Mr Stern on Wednesday night is really quite incriminating, primarily or rather only because *Debbie* never mentioned it."

"Yes, she kept that very quiet about that." Agreed Nick.

Amanda rose to her feet; the dressing gown slipped open provocatively. "Look," she said. "Why don't we go and chat to Debbie. She will have no idea that we are suspicious. I'll be able to tell you if she's guilty or not."

Nick grabbed Amanda and kneeling in front of her pulled her towards him and kissed her bare tummy.

"Woman's intuition again?"

Amanda rubbed Nick's tousled hair. "I'll just know," she said dreamily.

Inspector Down's pressed the lever on the squawk box.

"Sir!" Sergeant Price answered cheerfully.

"Send Sergeant Simpkins in please."

"Wilco!"

Downs scowled at the box. That desk sergeant was too flippant by half.

Simpkins knocked and entered the room. David Robinson and Jackie were still sitting uncomfortably opposite the inspector's desk.

"Young Robinson here has some interesting information for us," said Downs, gesturing to David. "Basically these two are having an affair and they have been using the empty cottage opposite Albert Stern's house for their liaisons. Indeed they were having just such a liaison the night that Mr Stern was murdered. Mrs White here was being blackmailed by our Albert and went to discuss the matter with him on Wednesday night, having first sent Mr Robinson here to sleep with sleeping pills in his wine."

Simpkins raised his eyebrows.

"Why did she do that?"

Jackie opened her mouth to speak but Downs interrupted her.

"Because she claims she didn't want Mr Robinson to know that she was being blackmailed, thought she might lose him."

"Sounds a complicated way of doing things to me," said Simpkins sceptically.

"It's true!" Jackie protested. "Do you think I would make up a story like that?"

Simpkins shrugged.

"Actually I believe her," said Downs. "Mrs White is smart enough to make up a better story than that if she'd wanted to." Jackie flushed slightly. The Inspector continued. "However Mr Robinson saw something of interest from the cottage window that night." He gestured again to David. "Tell Sergeant Simpkins what you saw."

David's mind went back to the hazy moonlit night, he sat up as he explained.

"Well, Jackie had just gone to the bathroom. I was just looking casually out of the window. You know, I just pulled the curtain back a bit to see the outside world. Actually I was thinking what a perfect night it was. The remains of a sunset; haze from the river and a glorious full moon. Anyway, just as I was about to drop the curtain I saw this figure run across Mr Stern's lawn, back towards the road."

Simpkins raised his eyebrows. "What sort of figure and where was it running to?"

David thought again, trying to concentrate on the shadowy image from the night in the cottage.

"Well.. It was small I suppose and slightly hunched."

"Would you say the person was male or female, young or old?"

"I suppose..no wait, I was going to say old but that's just because they were small. I couldn't say the age. Just that whoever it was moved pretty quickly, you know, urgently."

"And the direction?" Encouraged Sergeant Simpkins.

David cast his mind back again. "Yes that's a point, they weren't attempting to run up the road. I suppose the best I could say is that they were running towards the two cottages. You know, I suppose the alley-way between them."

"You mean between your cottage and Mrs Cummings, next door?" Simpkins looked at Inspector Downs. "Interesting!"

Downs leaned back in his chair. He turned to David and Jackie.

"Ok you two can go and if you continue to co-operate I won't go out of my way to inform your husband Mrs White."

Jackie breathed a grateful sigh of relief.

"There is a condition though," added the inspector.

"Anything," agreed Jackie quickly.

Downs looked sternly at the pair of them. "I don't want a word of this breathed to anyone. Do you understand?"

The pair nodded.

"Not to the papers, your friends, the TV, anyone! Also don't leave town."

They nodded again. "Agreed," said David.

"You appreciate the consequences?" He looked from one to the other.

"Don't worry inspector," said Jackie. "We know where we stand."

"I want your mobile on at all times and if I call for you come straight here ok?"

Jackie nodded again.

"Be off with you then. I may be calling you in tomorrow."

David and Jackie made for the door as they opened it the inspector called again.

"Remember!" He eyed them sternly. The couple closed the door behind them and breathed a sigh of relief. They looked at each other.

"Come on," said Jackie with feeling, "let's get out of here. We've seen enough of this place and I need a strong drink."

Solomon Weinstein sat at a table in the Melbury Library. Whilst the rest of the town were absorbed with the 'Beekeeper Show murder' investigation, he had other things on his mind. In front of him were strewn all the legal books and documents he could find relating to unfair dismissal. In point of fact there was more to his legal action against Bernie Small than met the eye. He really did not enjoy being a garage mechanic anyway. His ambition in life was to be taken on or sponsored by a legal firm and to work up in the profession. He had his eye on one in Ixdon; 'Manley and Cohen'. He had already spoken to Mr Cohen and he felt that if he could make a good job of representing himself on this case he might persuade the firm to recruit him. Solomon also wanted to get one over Bernie Small. He didn't mind being teased and he liked a good joke, but the one Bernie made about his own father having died in a concentration camp.. by falling out of the gun tower, drunk, was too much. He would get his revenge.

Solomon scribbled some notes on a pad then looked up as he became aware of a portly presence at his table. Bernie Small looked down confidently amused.

"Ah young Einstein, 'thought I'd find you here."

Solomon looked irritated. "The name," he said, "as you very well know, is Weinstein, *Weinstein* with a 'V', not *Einstein* with an E, so please call me by my correct name, anyway what do you want? I'm not going to drop the case if that's what you think."

Bernie smiled wickedly. "I've just come to tell you we're in court tomorrow. My attorney (he liked the grandness of the term) Rupert Crook's partner Mr Tritton, has brought your case forward."

Solomon looked annoyed. He put on an exaggerated Jewish accent and spread his palms.

"What's this then? First you fire me, now you're my agent?"

Bernie chuckled. We're in front of Eb' Wedgewood so I hope you can shout." He chuckled again as Solomon's hand went to his brow. Bernie looked at the books strewn on the desk. "Hope it gives you enough time." He said. "Anyway must go, see you tomorrow."

Bernie headed noisily for the library front door, ignoring the disapproving looks from various people, sitting studiously around room. He walked out onto the sunlit Melbury high street and smiled to himself. For the second time that week he took a deep satisfied breath of the dry harvest air. Things generally, he thought, were looking up.

Solomon went back to work. 'Tomorrow!' He thought. 'If that crafty devil thinks he could get one on me by rushing he's got another thought coming!'

He picked up a small red booklet in front of him entitled: 'Discrimination In The Workplace,' and flicking it's pages, industriously started making notes.

Chapter 17

"What do you make of our running figure then?" Downs asked his colleague.

Simpkins looked thoughtful. "Well, It doesn't fit with Frank White or Lenny James, you couldn't have called either of them small."

"True," agreed Downs. And Ronald Finch was going the other way, through the woods."

"Bernie was staggering up the high street." Added Simkins.

They were both thoughtful for a moment. Then Downs spoke again.

"Well, barring Mrs White and Robinson himself that leaves, um.."

"Deborah Smith, the barmaid." Simpkins filled in the missing name.

"Deborah Smith," echoed the inspector.

"Albert Stern's only nocturnal visitor unaccounted for." Added Simpkins. "And she is small. She would fit Robinson's description of the running figure. Constable Ellis has told us that she went to the cottage that night. In fact she is the only person we know who was in the cottage and could fit the bill."

Downs considered this for a moment.

"But she had no motive to kill Stern." He protested.

"None that we know of, but why was she there?" Said Simpkins I think we should bring her in. It's the only way we'll find out for sure."

Downs groaned and rubbed his bruised cheek again. All he really wanted was some more concrete evidence to nail Ronald Finch. "I suppose so," he agreed. "Let's get Price to pick her up now."

As the inspector and Sergeant Simpkins left the office a huge commotion greeted them in the corridor by the front desk. Sergeant Price was physically restraining Rupert Crook, who looked hot and flustered in a heavy black suit. Crook was protesting loudly.

"I must speak to the inspector! This is an outrage! A grave injustice is being done!"

Downs strode purposefully up the corridor.

"Let him go sergeant!"

Price released Crook's jacket, which was now extremely crumpled.

"Sorry sir, but you said.."

Down's held up his hand.

"That's alright Sergeant Price" He turned indignantly to address Mr Crook, who was attempting to unruffle himself and straighten his tie. "What is the meaning of bursting in here and causing all this disturbance. What is going on?"

Rupert Crook adjusted his black-rimmed glasses back to the horizontal and assumed an air of dignity.

"You have no right to hold my client a moment longer." He asserted pompously, "I have strong evidence that could implicate a number of other people..for a start Albert Stern was blackmailing both Frank White and his wife. A classic motive for murder." He prayed secretly that the expensive information from Bernie was correct. "Furthermore.."

Jason Damagio strained at the door to hear the conversation. Down's caught sight of him.

"Get him out of here!" He yelled.

Sergeant Price, already exhausted from restraining Mr Crook, advanced wearily on the reporter.

"Furthermore," added Crook, "you have made no effort to question an obvious witness in this case. This is gross incompetence and I shall be reporting it."

"What witness might that be?" interrupted Simpkins, slightly amused at the sight of the angry dishevelled solicitor.

"Why, Albert Stern's daughter of course! Don't you read the paper?"

Downs looked at Simpkins for enlightenment, the latter raised his eyebrows suggested that none would be forthcoming. Downs made a mental note to read that day's Norwich Standard. In fact, due to Nick King's late night call, only the late editions of the paper carried the item: '*daughter grieves*'.

And who might Albert Stern's daughter be Mr Crook?" Asked Downs unenthusiastically, an air of unrestrained cynicism in his voice.

"Why Miss Deborah Smith," replied Crook, indignantly. "Debbie, the new barmaid at the Bell."

Father Simpson listened with interest as Doctor Rotton finished his description of the usefulness and effects of Paclitaxel. He was as confounded as the doctor, especially as it made his own theory look less likely. They both sat silently for a moment.

Doctor Rotton broke the silence.

"What about your story then father. What are these 'facts' that have come to your attention?"

Father Simpson looked doubtful. "I don't think they make sense in view of what you have told me." He paused for a moment, thoughtfully pressing his palms together and tapping his forefingers against his lips. Then, with great deliberation he continued.

"Doctor Rotton; Is there anyway that the pathologist could have been wrong. I mean is it possible he could have mistaken something else for this drug. Could there be a more simple explanation? Some other cause of death?" He was considering how in the press medical practitioners still, albeit rarely, made headlines over mistakes or sometimes critical errors. "After all," he added. "No one is infallible."

"Indeed you are right!" Rejoined the doctor. "The medical profession makes many mistakes. They say that one in six hospital beds are occupied by patients who have been made ill by their treatment!"

Doctor Rotton lifted his generous figure from the chair and walked across to the window. "I suppose it's possible there has been a mistake but I know the pathologist, William Hadley. He's very good, has a great reputation. He is quite familiar with drugs used in oncology. He's probably found traces of them in the poor victims of cancer that he may have performed post-mortems on. Besides, what would be similar to Paclitaxel.."

His voice faded as he gazed out of the window. The churchyard yew tree swung and rustled in the strong breeze again. The subliminal thought that had stirred earlier, urged by the priests question, now sprung to the front of his consciousness.

Father Simpson stood up to find what had so distracted the doctor. He strained to look out the window, which was being successfully blocked by Andrew Rotton's large figure. The doctor continued to stare at the tree.

"Of course!" Exclaimed the doctor. "The yew tree!"

Father Simpson was lost.

"What about it?" He asked, peering bemused at the branches swaying in the breeze.

The doctor turned around, his eyes shone with excitement.

"Quick! Do you have an encyclopaedia? Get it quickly!"

The baffled priest thumbed across a shelf and pulled down a large red-bound book. Doctor Rotton grabbed the book and quickly flicked through its pages to those indexed with the letter 'T'. Then he narrowed down his search, turning the leaves carefully. Finally he stopped at a page and excitedly scanned its contents.

"Here it is!" He exclaimed, pointing at a paragraph: *Taxus bacatta!* The English Yew..its bark is poisonous!"

The Priest looked, curious, but unenlightened, at the page.

"The *taxel* part of the name Paclitaxel refers to its origins." Explained Doctor Rotton. " It is made from the bark of the Pacific Yew." The doctor slapped his forehead. "Why didn't I see it before! You see yew has medicinal properties. For example the American Indians used yew bark for treating skin cancer, but like many things it is poisonous if care is not taken. Look!"

He pointed to a paragraph; "Caesar records that the Gaelic chieftain Cativolcus was killed by drinking an infusion of yew bark. Yew has been a poison for centuries!"

"So what you are suggesting is that Doctor Vandersteen was killed by drinking an infusion of yew bark and that the pathologist mistook it for this drug Paclitaxel?" asked the priest incredulously.

"It is possible isn't it? Asked the doctor. "I mean I just don't believe that a GP would kill himself by means of this drug. Yew poisoning may offer a solution don't you think?"

"It also poses another question." Added the priest.

"First things first. Where is your phone? I'm going to call Mr Hadley. We'll take it from there."

With the news that Deborah Smith was the sole heir and beneficiary to Albert Stern's estate, the contingent sent to question her was on a scale similar to that sent to apprehend Frank White. Sergeant Price was left in charge of the police station, whilst Ellis drove Simpkins and Inspector Downs to the Bell Hotel. Seeing the entourage leave, Jason Damagio grabbed his director, jumped into the outside broadcast van, and set off in hot dusty pursuit.

En-route to the hotel, much to Inspector Down's displeasure, Simpkins was explaining how statistically most murders were perpetrated by kinsfolk of the victim.

"Most," conceded Downs. "*Most*! It doesn't mean *all*. Right now we only want Miss Smith for questioning. Don't forget Ronald Finch is still our main suspect.."

He sounded unconvincing, and felt strangely nervous as the car drew up outside the hotel.

Fran Todd, standing at the Bell Hotel's oak reception desk, was talking to Nick King and Amanda. All three looked startled as the police contingent burst unceremoniously through the front door. Inspector Downs approached the desk and looked suspiciously around the reception area, as if expecting to see a felon.

"Mrs Todd!" The inspector spoke stridently. "I wish to speak to Miss Deborah Smith, I believe that she works here." Sergeant Simpkins pushed open the door to the bar and looked casually inside. Jackie White was in the corner with David, downing her third gin and tonic. She looked up and rolled her eyeballs when she spotted the policeman. Constable Ellis, hovering by the front door, managed to eject a protesting Jason Damagio.

"Inspector!" Exclaimed Fran. "I've just told Mr King here, Debbie had a phone call about twenty minutes ago. She said she had to go, dropped everything and just disappeared. Larcum is well displeased. He's had to work her shift through lunchtime.."

"Do you have any idea..?" Nick and the inspector spoke simultaneously.

Downs looked menacingly at Nick.

"Do you have any idea," he continued, with exasperated patience, "where Miss Smith may have gone?"

Before Fran Todd could answer, another commotion heralded the appearance of Doctor Rotton, as he burst through the hotel entrance. Doctor Rotton was flushed with the exertion of tracking down the inspector. Accompanied by Father Simpson he stood panting in front of the gathering at the desk.

"Inspector! Inspector! Thank goodness I've found you."

He paused for breath whilst Downs looked at him in astonishment.

"Inspector." The doctor continued. "I have important information for you. The post-mortem. I spoke to the pathologist." He paused again, puffing. "We have a new theory.. It wasn't the drug Paliataxel at all.. It was yew!"

Downs look turned to incredulity.

"Are you mad doctor? What are you on about?"

"Doctor Vandersteen!" Explained Rotton. "It was yew!"

Downs shoulders slumped, he paused to allow the statement to sink in.

"Oh well! At last!" He exclaimed with heavy sarcasm, glancing around the assembled gathering. "Of course! I've arrested or detained half of Melbury; including an old gardener, a wealthy businessman, half of his associates *and* a drunken garage mechanic, when, if only I'd considered it, it was me all along!" He looked around again, wide eyed. "What a fool I've been. I haven't even interrogated myself, yet there I was all the time! The culprit! Right under my own nose..." He warmed to his theme, still staring around in mock amazement.

"I can see the headlines now: 'After eliminating most of the population of Melbury in his investigations, Inspector Downs came to the inevitable conclusion that he himself must be the murderer.' Yes I think.."

"I think the doctor is referring to the tree," interrupted Simpkins respectfully.

"Yes! Yes! That's it," agreed Rotton, excitedly. "The poison was not Paliataxel but yew! The drug is basically an extraction from yew bark. The pathologist confesses that he was surprised at just what a reaction Doctor Vandersteen had to the drug. He agreed that a crude distillation of yew could cause the effects that would seem extreme compared to the purified drug, and that a yew distillate could fool the assay that he used as a screen. He freely admits that yew poisoning is a likely alternative. In my opinion, and in view of the fact that there was none of this drug in the vicinity or reported as having been obtained locally, yew poisoning is the more likely cause of death."

Downs, feeling rather foolish, considered this for a moment. Before he could comment Father Simpson spoke.

"Inspector," said the priest calmly. "I presume that you are here looking for Miss Smith. Do you have any idea where she is?"

Downs turned inquisitively to Mrs Todd.

"That's just it inspector, she got this phone call about half an hour ago now and just zoomed off, all of a rush. I don't know where to. It's not like her I must say."

"I think I know where she's gone," said Father Simpson. "And if I'm not mistaken she might be in grave danger. You had all better follow me. We have no time to lose."

Chapter 18

Jason Damagio stood outside the Bell feeling very miffed. "Bloody cheek," he said. The film crew were busy tidying up the equipment that had been hurriedly thrown into van prior to their hasty exit from the front of Melbury Police Station. "Can't even go into a hotel now. I'm sure this is illegal." He spotted Jackie White through the bar window and brightened up. "Andy! How about a swift half while we're waiting.."

His director was about to make an acerbic comment when the group that had been gathered by the hotel reception desk poured urgently out onto the street. Father Simpson and Doctor Rotton ran to the priest's small Renault. The policemen followed them out of the hotel and climbed into the police car, a bright red Ford Sierra, which was parked directly outside. Ellis started the engine and waited for Father Simpson to move off. The haste and serious intent expressed by the group conveyed to Andy that something important was happening.

"Quick!" He turned to one of the technicians. "Run the camera and somebody start the van! I want to follow this lot, something's going down here!"

The cameraman filmed the departure of the police car, then he lifted the camera onto the back of the van and hastily scrambled inside. Meanwhile Inspector Downs and Simpkins sat, somewhat confused, in the rear of the Sierra.

"What do you make of this sergeant?" Asked Downs, trying hard to keep up with events.

Simpkins was equally mystified. "We seem to be heading back toward Albert Stern's cottage," he observed, peering ahead at the directions being taken by Father Simpson and the doctor.

The black Renault had turned right over the stone bridge and was heading towards the edge of town. It pulled up suddenly, just short of Albert Stern's house.

Father Simpson leapt out of the car, crossed the road and began banging on the door of a white two-storey cottage. As the police arrived, the priest started knocking again, this time more urgently.

"Inspector!" Exclaimed the priest. "I will explain everything later, but right now I have to ask you to break this door down!"

Downs looked aghast, but Sergeant Simpkins, sensing the urgency in Father Simpson's voice, wasted no time and leaning back kicked hard against the lock of the flimsy front door. A modern door would have offered more resistance, but the after a second kick the old door gave way, to the sound of splitting wood and wrenching metal. Simpkins rushed into the house closely followed by the priest. The cool interior of the cottage was strangely quiet after their violent entrance. Simpkins stood in the silent empty hallway and looked at the priest.

"I hope you know what you're doing!" He hissed. Somehow the silence forbade raised voices.

Father Simpson brushed past Simpkins and pushed open the lounge door on the right. Mrs Cummings stood calmly near the back of the room, her hand clasped in front of her. In a chair by her side Debbie lay slumped back with her eyes shut. Debbie's pallid complexion told the priest all he needed to know.

"Quick, call an ambulance!" He shouted, "Doctor Rotton! In here quickly!"

"It's too late for her," said Mrs Cummings, looking with detachment at Debbie's supine figure. "She'll be gone soon.." Her lips tightened and her face quivered with the grief of a painful memory. "Just like my little Katie."

Simpkins ran to the telephone that he had seen in the hallway. Doctor Rotton knelt in front of Debbie, taking her pulse and holding his hand to her forehead. Inspector Downs stepped into the middle of the room, trying to make sense of the scene before him.

"What the devil is going on here?" He demanded.

Father Simpson stroked Debbie's dark hair tenderly and looked up at Mrs Cummings.

"You have allowed great evil into your soul Edith Cummings! You have stretched the powers of Christian understanding beyond reason. What have you done to this poor girl?"

Mrs Cummings swayed back and forth, keeping her hands locked together. Singing gently.

"*Sweet cisely she gave to me.*"

"What the blazes is going on!" Inspector Down's repeated his demand.

"*To stop the pain of dear Katie,*" continued Mrs Cummings, seemingly oblivious to her surroundings. A tear rolled down her cheek.

Father Simpson picked up a cup lying on its side. Next to Debbie's languid hand. He sniffed the cups remaining contents.

"Sweet cisely?" He addressed the doctor. "What's that?"

"Andrew Rotton looked blankly at the cup.

"It's Cow Parsley, chipped in Constable Ellis. "You know, the stuff growing by the roadside. I remember my mother used to call it cisely, or sweet cisely, something like that."

"Never mind!" Exclaimed the doctor. "It's toxic! She's been poisoned! That's all that matters."

Debbie stirred on the chair and groaned, she lolled sideways pulling her knees toward her stomach.

"Go and get some blankets." Shouted Doctor Rotton to Ellis. Sergeant!" he turned to Simpkins. "Quickly! Make up a strong solution of warm salt water!" He put his hands under Debbie's armpits. "Inspector! Help me to get her on the couch and keep her comfortable until the ambulance arrives. I'll have to call Ixdon casualty unit and tell them what to expect."

Father Simpson approached Mrs Cummings.

"There is no need for this girl to die at your hands like this. It won't bring back Katie or your husband. Now tell me, it's not too late, what did you give her exactly and what can we do to save her?"

Mrs Cummings continued to rock back and forth, humming a curious cracked tune and staring vacantly at the floor.

The priest grasped at a chain around his neck and produced a small pewter crucifix. He held it in front of her, shaking it to emphasise his point.

"Redemption Edith! It's not too late! Tell me!"

Inspector Downs lowered Debbie onto the patterned orange couch.

"What's going on?" He insisted, directing his remark towards the priest. "Are you telling me that Mrs Cummings has tried to kill this girl?"

The wail of an ambulance siren pierced the dramatic tension of the room as Simpkins appeared from the kitchen holding a glass of hazy liquid. Doctor Rotton took the glass and sat Debbie's pale frame upright. "Give me a hand sergeant!"

Simpkins helped to support the girl whilst the doctor held her mouth open and poured the saline solution into her throat. He firmly held her jaw shut and gently massaged her thorax to induce an involuntary swallow.

After a quarter of the glass had gone Debbie suddenly lurched forward and threw up over the carpet in front of her. Doctor Rotton held her stomach as she continued to retch. "Hold her!" Ordered the doctor. He poured the remaining salt water down Debbie's throat, repeating the rough exercise of holding her mouth shut. Debbie swallowed again, choking as she did so. Then, with a painful rasping noise, she coughed and vomited again. The room reverberated to the pitiful noise. Doctor Rotton rubbed her back tenderly to soothe her.

"It's alright Debbie, you're ok."

Debbie continued to gag. Her distress upset Father Simpson greatly. He turned to Mrs Cummings with unbridled anger.

"Look what you've done! You wicked woman, have you no pity! Did you really want to cause this girl all this pain?" Mrs Cummings looked at Debbie dispassionately. Hatred glittered in her eyes. "She's the fruit of the evil vine isn't she?" Her voice cracked and she sobbed. "Why should she live while my Katie lies cold and lonely for all these years."

Gradually Debbie's retching eased. Her stomach was empty yet still she gagged. Finally she stopped and lifted her head to look, with red moist eyes, first at the Father Simpson and then at the doctor.

"Wha..What's happening?" She asked weakly.

Inspector Down's looked distastefully at the green vomit, which had splattered his shoes.

"I was rather hoping somebody might tell me that," he said, optimistically.

The BBC van arrived at Mrs Cummings cottage just as Simpkins had finished kicking down the door. Nick King and Amanda stood outside the entrance; Nick was talking urgently into his mobile telephone. Andy hastily organized Damagio in front of the camera.

"Right!" Said Andy excitedly, roll the camera, start talking Jason."

Damagio looked alarmed.

"What shall I say?"

"Just say what's happening," Said Andy irritated. "This is break-ing news! Be a pro! One take, no rehearsal!" He turned to the van and shouted.

"Brian! Call Norwich. Tell them we've got breaking story and that we need a courier to get the film back for the early news!"

"One take!" Jason was horrified; he always needed a couple to get it right.

In the distance an ambulance siren wailed towards them.

"Right!" Said Andy, "Roll the camera, sound check ok Dave?"

A technician with earphones gave a thumbs up.

"Action!"

Jason stood inertly. For a moment his expression was that of a rabbit caught in a car's headlights. Andy waved his hands encourag-ingly, urging Jason to talk. Finally Damagio began.

"Er, today a major development in the 'Beekeeper Murder' inves-tigation has, er, developed." He looked lamely at the director then continued.

"Presently, the main suspect, Ronald Finch, is in the Melbury Police Station. He is charged with Murdering Albert Stern, his old adversary in the annual Melbury Beekeeper Show. Despite this how-ever, the Melbury police, under the authority of Inspector John Downs, have continued to interview and detain various Melbury citizens in-cluding a local businessman, Frank White, his wife and her assistant David Robinson. A few moments ago.." Jason turned dramatically towards the white cottage. "Inspector Downs and his colleagues ar-rived at this cottage in search of a Miss Deborah Smith, a young woman who has recently been discovered to be the murdered man's daughter. In a dramatic development, the police have broken down the cottage door and are presently.."

Jason's voice was drowned out by the noisy arrival of an ambu-lance outside the front of the cottage. The vehicle screeched to a halt amidst a cloud of dust. Peace resumed as the siren ceased though the blue lights on the top of the vehicle continued to flash dramatically. Two paramedics deftly retrieved a stretcher trolley from the back of the ambulance and rushed urgently into the house.

Inside the cottage Doctor Rotton helped the paramedics lift Debbie onto the stretcher.

"I'll go with them," said Rotton curtly.

"Is she going to be alright?" asked Father Simpson, worried. "I mean should I come?"

The Doctor smiled wryly.

"I don't think she will need the last rites if that's what you mean William." He grimaced towards Mrs Cummings. "No thank to the poisoner over there though. I think you had better arrest her inspector. I will leave Father Simpson to explain."

Constable Ellis, seeing the attention the press were going to give the medical team, stepped outside to control the crowd.

Edith Cummings struck fast. Ellis had been standing close to her before his exit. Now, relatively unsupervised, she moved carefully towards a dark oak cabinet by the wall. On the top of the cabinet lay a brass oriental letter opener, curved in the shape of a dragon, its body and feet forming the handle of a knife. She grasped the weapon and lunged with sudden agility towards the stretcher. Before anyone could react she had taken the two steps that brought her in range. Snarling viciously she held the knife above her head with both hands and brought the weapon swiftly down towards her target.

Sergeant Simpkins was the first to react. Realizing the danger, he dived forwards and propelled the stretcher trolley towards the door, taking the paramedics and Doctor Rotton with it. The letter opener missed its intended victim and instead, tore sickeningly into the shoulder of one of the ambulance men. Mrs Cummings tried to renew her attack on Debbie but Father Simpson desperately held her back and Inspector Downs lunged forward to get his arm around her neck. Between them they wrestled Edith to the floor; it was all over in seconds. Downs yelled for the restraint devices to be brought from the police car. The paramedic sat in the corner, clutching his shoulder, groaning. Blood soaked his uniform.

Simpkins appeared with a pair of handcuffs. He snapped them on Edith Cummings wrists and pushed her roughly to the corner of the room. Doctor Rotton, having recovered from being propelled across the cottage, was attending to the injured man.

"How is he?" Called the inspector.

"It's a nasty injury," said Rotton, tentatively opening the medic's shirt collar. "I think we had better get them both in the ambulance and over to Ixdon. Give me a hand here."

The remaining paramedic and the doctor lifted the wounded man up and carried him towards the cottage door. Outside there was pandemonium. A crowd of Melbury residents had made its way to the cottage and they blocked the way to the ambulance. The fracas inside the building, followed by the appearance of the wounded medic and Debbie on the stretcher, caused gasps of dismay. Jason Damagio continued to talk excitedly into his microphone. Andy looked on with disbelief as the broadcast developed and he had to admit, Damagio was rising to the occasion.

Doctor Rotton climbed into the ambulance behind the stretcher, ignoring the BBC microphone thrust in his face. A cloud of blue fumes enveloped everyone in the road as the ambulance driver started the vehicle's engine. Then, with an ear-splitting scream, the ambulance siren burst into life and the vehicle the sped towards Ixdon, it's blue lights still flashing.

Back inside the cottage Inspector Downs gathered his thoughts and tried to resume control of the situation. He looked, almost disbelievingly, at Mrs Cummings sitting handcuffed in the corner. Then turned to glare accusingly at Father Simpson.

"Alright father! I want an explanation, from the beginning and I want it fast. I am not entirely convinced that you cannot be arrested for withholding evidence, regardless of you status as a priest! Before I charge this woman for poisoning and assault you had better start talking."

Inspector Downs was clearly furious as well as being totally confused.

"To save you the trouble later." Father Simpson spoke calmly. "You had better also charge her with the murders of both Albert Stern and Doctor David Vandersteen."

Downs looked blankly at the priest. He was becoming used to surprises.

"Go on."

The priest walked to the window and turned to look at Mrs Cummings.

"I have not been withholding evidence inspector. It was only this morning that all the parts of the riddle fell into place."

Father Simpson paused to gather his thoughts.

"Mrs Cummings murdered Albert Stern because she hated him." He said simply. "About twenty years ago, Albert Stern was about to retire from the air force when he was seconded to Norwich for public relations duties. Apparently he was very good at pouring oil on troubled waters and the RAF, for various reasons, were not popular in the area."

The priest looked at the woman on the floor again. She glared back at him angrily.

"Anyway it was whilst working in Norwich that Albert Stern met Katie Cummings, Mrs Cummings twenty five year old daughter."

"Curse the day!" Edith spat the words out. Father Simpson continued.

"It may seem unlikely, with a near thirty year age difference, but Katie and Stern had an affair."

Sergeant Simpkins interrupted. "With respect father, how do you know all this?"

"I am a good friend of Patrick O'Byrne, the parish priest of Mrs Cummings old diocese. Father O'Byrne became involved with counselling Mrs Cummings husband. Anyway, let me carry on and it will become clear."

He gathered his thoughts again.

"Katie Cummings was a very attractive but unstable girl. Unknown to Albert Stern she had a history of emotional problems. From her early twenties she had suffered from neurosis and depression; indeed she had been receiving treatment for a year before the couple met. Anyway, apparently she fell in love with the charming Albert Stern and she also, unfortunately, became pregnant."

The priest glanced at Mrs Cummings who fixed him with a malevolent gaze.

"Stern suggested that she terminate the pregnancy. Katie protested, but she thought that if she did not Stern might leave her, so, against her wishes, she had an abortion."

Simpkins and the inspector listened attentively; the room was very quiet.

"In due course Stern left Norwich and in the process stopped his romance with Katie Cummings. Katie became clinically depressed, both due to the abortion and due to Stern leaving her. Despite receiving treatment, she was inconsolable. Eventually she took her own life by leaping from the cliff top at Cromer."

"Poor girl," muttered Simpkins.

"Yes, it was tragic," agreed the priest. "But there is more. Katie was the Cumming's only child. Her father adored her. After her suicide he started drinking heavily. Then, one night, after a bout of heavy drinking he crashed his car into a tree. As a result he was brain damaged and spent the rest of his life in a wheelchair, being cared for by Mrs Cummings here." He nodded towards the forlorn figure in the corner.

"And she blamed all her misfortune on Albert Stern," concluded Simpkins.

Father Simpson nodded.

"A while ago Edith's husband died. That is when she first moved to Melbury to live in the cottage opposite Albert Stern."

"Surely Stern would have known her?" pointed out Inspector Downs.

"They had never met," said the priest succinctly. "I gather that Mrs Cummings did not approve of her daughter seeing an older man."

Mrs Cummings became agitated, straining against the handcuffs.

"I hope he rots in hell!" She hissed.

"So Mrs Cummings moved to Melbury to plot the murder of Albert Stern?" Asked Sergeant Simpkins.

"Not quite," replied the priest. "She seemed content just to watch the object of her hatred. She was receiving treatment for her own depression from Doctor Vandersteen. I discovered, from reading his medical notes this morning, that she had discussed her hatred for Stern in great detail with the doctor. But only she can tell us what eventually drove her to kill the old man."

Inspector Downs looked at Edith puzzled. "How do you know for sure that she killed Stern? We have no conclusive evidence."

"Because," said the priest, "she also killed Doctor Vandersteen."

Downs looked none the wiser. The priest continued patiently.

"There was only one person in Melbury who could have connected Edith with the death of Albert Stern and that was Doctor Vandersteen. He had listened for months to her outpourings of hatred for the man. Indeed he had even had such concern for Albert Stern's safety that he went to warn him of his imminent danger. On the very night in fact, that he was killed."

"Of course!" Exclaimed Simpkins. "We've been trying to fathom out why the doctor visited Stern that night!"

"Once she had killed Stern." Explained the priest, "Mrs Cummings had to get rid of Vandersteen."

"If Albert Stern had been warned he must have been prepared." Pointed out Downs, how could she have attacked him with a knife then? He would have been ready!"

"She didn't want to attack him with a knife did you Mrs Cummings?" Edith remained impassive. "She wanted to poison him. Like she did Doctor Vandersteen. She was an expert at herbal medicine don't forget. She knew how to make any number of natural poisons. But when she went across to Stern's house she found him already unconscious."

"Bernie Small!" Chipped in Simpkins.

"Yes." Agreed the priest, "Bernie had left after Stern fell and struck his head. Mrs Cummings took advantage of the door that Small had left open and entered the house. Seeing Stern unconscious she went to the kitchen for a knife."

"He wasn't unconscious." Edith Cummings voice sounded bitter, they all turned to look at her.

She looked back around the room.

"He was crawling. Crawling towards the hallway. Just like the worm he was. I stuck it in him there and finished him off." Her voice petered off quietly.

"It was just like killing vermin."

Father Simpson looked at her pitifully.

"What drove you to eventually kill him Edith. You had resisted it for so long?"

Mrs Cummings gave a hollow laugh.

"It was the girl," she said. "She was young, like Katie, I thought he was at it again. I wasn't going to let him do that to another poor girl. Ha.. I wasn't to know it was the swine's daughter. I wish I'd been able to kill her too, just like he did my little Katie.."

She began to weep.

"And how did you poison Doctor Vandersteen?" Asked the priest quietly.

"I got some bark from a yew tree," Edith sobbed. "Phoned him and told him I had made something for his migraine. I took it over. Very grateful he was, drank the lot. Some doctor.." She shrugged. "Then I left a note. Thought since he was always so depressed it might look like suicide."

"What about Vandersteen's cut wrists?" Asked Simpkins.

"I went back." Said Mrs Cummings simply. "He was too sick to lock up. I just walked in. I had to be sure he was going to die. I wasn't sure he'd drunk enough poison so I slashed his wrists to be sure." Her voice lacked remorse. Inspector Downs looked at her with disbelief.

"It was poor reward for all the counselling and help the doctor gave you," observed Father Simpson.

Edith Cummings shrugged.

"He was as unhappy as me. I probably did him a favour."

The priest looked at Mrs Cummings piteously.

"Having killed Doctor Vandersteen Edith tried to cover her tracks," continued Father Simpson. She knew that the doctor would have made notes of her conversations with him so she destroyed a number of files, including of course her own."

Mrs Cummings shifted uncomfortably.

"What she didn't know was that Doctor Vandersteen had started backing up his medical files on a computer. It was there, on the surgery computer, that I found the record of Doctor Vandersteen's concern for Albert Stern's safety."

The inspector had had enough.

 "Let's get her down to the station," he said curtly. He walked across the room and pulled Mrs Cummings upright. "Come on sergeant."

As they pushed Edith towards the door, Downs stopped and looked respectfully at Father Simpson.

"Good job father, I owe you."

Father Simpson shook his head.

"Just remember inspector. She is a very sick woman. This is no ordinary murderer."

As the inspector emerged from the cottage, a crowd surged forwards.

"He's got Edith in handcuffs!" Shouted Jenny Larcombe excit

edly.

Jason Damagio tried to push his microphone through the crowd. Nick King called out.

"Inspector a statement! Please!"

Downs held up his hand as he and Sergeant Simpkins propelled Mrs Cummings towards the police car.

"I will issue a full statement from the police station." He pushed the woman into the back seat. "In about an hour." he added over his shoulder.

Constable Ellis had given up his fruitless task of trying to control the crowd and had leapt into the driving seat of the Sierra. Sergeant Simpkins squeezed in to the back seat. Mrs Cummings sat dwarfed between the two policemen. Finally the Sierra's doors closed emphatically and with another cloud of Melbury dust, the car sped off towards the police station.

The desk sergeant greeted the inspector anxiously.

"Inspector Mr Crook is being very difficult. He is threatening to sue the whole police force! He says that we have no right to hold Ronald Finch!"

The sergeant looked curiously over the inspectors shoulder. Mrs Cummings, her hands handcuffed in front of her, stood, held firmly, by Sergeant Simpkins.

"He's right!" replied the Inspector briskly. "Help Sergeant Simpkins take Mrs Cummings to the interview room and then we will allow Ronald Finch and Frank White to go." He turned to Simpkins. "I'll be with you in a minute. I'm just going to put a call through to Chief Superintendent Ross."

Simpkins allowed himself a smile.

"Yes sir." He led Edith down the corridor and called over his shoulder. "I think we can tell him that we don't need the murder squad tomorrow."

Inspector Downs walked down the corridor towards the cells. As usual, the conversation with Chief Superintendent Ross had not been easy. Convincing Ross that the murderer was not in fact an old man who was fond of gardening, but actually an old woman who was keen on herbal remedies had been arduous to say the least, especially as she was a double and almost a triple murderer. Finally however

Ross seemed to be satisfied, with the caveat that he found Downs's methods of investigation rather unconventional and that he was coming down himself to see what was going on.

Sergeant Price unlocked the door to Ronald Finch's cell. Ronald looked up from his bed, startled. Whenever Inspector Downs appeared it was usually bad news.

"Mr Finch," began the inspector. "I want you to know that all charges against you are now dropped. Thank you very much for helping us with our enquiries, you are now free to go."

Ronald looked bewildered.

"Free to go?" He said, surprised. "You don't think I killed Mr Stern anymore."

Downs smiled.

"We know that you didn't Mr Finch and I apologize for putting you through this experience. As you must know we can leave no stone unturned in these investigations."

The inspector held out his hand.

"Good luck Ronald."

Finch shook Down's hand limply.

"If you walk up to the front desk," said Downs, "you should find Mr Crook waiting. I think that he will take you home to your wife."

Ronald picked up his jacket and glancing at the two policemen, walked stiffly out of the cell and up the corridor.

Sergeant Price looked admiringly at the inspector.

"Very tactfully handled, I must say sir!"

"Thank you sergeant," acknowledged Downs ruefully. "I have a feeling the next one will not be so easy."

Frank White was unperturbed when the two policemen entered his cell. He stretched out on the spartan bed and then sprang to his feet.

"Just like old times," he said nodding at the bed. "Very comfortable. Mattress is a bit thin but much better than the scrubs." He glanced at Downs. "What can I do for you inspector? You're not going to let that dog Simpkins loose on me again are you?"

Downs shook his head. "No Mr White. I have come to thank you for you assistance and to tell you that you are free to go."

Frank's eyes narrowed.

"That's it! You publicly humiliate me and expect me to just go off as if nothing had happened?"

"I am just going to say that I will have forgotten what I have learned about you, if you accept my thanks and leave with the minimum of fuss. I would like everybody to resume their lives as if nothing had happened."

Frank White considered this.

"Have you found the killer?"

Downs nodded. "I have. You will hear all about it soon. Meanwhile, do we have a deal?"

The inspector held out his hand.

White looked at the outstretched palm for a moment, then laughed loudly.

"I have to hand it to you inspector," he said, shaking his hand. "You have a strange way of doing your work." He laughed again. "But yes. I'm out of here! I've got a business to run!"

Frank White picked up his jacket from a chair in the corner.

"Well well," he said, shaking his head. "So old Finch did it after all."

Downs smiled ruefully,

"Not quite," he said, "but as I say, you will find out soon enough."

Chapter 19

Ebenezer Wedgewood stood at the window of his office in the Melbury magistrate's court looking, with ill humour, at the scene outside. The town, it seemed, had been taken over by the country's media and the local population was actively participating in the whole circus. In fact it was probably safe to say that Melbury had ground to a halt. Ebenezer had not even been able to get his hearing aid properly repaired because the shop that serviced it had been closed. Instead, he made his clerk borrow an inferior hearing aid from his mother who lived in Spittle Street. Much to his mother's chagrin the clerk had effectively requisitioned the device. Ebenezer shook his head and walked back to his desk.

Eb' Wedgewood had been a magistrate for three decades. In his younger days he had actually been quite good, but now, at eighty, some of his faculties were not as keen as they used to be, particularly his hearing. He retained his position in Melbury, largely because no one else wanted to do the job. The legal matters up before him were so mundane and Melbury was usually such a dull town, that despite his handicaps, 'Eb' managed, generally, to cope quite well.

One of the reasons for his success appeared through the office door. The Melbury magistrates clerk, Earnest Pugh, a small bespectacled man, walked in clutching some files. He greeted Ebenezer respectfully.

"Good afternoon sir, how was lunch?"

Ebenezer leaned forward tapping the new hearing aid. "Eh?"

The clerk raised his voice. "Lunch sir, how was it?"

The magistrate grunted. "Ah, Lunch, very good, excellent in fact."

Actually lunch had been a bit too good. Ebenezer had, reluctantly joined a group luncheon hosted by the press, and whilst not a very active participant in the conversation. He had taken full advantage of a large meal and a glass or two of not bad claret.

"Bored me to death mind," he added. "Going on about this murder thing, all these people dying all over town. Getting sick of it I am. Even the police inspector's managed to drown himself."

Earnest looked confused, "I beg your pardon sir?"

Ebenezer grunted, "Don't know the details, some fellah called, said the inspector's drowned."

The clerk, who was convinced that Ebenezer was beginning to lose his marbles, sympathised. "Yes sir, anyway, something more mundane this afternoon."

He placed a neatly typed document on the desk in front of Ebenezer. Mr Pugh took great pride in the smooth running of the magistrate's court and in deference to Ebenezer's reduced faculties, he always presented the magistrate with a simple explanation to the days activities. In fact the system worked quite well and with the clerks assistance, Ebenezer usually managed to deal with his responsibilities adequately.

"First," continued Mr Pugh, "we have a matter of the two brothers accused of stealing cabbages from a farmers field. Ronald and Arthur Case."

Ebenezer's face began to flush. "Oh yes! Stealing cabbages! There is too much of that sort of thing going on 'round here!" As the owner of a small holding himself Ebenezer felt particularly strongly about the matter. "I don't believe anyone buys vegetables in Melbury anymore. They just steal 'em. Should be flogged, the lot of 'em. Bloody disgraceful!"

The clerk looked slightly alarmed as the magistrates colour turned purple.

"These two were caught red handed weren't they!" Ebenezer Continued. "Read it in the papers!"

"I don't think that you are supposed to know that sir." Mr Pugh squeezed his palms together obsequiously. "But anyway, I do believe that they *were* caught in 'flagrante delicto' so to speak."

Ebenezer tapped his hearing aid.

"Eh! Fragrant what?"

The clerk bowed slightly.

"Nothing sir, just that I do believe that the brothers had the items, so to speak, in a sack when apprehended in the field, as you say."

Ebenezer cleared his throat. "Hrrumph! Quite! Well no doubt the law will take its course. What else?"

The clerk produced a small buff file. "Next we have a claimed unfair dismissal, made by a gentleman called Solomon Weinstein against his former employer Bernard Small."

The magistrate grunted again, looking at the document in the file.

"Mr Weinstein," added the clerk, "will be representing himself."

Ebenezer made a disparaging snorting noise. "Amateur's!" He said with feeling. "Shouldn't be allowed!" He turned to the clerk and gestured toward the door with the back of his hand. "Look you carry on. I'll see you through there in a few moments."

The Clerk disappeared and Ebenezer stood and went back to the window. He was thinking about the vegetables growing on his small-holding. Perhaps, he thought, he should buy a big dog..

The church clock struck, bringing Ebenezer back to the present. He stood in front of the office mirror, straightened his tie and jacket, and then walked purposefully towards the courtroom.

Rupert Crook was doing a very thorough job presenting Bernie Small's defence against the unfair dismissal of Solomon Weinstein. The two accused brothers had not appeared, so the clerk had hastily rearranged the court timings. The unfair dismissal hearing kicked off first and a court orderly was sent to track down the Ronald and Arthur Case.

Ebenezer Wedgewood sat motionless on his seat behind the bench on the magistrate's court. Motion was fairly difficult for Ebenezer anyway because, as always, his substantial girth was jammed against the bench in front of him. Today however, he was particularly still, his palms together against his lips, eyes half closed, the picture of intense concentration.

In fact, Ebenezer Wedgewood was asleep. His pinioned stomach holding him in an upright attentive position. The effect of a large hospitable lunch, a warm soporific courtroom and Rupert Crook's droning was inevitable. In fact without even those factors, the odds on Ebenezer staying awake were small. Young Solomon Weinstein had been so nervous when presenting his evidence, that his voice had been reduced to a squeak. Ebenezer's requisitioned hearing aid was simply not up to the job, so the magistrate had started the afternoon by looking curiously at Solomon's earnest mouthing at the bench.

Then there was the bee. It started at the window by the magistrates right shoulder, trapped and struggling uncomprehendingly against the glass, determined to return to it's normal world. At first the bee had been unobtrusive, but as it's fruitless struggle became more intense, the note of it's thrashing wings moved up an octave. An octave in fact that put it in perfect harmony with Rupert Crook's dull monotone. Between them, Rupert and the bee created a soothing cyclic hum, that even the most determined insomniac would have had trouble resisting.

The clerk to the court, having decided that the bee was creating too much of a distraction, walked over to the window and took aim with a hefty document from his desk.

Thwack!

The bee, feeling the added threat to it's welfare, increased it's efforts to escape, creating such an angry noise that Rupert brought his summing up to a rapid close.

Thwack! The clerk missed again, but his second attempt had the effect of startling Ebenezer Wedgewood back to the land of the living. He jumped in his seat, his eyes opening suddenly. Fortunately for Ebenezer, such was the distraction of the mortal combat between the clerk and the bee, that no one noticed. As the magistrate tried to take in the events around him, the clerk prized open the stiff courtroom sash-window and with an exhausted high-speed dash, the bee fled to safety.

Ebenezer quickly tried to catch up. He had totally lost track of events and in his panic he totally forgot about Mr Pugh's hurried explanation regarding the revised court timings.

Rupert Crook gazed expectantly at the bench. Ebenezer looked around and surreptitiously slid the clerks neatly typed itinerary in front of him. He glanced at the clock at the back of the courtroom and then at the timetable on the paper. It was two forty five; the session had started at two. Ebenezer glanced at the first item on the itinerary. It was clear to him that he had been presiding over the two brothers accused of stealing vegetables. He glanced up at the expectant Mr Crook who was standing shoulder to shoulder with Bernie Small. He never prejudged a hearing, but he was quite familiar with this case. The two brothers had been caught red handed; there was no doubt that they were guilty. Ebenezer quickly decided, somewhat uncomfortably, that he could see that justice was done and save face at the same time.

He fixed Rupert and Bernie with his most magisterial gaze.

"Do either of you two gentlemen," he began sternly, "do either of you two gentlemen have any idea what a cabbage costs in the shops these days?"

Mr Crook looked blankly at Bernie and then at the magistrate. The clerk, Mr Pugh, sensing something was seriously amiss, began to sweat profusely.

The silence annoyed Ebenezer. He hated dumb insolence.

"Well!" He boomed, "*Do you!*"

Rupert Crook was lost. "Well, er no," he replied, "but I don't…"

Ebenezer leaned forward intimidating.

"What? Speak up!"

"Er no..but really.."

"*I'll bet you don't!*" Roared Ebenezer angrily. "I bet neither of you have ever bought a cabbage in your lives! Just Steal 'em.. Do you realize how much work goes into growing one cabbage! *Do yer! Eh.*"

The clerk began to panic, he realized what was happening and rushed to the bench.

"Wrong case!" He hissed loudly in the Magistrates ear.

Ebenezer's hearing aid began producing feedback. He tapped it hard with his forefingers and glanced again at his itinerary. Had he missed something? He saw the names on the sheet..

"Ron Case," he said staring hard at Rupert and Bernie again.

"No!" The clerk hissed in his ear again and pointed at his itinerary. "It's the other case!"

"And Arthur Case." Said Ebenezer, looking strangely at his clerk and then back at Rupert, "are guilty of the most heinous.."

"No! No!" The clerks voice was raised by now. His finger stabbed at the itinerary, "You've got it wrong, call a recess!"

Ebenezer looked uncertain now. He blinked unhappily. "Anyway, before I continue we will have a short recess. Everyone back in here in twenty minutes!"

Bernie, Rupert and Solomon picked up their papers and made their way to the door.

"What was all that about?" Hissed Bernie.

"I've no idea," shrugged Rupert. "I think the old boy's gone completely loopy."

The Bell hotel was once again a scene of bustling excitement. As Ebenezer Wedgewood had observed, Melbury had practically come to a standstill. The townsfolk were totally preoccupied with the arrest of the 'Beekeeper Show murderer' and almost anyone, it seemed, was available to express their opinion to the gathering throng of press and media.

Jenny Larcombe, whose haberdashers shop hadn't been open for days, was, as usual, holding court.

"I always knew there was something strange about that woman," she confided. "Look how she used to stare out that cottage window every night."

"I thought you were convinced that Mr Finch was the killer." Pointed out Roy Barnes. "You've been going on about it all week."

"I just said he didn't like old Stern that all," said Jenny defensively.

Mrs Baker, clutching her customary sherry leaned forward. "I always thought Edith Cummings was evil," she said ominously. "Look at that thing she organised with moths when we all got bitten. If that wasn't evil I don't know what is."

"Rubbish!" Ivan Hillsdon joined in. "Let face it, we all thought Ronald Finch was guilty. We owe him an apology."

"He was guilty of spying on Mr Stern's garden," pointed out Fran Todd from behind the bar.

"And if that's the worst thing that ever happens in this town in the future we should all be grateful," added Roy. "I think it's nigh time this town went back to a bit of peace and quiet.."

Back in the Melbury magistrates court Earnest Pugh had patiently explained the situation to his boss. The clerk had convinced Ebenezer that despite Solomon Weinstein having bravely presented his case, there was no justification for a finding of unfair dismissal. Although the magistrate hadn't heard a word of the case himself, he trusted his clerk's judgement. Ebenezer readily agreed to a face saving solution offered by Mr Pugh. The courtroom reconvened.

Bernie, Rupert Crook and Solomon looked anxiously at the magistrate as he squeezed his girth behind the bench. Having settled down Ebenezer coughed, shuffled some papers and turned to address Solomon. The magistrate decided that it was best, on balance, not to refer to his previous diatribe on the price of cabbages.

"Mr Weinstein," he began. "From the evidence we have heard today," Ebenezer was aware that the phrase only inferred that he himself had heard any evidence. "From the evidence we have heard today, I'm afraid that I cannot find for a case of unfair dismissal."

Solomon looked crestfallen. He had worked very hard assembling his presentation. To add insult to injury Bernie Small leaned forward, beamed across at the room and gave Solomon a cheerful wave.

Ebenezer continued briskly. "Therefore I find for Mr Small." The magistrate, anxious to leave, stood up. "Thank you gentlemen, this session is now over."

Ebenezer gratefully gathered his paperwork and hastily headed back to the safety of his office. He was going to have some pretty strong words with a certain hearing aid specialist, very strong words in fact.

As everyone began to leave the courtroom, Mr Pugh intercepted Solomon.

"Mr Weinstein! Excuse me, may I have a quick word."

Solomon was in no mood to talk to anyone, he stopped and looked unhappily at the clerk.

"I had a case! This is unjust!"

Mr Pugh was unsympathetic.

"Actually I don't agree, however I was most impressed with the way you presented your arguments, you obviously did a lot of research."

"I did." Agreed Solomon aggrieved.

"Look," Said Mr Pugh. "I'm aware of your ambition to go into law. I happen to think that you have a future in the profession."

Solomon shrugged, "I appreciate what you say Mr Pugh but losing this hasn't helped much."

"Not at all," Rejoined the clerk. "you can't always win. Anyway I am going to write a letter for Mr Wedgewood's signature, addressed to Manley and Cohen at Ixdon. I'm going to recommend that they take you on as a trainee."

Solomon's face lit up. "Do you think you could get Mr Wedgewood to sign it? I got the impression that he didn't like amateurs representing themselves."

Mr Pugh smiled wryly.

"Oh, I think he'll sign it.."

He glanced smugly towards Ebenezer's office.

"I think he'll sign it alright..Mr Wedgewood has had a difficult day..and he owes me a favour or two.."

The Funerals of Albert Stern and Doctor Vandersteen were a public affair. The two men were buried in the graveyard next to Melbury's main church. Business in the town came to a standstill as the procession carrying the two coffins proceeded through the centre towards the cemetery. Solemn crowds thronged the pavements; heads bowed as the black hearses drove slowly by. Even the garrulous Jenny Larcombe was moved to silence as the vehicles passed.

Although the church was anglican, the vicar had felt it appropriate to ask Father Simpson to say a few words. The two hardwood coffins straddled the aisle of the packed church as Father Simpson climbed the short winding staircase to the pulpit. He surveyed the congregation.

"It is most heartening," he began, ignoring the feedback from the microphone in front of him. "To see so many mourners here today. Here, to lament the violent deaths of two of their fellow Melbury citizens." He looked at the two coffins. "Two very different citizens. One, a doctor, dedicated to the welfare of his fellow human beings, even, in the final event, to the welfare of his future killer. The other," he glanced at Debbie, still not completely recovered from her ordeal, sitting pale and beautiful in the front pew. "The other, a colourful and dynamic man who lived life to the full.." Father Simpson gripped the edge of the pulpit. "Maybe Albert Stern was not, in the purest definition of the words, a good man." He paused to allow the thought to sink in. "His life was, perhaps, controversial. He was, like everyone here, a sinner." The congregation shifted uncomfortably. "But, in the final analysis, it could be said that he contributed much to the life of Melbury. He was, despite his flaws, the sort of man, without whom the world would be a duller place." Father Simpson looked at Debbie again; she smiled weakly. "Remember Albert Stern then, for his love of life, and for the way that he delighted us all with his magnificent and beautiful entries to the annual Beekeeper Show."

There was a subdued murmur of agreement. Debbie began to sob loudly. Mrs Finch put a comforting arm around her. Bernie Small, still smarting from his unpaid gambling debt, muttered under his breath. Mrs Small elbowed him smartly in the ribs.

"Both these men," continued the priest, "were killed because evil was allowed to manifest itself in the form of a misplaced sense of revenge. You all know how this small community has been affected by the actions of one woman. A woman who, either due to her own insanity, or by her willingness to entertain evil, or perhaps both." The priest's voice was raised to make the point. "Made the perverse decision to commit murder."

The congregation shifted uneasily again.

"This reminds us all of our own duty to guard against evil. Evil exists and these coffins give testimony to it." He paused for a moment, allowing the point to sink home.

"It is now our duty," he said quietly. "To restore this town to its former peace, and to pray for the souls of David Vandersteen and Albert Stern."

The coffins were carried out of the cool church out into the brilliant sunshine. The whole population, it seemed, were there to pay their respects, feeling guilt perhaps, that such deeds had been carried out in their own town. As the crowd thronged to the churchyard, the funeral cortege proceeded solemnly back through the streets. Never in its history had the old weaving town seen such a display of unity and sympathy.

As the coffins were finally laid to rest, the crowd slowly dispersed. Leaving two gravediggers to finally shovel the mounds of red soil onto the dark polished boxes.

Larcum Todd had laid on a small buffet at the Bell Hotel. After the funeral many of the townsfolk gathered in the bar, the normal high spirits of the hostelry absent as the Melbury citizens tried to come to terms with the events of the last few days. In the dining room, the official guests and mourners were gathered. Fran Todd moved amongst them with a tray of sherry.

Frank White, in an unsuitably buoyant mood was standing next to his wife. He had the air of a man who had seen his life ruined and restored again and could not believe his good fortune. Jackie meanwhile was morose, having earlier agreed with David that their affair should cease, for now at least.

Debbie, as Albert Stern's daughter, was the centre of sympathetic attention. She finally broke away from the crowd and walked across the room to Father Simpson. She grabbed his arm.

"William!" She hissed excitedly. "Frank White has said that he will pay off all my father's debts! That means I won't have to sell the cottage. I can live there and stay here in Melbury!" She squeezed his arm. William Simpson felt a tingle of excitement himself. He had resigned himself to being attracted to Debbie and had decided that he wasn't going to feel guilty about it.

"I thought he might," mused the priest.

Debbie looked at Father Simpson accusingly. The priest grinned. "I simply asked him if he would consider a contribution. I think he felt it was in his interest. There are rumours you know, that 'Frank' White is not 'Lily White'. He is keen to be seen as a good Melbury citizen."

Debbie looked at the priest's mock innocence. She was, she thought, very happy to be staying in Melbury.

"You!" She hit his arm playfully. "You spoke to him! You black-mailed him!"

A tall presence interrupted the conversation. Inspector Downs, accompanied by Maddie, appeared at her shoulder.

"Good afternoon Father." Downs nodded courteously to Debbie, "Miss Smith, my condolences."

"Inspector! And Maddie!" Father Simpson greeted the couple. "What is the news on Edith Cummings?"

"Well, pending a psychiatric report. She will stand trial in Nor-wich Crown Court in a couple of weeks," replied Downs.

"But the other news is that John is staying here in Melbury," added Maddie, clearly delighted. She linked her arm through the inspec-tor's.

"Why should you not stay?" Asked Father Simpson.

Downs looked rueful. "Well, to tell you the truth, a day or so ago. I thought that I might end up being posted to a remote job. Chief Superintendent Ross is not my greatest admirer and if I had messed up this investigation my card would have been marked."

"Well you didn't mess it up!" rejoined Debbie.

"That's just it," added the inspector. "Because of the media cover-age and the successful outcome, I have been invited to work in New

Scotland Yard on detective duties."

"That sounds like a career move to me." Commented Father Simpson.

"Downs looked at his feet uncomfortably. "I'm no great detective William." Without you intuition and help I would probably be on my way to the Hebrides right now."

"That's not true!" Exclaimed Debbie. "You conducted a very thorough investigation."

Downs shrugged.

"Possibly. Anyway, I have recommended Sergeant Simpkins for promotion to the job."

John Downs looked at Maddie who positively glowed in his company.

"Besides, I think that I am at home here in Melbury. There are things here I can do. I can make a difference."

"And we will be delighted to keep you here," enthused Debbie. "You are our Police Chief.

Father Simpson and Maddie concurred, and the inspector, unused to flattery, flushed happily.

As the afternoon came to a close people began to drift away. Nick King and Amanda had left the Bell and walked over the bridge and down to the river. They were to check out that evening, and felt strangely sad about it.

Nick held Amanda's hand as they stepped slowly along the bank.

"Weren't they all wonderful, turning out like that," said Amanda. She had been moved by the town's reaction to the funeral.

Nick agreed. "Yes, it's quite a town."

"We'll come back here wont we?" Asked Amanda, turning to face Nick and standing close to him. Nick put his arms around her.

"Sure we will."

It was becoming dark. An enormous harvest moon grew on the horizon.

"Look how the moon throws its light on the countryside," marvelled Amanda.

Nick looked at the orb and smiled.

"So shines a good deed in a naughty world." He replied happily.

Amanda looked up at him. "What?"

"Merchant of Venice," laughed Nick grabbing her hand and pulling her back to the bridge.

"I did it at school, don't worry, come on, let's get going." He stopped for a moment and kissed Amanda gently.

"And thanks," he added. "I couldn't have been here and done this without you."

Amanda felt a surge of happiness. She squeezed his hand. Nick turned away and they walked in contented silence back to the bridge.

The Beekeeper show took place a few days later. The show, as planned, was combined with the womens' institute fete. It was a splendid affair, attracting more visitors than ever.

Mrs Rotton, hastily elected as the chair of the Womens' Institute, worked on the White Elephant stall and Jenny Larcombe ran the wheel of fortune. The wheel still kept falling off but somehow it didn't seem to matter this year.

There were all varieties of the produce of the Suffolk countryside including at least ten different types of honey. There were cakes, fudges, scones all manner of home produce. In an annex local artists displayed their exhibits and carvings and all this was to the cheerful background sound of various local bands.

The horticultural exhibits were magnificent.

Ronald Finch won the first prize in the flower and vegetable section. Under strict instructions, Mrs Finch has been tending Ronald's pom pom dahlias whilst he had been in the police station.

Ronald had accepted the congratulations of his fellow competitors. His wife in particular was delighted. Especially as it made her life easier if Ronald didn't sulk for weeks after the show.

Now he stood silently in front of his exhibits. The red rosette, resting on the dahlias, proudly displayed his first place status. He was pleased of course, but he knew something was missing.

Ronald looked around the room. He felt sad. Even after years of resentment and hostility, he had to admit, the show really was not the same without Albert Stern: tall and proud, preening himself in front of his leeks and carrots.

The Beekeeper Show